Moon Child

Gaby Triana

All rights reserved. No part of this book may be reproduced in any form or by any electronic or mechanical means, including information storage and retrieval systems, without permission in writing from the publisher, except by reviewer, who may quote brief passages in a review.

ASIN: B08N3D1J8R (eBook Edition)

ISBN: 9798705802340 (Print Edition)

Characters and events in this book are fictitious. Any similarity to real persons, living or dead, is coincidental and not intended by author.

Cover art copyright 2021 by Lynne Hansen, LynneHansenArt.com

Printed and bound in the United States of America

First printing February 2021

Published by Alienhead Press

Miami, FL 33186

Visit Gaby Triana at www.gabytriana.com

MOON CHILD

She was, in fact, a child of the moon. Wandering around aimlessly in the dark. Bringing light to everyone around her.

– s & a

Prologue

The little boy's flower was made of yellow tissue paper for the petals and orange construction paper for the center. It was cinched at the base and fastened with a green pipe cleaner for a stem. A cutout construction paper leaf was taped to the middle, giving it, he thought, a realistic appearance.

He twirled it between his fingers. It was the most beautiful thing he'd ever made.

"Go show it to Mommy," Miss Katie said.

The boy pushed back on his wooden chair, which scraped against the cobblestones. He skipped out of the garden room where Miss Katie taught Art a few times a week. The boy loved it because he could see the moon high above them through the glass ceiling.

Bobbling into the hallway that stretched through the middle of the big hotel, the boy headed toward the kitchen. It was his mother's turn to help make dinner with the other ladies. His flower would undoubtedly make her happy after such hard work. He loved nothing more than making his mama smile.

Ever since they'd arrived at the resort, life had been magical, if a bit strange. In the mornings, they sat outside to greet the sun. At night, they danced in circles, holding hands, around a fire under the moon. The women dressed in bright colors and wore their hair long, tiny flowers pinned to the strands. They wove tales of gods and goddesses, of mythical creatures, of trees and fairies, totem animals, and spirit beings who watched over them.

In time, he would learn to see them, they assured him.

What the boy never told them was that he already could. See the spirit beings, that is, in the upstairs rooms while they had cross-legged quiet time on the floor. The see-through people always stared at him with gaunt faces and soulless eyes, whispering concerns about the creature who wouldn't let them pass. The clouds surrounding them were always dark silver or black. The boy was certain these beings were different than the ones the ladies had meant.

He was thinking about this, hoping he wouldn't run into one of them now in the hallway, when an odd smell rose into his nostrils. Slowing, he inhaled a sweet, rotten aroma, like burnt electricity that did not smell like dinner. He paused outside the kitchen door, peeking around the door frame. The women standing by the stoves, ovens, and worktables smelled it, too. They sniffed the air curiously, speaking in hushed tones.

"Is that..." they asked each other.

His mother stood at the long worktable shaping bread loaves. She reached for a towel to wipe her hands clean. She looked over and saw him. "Honey, stay outside..." She and the other women hurriedly put down their utensils, abandoning their bowls.

The boy held up his flower. "I made you this."

She didn't look at it. She was trying to listen to all the women's orders at once. "Honey, Mommy said to go outside," she instructed.

The boy heard something in his mama's voice he'd never heard before, an emotion, a hiccup he couldn't name. "But—"

"*Now!*"

The boy staggered back, as he watched the women scatter like ants. He knew the smell was to blame for their change in niceness. His mother would never *not* appreciate his art.

Without warning, a blast of spitting light and heat burst from the kitchen, searing his tender skin. The boy fell to the ground, covering his face with the crook of his arm. A noise rang in his ears. The explosion's wind blew his flower right out of his hand. He snagged it, scrambled to his feet but was knocked down again by an unseen force.

The kitchen doors slammed shut by themselves.

"Mommy!" he screamed.

On his belly, he tried to push open one of the doors when sheets of black smoke began pouring out from underneath. On the other side of the doors came the pounding of women begging to be let out. There was screaming. Coughing. The smoke burned the boy's eyes and face, so much that he had to duck his face into his shirt to protect them. He tried to push the door open again, but the metal panel on the bottom burned his fingertips.

He cried out, drew back his hand, tried kicking the door instead. It wouldn't budge. The door shook and rattled, as fists pounded on the other side.

Suddenly, one door swung open. One of the women ran out covered head-to-toe in yellow flames that stuck to all her clothes. Half her hair had burned off her charred scalp. One hand at her own throat, the other stretched out to him, she coughed and sputtered and collapsed beside him. A single blue eye stared at nothing.

A set of strong arms scooped him up and whisked him away. Miss Katie ran with him, as she hurried to corral the other screaming kids. They fled through the lobby out the front doors until they were a safe distance away, until Miss Katie couldn't carry him anymore. She set him down to catch her breath. The children gathered, clinging and crying against her bell-bottoms.

The boy watched as a monstrous fire consumed the roof.

Smoke billowed out the top of the building into the evening sky, pluming toward the moon. The flames reminded him of a sea creature's tentacles wrapped around an ill-fated submarine. He watched in morbid fascination, waiting for his mother to come running out and scoop him up.

When she didn't, he hugged Miss Katie's leg and dried his tears on her pants.

She never even got to see his flower.

ONE

From His cross on my pink wall, Jesus stared at me. Painted blood dripped from His palms, feet, and side where they'd pierced Him. I'd always understood the message behind His dejected gaze—*Be good, so I won't have to do this again.*

There were sparklier versions of the Holy Cross, of course, but my grandmother bought all her religious effigies at Dollar Tree in Little Havana, where tall glass prayer candles wrapped in plastic images depicted Jesus's heart beating on the outside of His body, glowing like the sun, eyes trickling with crimson tears.

Underneath Him, atop my bookcase peppered with lit candles, was another childhood staple—my ceramic Virgin Mary lamp. It was painted pastel blue and gold, and at night, switched on, the Holy Mother, with her incandescent bulb buried deep inside, radiated nightmares. Her youthful appearance was replaced by the yellowing crevices of her cloak. Her cheek lines resembled a forest hag's. As a child, I called her Scary Mary.

But it wasn't just her appearance that creeped me out.

An unwanted, intrusive thought always flitted through my mind whenever I touched her. It was my grandfather, sitting at his office desk, signing the greeting card to go with the lamp, which was to be my First Communion gift. He nervously awaited...something. I never knew what exactly, or why it unsettled me.

Tonight, I turned her on—quickly so my fingers wouldn't conjure up the image.

I sat down cross-legged and took out the square basket containing my tools: a black candle to symbolize tonight's New Moon, my abalone shell, my palo santo, my lighter, and my tarot cards wrapped in red silk. I laid it all out across my worn pink and purple rug woven with shreds of glittery thread. Then I waited.

In the corner of the room, a glow-in-the-dark peel-and-stick full moon emitted a soft, green glow, as I waited for my grandmother to finish closing up for the night. Soon, all was quiet. *Here we go...* I lit the candle first, then picked up the three-inch stick of palo santo, charred on one end from multiple use, sticking it into the flame. It crackled as it caught fire.

For a moment, I heard Abuela shuffling through her room next to mine, as she entered her bathroom, slippers padding across the tile floor. My breath caught in my throat. I heard sink water rushing through the walls, then the springs of her bed creak as she settled again.

Taking a deep breath, I blew on the lit end of smoldering wood. The flame went out, releasing a thin stream of smoke into the air, unpredictable curls swirling as it rose. I wafted the smoke over the cards, clearing them of stagnant energy. I would've used sage to cleanse them, but sage smelled like weed, which definitely would've brought Abuela investigating.

"Smoke of air, fire of wood, cleanse and bless these cards for good. Tell me what I shouldn't or should..." I whispered.

Tomorrow was the *Youths for Jesus* retreat, a two-week camping thing my church did every summer out in the Everglades. I was supposed to be praying to the Virgin for a successful trip. Instead, I was hoping tarot cards would fix my life.

I'd been a member of *Youths for Jesus* for thirteen years now. I couldn't remember a time when Ministerio Jesus hadn't been a part of my landscape. Confraternity of Christian Doctrine classes, First Communion, Confirmation, youth group picnics, youth group assemblies, youth group retreats, and everything in between. There was no escaping church. Not when your grandfather had been the school's principal for twenty-four years.

Tomorrow, they'd be making me an assistant leader. I knew, because Camila, my best friend, already a YFJ leader, told me after their meeting two nights ago. I was supposed to act surprised and be happy about this.

"Just telling you so you can be ready," she'd said.

I'd feigned excitement.

After Camila went home, something inside of me died. I'd been naïve to hope this retreat might be my last. After all, I was starting college in August. I wouldn't have much time to devote anymore. But no—they were reining me in tighter. Closer. I could almost feel the invisible choke collar around my neck.

I stopped shuffling the cards. "What do I do?" The air conditioner turned off, as an eerie quiet settled through my room.

Who was I talking to? God? I wasn't sure anymore. Maybe my own conscience. Maybe the Universe *was* God. So were these cards, this candle, this room, these walls, the cross around my neck that my father gave me. All of it. Maybe everything was made of the same energy, vibrating at different rates. Maybe religion was a thing of the past, and it was time to follow my own beliefs.

I lay down the first card—the Ace of Cups, a tall, silvery Holy Grail overflowing with glistening water. It symbolized new beginnings, an emotional new start. Was tomorrow the beginning of a new life in the ministry? If so, I didn't want it.

But how could I get out of it? Saying no to my parish would be like denying my family. There was no easy way out. If I didn't show up in the parking lot at 7 AM tomorrow, there'd be hell to pay.

I lay down the second card—the Fool, a naïve young man

teetering on the edge of a rocky cliff, his dog trying to warn him of the dangers ahead. I sniffed a laugh. "Yeah, no shit."

I held the last card in my fingers.

Suddenly, I heard Abuela's door pop open, followed by the hallway's fluorescent light glowing underneath my door, the scraping of slippers along the floor. I grabbed a pillow I kept nearby in case this should happen and quickly covered the cards and shell. She knocked then flung open my door.

"O, estás despierta?"

"Obviously, I'm awake, Abuela. I'm on the floor." I added a smile, so she wouldn't think I was sassing her.

"Valentina, what's burning?" She stepped in, the edges of her bata de casa swishing against the floor. She sniffed the air like a police dog.

My heart pounded. If she saw the tarot cards, she'd tell me I was asking for trouble. They were not a sanctioned part of our faith. "Uh, I opened the window. Maybe smells came into the room?" I lied. I'd been lying for a while now. They gave me no choice when my real words were never the ones they wanted to hear.

She scanned the room with sharp green eyes, which fell on Scary Mary. "Ay," her tone brightened. "Qué linda la lamparita." She moved towards it, her foot a couple of inches from my hidden card spread. Her fingers gingerly touched the lamp. "I remember when we gave it to you. How come you never turn it on?"

"I mean, look at her, Abuela."

"But it's so pretty. Cuco used to leave it on for you every night."

"And I used to turn it off the second he'd leave." I never told her about the weird thoughts I'd have whenever I'd touch it.

She sniffed again. "It's stronger around here."

"It's the candles. They're cedarwood. Actually? I'm praying

right now, so could you..." I waited for her to realize she was intruding.

She shrugged and turned to go. But then, her slipper caught the edge of the cushion, dragging it a few inches. The corner of the Fool card slid out from underneath. Abuela stared down at it. She looked at me. It was hard to tell what she was thinking.

"What are you doing?" she asked suspiciously.

"Writing my retreat letter," I lied again. The "retreat letter" was an anonymous inspirational note we were asked to write every year on the eve of the trip. The letters got scrambled then passed out, and you were supposed to get someone else's letter while they got yours.

For the first time ever, I wasn't writing it.

Abuela scowled. I braced, but she only tucked the Fool back under the cushion with the toe of her slipper. "Don't you have to be awake early?"

"Yes. The sooner I finish, the faster I can get to bed."

She shuffled to the door, and for a moment, looked like she was going to say something. She began closing the door, giving me a tight-lipped smirk. "Goodnight, Vale."

"Nite, Abuela."

The door closed all the way...almost.

She opened it back up. "Vale?"

"Yes, Abuela?" I held my breath.

"I would not consult the esoteric, if I were you. God has laid out his plan for each of us. Your job is to follow that plan."

My heartbeat pounded in my ears.

"Catholics don't dabble in dark arts. You understand?"

I stared at her disapproving glare. I could tell her she was wrong, that I was eighteen and could decide for myself what I believed in, but did I want to start a fight at this late hour?

Quietly, I swallowed. "Yes, Abuela."

She waited a moment, gauging my sincerity. "Now, put those cards away and pray for forgiveness."

Forgiveness? For what?

I wasn't doing anything wrong.

"Okay," I said. "Goodnight."

She watched me another moment, then closed the door. I listened for all the sounds of her going back to bed, for all the good it did me the first time, then let out a major breath.

This was why I needed to come out of the broom closet. I couldn't read cards, sit under the moon, burn herbs, meditate, or any of the other unsanctioned things I did as long as I was in this house.

I couldn't keep living this way.

This wasn't a phase. I wouldn't be growing out of my spiritual curiosity anytime soon, no matter how wrong it seemed to them. The more I read, the more I learned, the less God could be a bearded, robed Father in the sky, judging everything everybody did. That didn't sound like love to me.

I couldn't become assistant leader either. I couldn't go on the retreat. I wasn't the person they thought I was. But my bags were packed, and Camila was expecting me to give her a ride tomorrow.

"What do I do?" I whispered. I was still holding the last card between my trembling fingertips. I slid it out from underneath my leg where I'd tucked it and flipped it over.

The Moon—Hecate the Crone, Goddess of the Crossroads, stood in the foggy road, holding a torch. Her silver hair flowed in the cold wind, signifying truth and power. The Moon card was about deception, intuition, secrets. Together with the Ace of Cups and the Fool, I faced a new beginning. Adventure and magic, but not without peril. Moonlight revealed hidden truths. And sometimes, like Scary Mary, we wouldn't like what we see.

I wrapped up the cards and placed them back in the basket, along with the shell and palo santo. Standing, I blew out the candles, then turned off my bedroom light. I was about to turn off Scary Mary, too, when I paused to stare at her dark, creviced wrinkles, under-eye bags that'd make any kid cover their head with a blanket.

"Do you agree?" I asked her.

Mary flickered in silence. Above her, Jesus wept. And above Him, dancing lamplight bounced off the crucifix, creating a shifting reflection on the ceiling. For a moment, it looked like a wolf, howling at the moon.

Two

The only thing that could wake me up early, besides school, was the occasional South Florida sunrise. Summery rays of golden light broke through pink and blue candy floss clouds. Temperatures were not yet boiling. One might even call it comfortable. Herons pecked the sawgrass for dragonfly breakfasts.

Seeing Cami again two weeks after graduation was also a plus.

In the car, she rambled about her sister. I didn't mind. It gave me something else to think about on the drive besides my predicament. "I told her, 'Silvie, stop giving yourself away for free. Don't you see that the reason he does this is because you let him? He's a taker; you're a giver. You guys are a recipe for disaster.'"

Taker. Giver. A repressed memory from last summer snaked through my mind, but I pushed it away. "You said that?" I asked.

Blurs of telephone poles whizzed past at fifty miles an hour. I couldn't stop thinking about the wolf mirage on my ceiling last night, the way it had danced and leaped and howled for just a moment before disappearing.

"Yes, she needs to hear it. Don't you agree?"

Cami loved making her older sister out to be a lost soul. I was sure it made Cami feel like the mature one, but Silvie didn't need a savior. Silvie was a free spirit, unafraid of living her life through trial and error. So what if things weren't working out with her boyfriend? At least she was living, owning her own mistakes.

"I think you should let your sister figure things out for herself." I stared ahead, fingers tightly coiled around the steering wheel. "It's her life."

"Ay, Vale, you always give her the benefit of the doubt."

"You say that like it's a bad thing."

We drove in silence, as she thumbed through her phone and laughed at whatever amusing snippet caught her attention. I toyed with the idea of telling her I was heavily considering ditching the retreat, dumping her ass curbside, then going home again. It would mean facing a million questions from my grandmother and mother, yes. And I'd have to admit lukewarm feelings about the way I'd been raised. Catholicism was more Cuban than coffee, croquetas, and media noche sandwiches all rolled into one.

Approaching the turn in the road, I slowed. Cami pointed to the familiar campground sign, freshly painted and adorned with flowerful landscaping. "I can't believe we're back. How did a year fly by so quickly?"

"We must've been having oodles of fun," I deadpanned.

Vehicles were lining up. Cami sat on the edge of her seat, waving at everyone digging out bags from their trunks. Familiar faces in green baseball caps and matching shirts displaying our "Live the adventure!" slogan over a cross made it all too real.

A dull soreness ached in my chest.

"What?" Cami asked.

"What?"

"You sighed. Are you nervous?"

"Nah, I'm good."

"Is it Antoni?"

"I already told you no." I scoffed. She asked me this the other night, too.

Antoni Piñeda, a youth group leader from our sister church, Sacred Heart, joined us on the retreat every year. Last year, I shared a super-brief "thing" with him. A year older than both me and Cami, Antoni and I were somewhat close. We sometimes held hands, talked late at night—innocent stuff. We even prayed, always at his suggestion. Everyone said we made a cute couple.

I was curious where it would go.

On the last day, he pulled me into an empty men's bathroom behind the chapel while everyone was out by the campfire singing hymns. Surrounded by urinals, it felt alien and wrong. I assumed he wanted to kiss me away from prying eyes. What was the big deal doing so in public? He was eighteen—I was seventeen. It wasn't like people didn't know we were an item.

Well, we did kiss. Awkwardly. We didn't click at all. Kissing Antoni was like getting my face sucked off by an octopus. To make matters worse, he kept taking my hand and sliding it across his crotch, which I might have considered later on, in a different setting, but we were surrounded—by urinals. Not to mention I kept having intrusive flash thoughts of him with a guy.

After a few agonizing minutes of me redirecting my hand and him trying to force romantic alchemy, he pulled away, stood at the sink, and unzipped his jeans. Then, he...groaned. And relaxed. He was done. I felt repulsed, shocked, cheated out of a legit experience. The worst part was the way he then ushered me out of the bathroom in a hurry, like *I* was his dirty secret. No regard for how I felt. *His* needs had been met. I'd been nothing but an accessory to him, a used baby wipe.

"Are you sure?" Cami's voice snapped me out of it. "Because I could understand. I'd feel weird seeing him, too."

It had taken me a month to tell Cami about the incident. But only Cami, because who else would believe that charming, beloved, squeaky-clean Antoni was an ass? I never told her about the intrusive thought either, because I didn't know what was causing them.

"I'm fine."

I was. It could've ended worse. If anything, I was grateful for the experience for opening my eyes to the dual nature of people. Because of Antoni, I was more careful before trusting. Because of Antoni, my feelings about this community had changed. Not that he represented the whole of Catholicism, or even men, but maybe he had. In a way.

The little cross hanging from my rearview mirror swung back and forth. I reached out and steadied it then turned off the engine. Cami and I gathered our bags and headed toward the compound, while moths frantically demanded exodus from my stomach.

If I stayed...fifty of us would pray together, sing together, cook, eat, and share devotion to God together *for two weeks*. Some, like Antoni, would fake moral fortitude. Father José, Father Willie, and Sister Agatha would run the show. Activities would bring us closer to God—supposedly.

Why, then, did I want to turn and run the hell out of there?

The greetings began, the hugging, the air kissing, the questions about how the school year went, the blessings in Spanglish, the assurances that God would save us. I floated through the motions like a scuba diver giving the all-OK thumb's up, even as my oxygen levels neared the red zone.

Clutching the little gold cross around my neck, I blinked back tears. *What would you do, Dad?* It'd been five years since I heard his voice, but I knew he'd want me to be happy.

"Vale!"

I turned. "Oh, Father Willie. Hello."

With his big-cheeked smile and lumbering gait, the middle-aged priest looked like a friendly friar. I'd loved him since I was a kid. He was one of the few genuine people left in the church who gave it a good name.

He folded his hands over his belly. "It's so good to see you. I was so very sorry to hear about your grandfather. I was in Guatemala on missionary work when it happened."

"It's okay. Thanks for remembering him." I faked a smile.

"He was a good man, a pillar of this community, but you already know that. And so proud of you." He reached out to tap my arm. "Always with high hopes that you'd lead the next generation into the ministry."

"I..."

If Father Willie could only see the vortex of uncertainty swirling inside my mind. I heard my grandfather's voice reminding me I could talk to Father Willie. Father Willie was good with kids. He was nonjudgmental and might provide wisdom and guidance. Sadly, nobody here could understand what it felt like to have the dark side of the universe breathing life into my soul every night.

"Bueno, see you at the campfire," Father Willie said, ignoring my inability to form a coherent sentence. "Don't forget your letter."

Ah, yes, because someone here might need my encouraging words. Me, for example. "I will. Good to see you, Father." I ducked my head and got out of the hall fast.

IN THE EVENING, Cami and Yeni, an elder leader, were busy setting up their cabin spaces. Yeni was pleasant, if a little overexcited about the shower caddy she'd bought to carry All Her Things. The moment she stepped out of the cabin to grab something, Cami nodded to my duffel bag on the bed.

"Aren't you going to unpack?"

"In a minute. Cam..."

I tried.

I waited for the right words to come.

"What is it?" Her deep brown eyes searched mine.

I couldn't even tell my best friend of fourteen years how I felt.

"Heyyy," Yeni drawled, poking her head into the cabin with a scandalous smile. "Did you see who's here? Antoni." She made wide eyes that made me want to punch her.

"Can you give us a minute?" Cami glared at Yeni. Turning back to me, she took my hands. In her heart, I saw love and understanding. "You haven't been okay since you picked me up. What's up?"

I shook her hands. "I don't think I can do this."

"Do what? The leader role? Vale, it's little more than you're doing now, and—"

"It's not the leader role, Cami."

"Then what is it?"

A familiar clanging sound rang, the dinner bell. There were cheers and laughter and lots of movement toward the dining hall, kid voices and adult voices all mixed together. Every cell in my body resisted it. "I'll tell you after dinner."

I walked out.

Cami followed, mystified by my sullen attitude.

Then I saw him across the center courtyard, talking to a group of boys, nodding at whatever anybody said, as though he actually cared. He was probably imparting advice from his frosh experiences. I didn't care. In fact, I hadn't heard from Antoni all senior year, further validating my belief that I'd meant nothing to him. I was quite proud of the fact that I'd managed to push the bathroom memory to the back of my mind. I'd done such a good job of it, in fact, that I sometimes questioned whether it actually ever happened.

I could feel his gaze on my back. I ignored it, as we filtered into the dining hall—kids, leaders, aged-out members all talking about summer plans. I heard myself telling Yeni how I was starting FIU in the Fall. That was true, but that was all I knew. No idea regarding major or career direction. Everyone else seemed so sure of where their lives were headed.

Yet, I remember the exact moment my uncertainty began unfolding.

It was last summer. I was in bed, casually scrolling through Instagram, looking for inspiration for senior pics, when I saw it—a filtered photo of a little black cauldron, thin smoke rising from its belly. The photo of the tiny iron kettle was framed by chalky sketches of stars, moon, and candles. Cradling the cauldron was a pair of beautiful slender hands with black, pointy, sparkly fingernails.

There was something gorgeously enigmatic about the photo. It was a whole mood.

When I checked to see who in my IG feed would have posted such a goth-inspired gem, I saw it was Savannah, a recent graduate from Ministerio High, a girl who, a few days after graduation, had begun wearing blue lipstick, gotten bicep tattoos, and was making amazing cosmic art of naked nonbinary people.

Savannah was different. In Economics, she gave the best answers. Once, Ms. Halley asked, "What are basic needs in life?" Kids answered the usual—water, food, shelter. Then, there was Savannah: "Sex."

Everyone either laughed or clutched their pearls. What a complete badass. I never understood why she was in Catholic school to begin with.

I dove into her profile to stalk the rest of her gallery and found myself spiraling down a rabbit hole of bottomless intrigue. Each photo was more beautiful than the next—crystals, oil burners, bundles of herbs that she dried herself in a massive armoire. Before I knew it, I was googling half the words she used in her posts— energy, manifestation, vibrations, Universal source.

I began following many of the same accounts she followed,

posts with hashtags like #witchy #witchesofinstagram and #metaphysical. I bought a Tarot deck along with several books to help me interpret them. I began learning about Buddhism, Celtic runes, law of attraction, stuff that would never fly in my household. We all knew that God was to thank for any good that came into our lives, not our *own* powers.

Until I made up my mind about how I felt regarding the new information, I kept it a secret. If I was going to worry my family, I'd wait until there was something to actually worry about. So far, I was only intrigued by this mystical new aesthetic. I wasn't about to run off and join a Satanic cult.

Then, last night I'd asked for a sign.

The silhouette of a wolf showed up. I believed in signs—always had. When a double rainbow appeared on a shitty day, I believed God was cheering me up. When a butterfly fluttered over me in the courtyard at school, I knew it was my dad checking on me. I didn't know what to make of the wolf, though.

At dinner, I felt like an imposter. Like I was watching someone else's life unfold behind a sheet of glass.

"I'm worried about you," Cami whispered. We were helping wipe down tables littered with corn kernels and spilled chocolate milk after dinner. Several yards away, Antoni stood with another clueless fool who thought he was so wonderful, trying to make eye contact with me.

"I'm worried about me, too."

"Can you tell me now? There's more to the story, isn't there?"

"What story?"

"The bathroom story," she muttered.

"It's not about him, I told you." Why Cami couldn't fathom that something besides boys might be wrong with a girl was a mystery to me. "Don't be upset with me, but I have to go."

She stopped wiping and stared at me. The sponge in her hand dripped milky water down her wrist. "What do you mean?"

"I should've said this before—I can't do this."

"Do what?"

"This. The retreat."

"Vale, it's fine. We're going to have a great time. We always do! We look forward to this every year. Come on." She took my hand. Someone greeted us. We smiled. But in her grip, I felt her fear that something was wrong, that I was leaving not just the retreat, but her.

I plucked the sponge from her hand and tugged her around the corner of the building. Outside, the sky had darkened to a velvety royal purple. "Cami, *you* look forward to this every year. I only came because of you."

"That can't be true. You love this. Unless you're suddenly good at faking?"

"Maybe I am."

I saw the hurt in her eyes and felt guiltier than I ever have in my life. I searched the sky for answers. No wolves in the clouds.

"Look, I don't know what's going on, but I can assure you it's nothing we can't resolve without God's grace. We can talk to Father Willie. Father Willie loves you."

"Father Willie can't fix this. Trust me, Cami. My brain's a mess..."

"What am I supposed to tell them? Valentina, they're naming you a YFJ assistant leader tonight!"

"Tell them I got sick." I took off toward the cabin to grab my bag. I felt like a complete loser for ditching, but it would've been worse to stay and fake it.

"I can't believe this." She lingered in the cabin's doorway. "What am I supposed to do without you?"

"We'll talk when you get home in two weeks, okay? I promise. I love you." I kissed her cheek and pushed past her rigid stance.

"Valentina Callejas, what...the hell..."

I shot through the courtyard and out the camp gates, largely unnoticed, like the ejected ghost of an accident victim, rising from its dead body into the unpredictable liberty of the universe.

"Vale..."

I turned and saw him—the impossibly handsome Antoni, lingering in my peripheral vision. He reached for my arm. "Hey, can I talk to you a second?"

"No. I'm leaving," I said, pulling away before he could touch me. "I'm sorry."

"Wait, really?"

Yes, really.

"Bitch."

I bolted out, chastising myself for apologizing when I had nothing to apologize for. He was the one who took advantage of me in a smelly bathroom, not the other way around. Talking to him would only call the memory back again.

The campers' laughter melted away. One of the leader's voices blared through the megaphone, announcing campfire time. I left it all behind. Explanations would be demanded of me, but I wouldn't worry about it now. Once I was off the compound, the chorus of swamp crickets cheered me en route to my car.

I started the engine and navigated the gravelly dark path back toward the highway. Once on the road, I let out an exhale and opened my window for fresh hot air. The break wouldn't last for long, though—I was headed home.

Three

When I pulled into my driveway, I turned off the engine and waited for my courage to replenish. No sense in delaying the inevitable. I grabbed my bag and made it up the walk, stopping outside the front door.

In the silence of the night, I could hear my grandmother and mother arguing *through the walls* from inside my mother's room.

"My fault? How?" Mom fought hard to keep her voice down.

Either she knew about me leaving the retreat, or my grandmother told her about the tarot cards in my room last night.

"Claro que sí. Who else's fault would it be?" Abuela said. "You're her mother."

Keys in hand, I pressed my forehead against the door and let out a sigh. I wished I could steal into the night like some mysterious bird, fly-fly-away until I could breathe again. But I wasn't raised to run from problems, and despite the fact I was about to get the third degree. I turned the key and entered the house.

"She's here," Abuela said. It took less than two seconds for both of them to appear in the foyer. "Gracias a Dios!" My grandmother saw me and glanced at the ceiling. "Valentina, where have you been?"

"Driving home."

Mom followed me through the living room. "I called you. You didn't answer."

"I know."

"We didn't know if you'd gone somewhere, if you'd gotten into an accident..."

"That's a bit much, isn't it?" I hurried to my room.

"Don't get fresca with your mother," Abuela said.

I cast my grandmother a tired look. I wasn't getting fresh. They were overbearing, overprotective parents with no reason to treat me this way.

"Sorry to worry you," I added. "No texting and driving. Isn't that what you always say?" Trudging into my bedroom, I tossed my duffel bag onto the bed, as they followed me in.

Mom and Abuela jammed my doorway. "Explain," Abuela demanded. "They called from the retreat and said that you left."

So, this was about me leaving the retreat. For some reason, I found that easier to deal with than explaining my interest in the occult.

"Of course, they did," I muttered. The trap was set. No matter what I said, did, or felt, it'd be wrong. I chose to play the fool. "I'm fine. Nothing to worry about."

"Fine, ni fine," Abuela scoffed. "Why did you leave the encuentro after I paid three hundred dollars for it?"

"Mami, really?" My mother shot Abuela a look.

I stood by my bed, checking the texts that had come in after my defection. "Is that what you're worried about? Don't worry, I'll pay you back for it."

"Pay me back," she laughed. "With what job?"

"I'll get one. I have all summer."

My mother attempted to gain control of the situation. "Valentina, why on Earth would you leave? Father Willie said you just up and walked out, right before the presentation. They were going to name you a leader."

"I know, Mom."

"What's going on?" Her eyebrows knitted together. I appreciated she wasn't drilling me like she did other times whenever my grandmother stood directly behind her, puppeteering her with invisible strings.

"I didn't want to be there. That's all there is to it." It felt liberating to say it so plainly.

"Is that how it is now with this generation?" Abuela asked. "You just leave a commitment when you're not happy? This is what I was telling you," she said to my mom. "No follow-through. After she promised Cuco that she'd lead the youth group."

"No." I glared at her. "I *never* wanted to make that promise. You made me tell him that."

"He was dying!" Abuela said.

"I *know* he was dying, Abuela. It still wasn't your promise to make. I should've made that decision, not you."

"It's what you always wanted."

"When I was ten, maybe."

"You loved him."

"I did love him, but I never wanted to be a youth group leader. I only said that to make him feel proud of me. It's what *he* wanted, what *you* wanted. Right, Mom?" I looked to the woman who should've been on my side here. Yet, all my life, she'd been a mediator between me and Abuela.

"Forget the promise for a second, both of you," Mom interjected. "That's not what this is about. What made you leave so abruptly? That's not like you, Vale."

"How do you know it's not?"

"What?"

"How do you know it's not like me?"

"Because I've known you eighteen years..."

"You knew Dad for how many? Yet didn't really know him." That might've been a low blow, but there it was. The whole world knew of their marital problems, why not say it aloud? My mother sucked in a sharp breath and started pacing my room. "Is this a phase? This has to be a phase."

"Yes, it's called adulthood."

Abuela stepped into the room disapprovingly, as though the very walls offended her.

"Sabe quien tiene la culpa, no?" she muttered to my mother.

"No, Mami, why don't you tell me whose fault this is?" Mom leaned against my dresser, seething under the surface. "I suppose it's my fault again?"

"Can you guys argue somewhere else? I need to be alone." I sat cross-legged on my bed and took a good look around. I was never more hyperaware that my room was that of a child. I suddenly wanted to tear it all down.

"We're not done with you," Mom said, and my grandmother's condemning scowl said it all. No matter what I did, I would never please her. Who could ever live up to the standards set on women by the Catholic Church? Especially women of my generation?

"El progenitor paterno," Abuela said. "The paternal progenitor" meant my father in code-speak. "He strayed, you let him."

"Me?" Mom clutched her chest. "You're pinning him leaving on me?"

"You knew what he was doing, yet you said nothing."

"You're one to talk!" Mom blurted. "Where do you think I learned the subtle art of turning my cheek from my husband's indiscretions?"

"That's part of being married, hija."

"That's part of being abused. I told him to leave. I was angry. Weren't you ever angry at Papi?"

"Your father never hurt me like that."

I laughed inwardly. Mom laughed outwardly. "That you know

of. 23 and Me didn't exist in your time. Besides, you're the queen of denial."

I sank my head, stretching the back of my neck. These arguments erupted every so often, prompted by something I did or didn't do right, but it was rarely about me.

"Your father was a model man," Abuela insisted.

I glanced at Scary Mary, holding her rosary beads. Keeping secrets to prove my grandmother wrong. Something was up the day he wrapped the little lamp as a gift. I was sure of it every time I touched her.

My mother scoffed. "Your ignorance is baffling. Let me talk to my daughter or wait outside." She turned to me and closed her eyes. "Vale, it's okay if you didn't want to stay at the retreat. I...I get it. It just would've been better to tell us beforehand."

"There's no talking to you guys. You do see that, don't you? How am I supposed to tell you how I'm feeling when I'm being judged for every little thing I do?" It wasn't just my grandmother either. My mother played an equal part by not setting limits in her own house.

When my father passed away four years ago, my grandparents came to live with us. That's what Hispanic families do—they merge. Mom said it was bound to happen. We take care of our elderly. But Dad passed while they were separated, and it was too much for my mom to handle, so she invited her parents to stay with us earlier than planned. Because I needed more to deal with after my father's death.

I played with the cross around my neck, the one he gave me for my 7th birthday. I immediately saw his handsome face in my mind's eye.

Then, Abuelo died in May, and it became just us women. I hated the fact that we couldn't seem to hold life together without men in it. I would've thought Abuelo's death could've brought the end of stringency, but thanks to Abuela, the torture continued.

"Nobody is judging you," Abuela said. Through her Cuban accent, it sounded like "djodjing." "But you know who is? La vecina de al lado. Your neighbor, Alicia, has seen you outside doing whatever it is you do at night, practicing Santería, or whatever."

"What?" I barked a laugh.

My mother raised her eyebrows. "You're practicing Santería, Vale?"

"Mami, where would I even learn Santería in this Petri dish I've been raised in? Besides, Santería is a religion, and the truth, if you really want to know, is that I'm tired of religion. I love God, but religion can go screw itself."

"Valentina!"

"Why would I jump from one to another?"

"Then what are you doing outside at night?" Abuela asked. "What are you doing in this room? With your cards and your candles? Don't tell me you're praying, because I know a lie when I hear one."

My mother's curious gaze held mine.

"It's just tarot cards," I explained. "She acts like I'm worshipping the Devil."

"What do you do outside then?" Mom asked.

"I sit. Under the moon. In nature. Listening to frogs and crickets. I burn a candle, a piece of wood, whatever. The point is I'm not doing anything wrong. It's just meditation."

"Like yoga?" Mom was genuinely trying to understand.

"No. I'll explain later."

"Everything you're doing is wrong. Everything." Abuela strolled up to my little bookcase and pulled out the square basket with all my stuff, my tarot cards, candles, crystals and palo santo. My bundle of sage, which to her probably looked like a thick-ass joint.

I jumped toward her, clamping my hands on the basket. "Stop, that's mine."

Abuela held up the sage. "Esto es brujería."

"It is *not* witchcraft. It's for clearing energy. Same thing during Mass when they ring a bell or burn incense. Same thing!" I implored my mother. "Why do you let her do this? You let her take control of everything. This is *our* house. Stop letting her talk to me this way."

"Vale, I have the same concerns," Mom explained. "I'm more than a little worried right now. I don't even know what my own daughter is up to."

"If I'm telling you I'm doing nothing wrong, I'm doing nothing wrong. If you're scared of this," I snatched the sage out of Abuela's hand, "it's because you don't understand it."

"I would understand it if you talked to me!"

"And I would talk to you if I could trust you!"

Her shocked expression was frozen on her face. For a year, I'd been wanting to talk to her, but she was unreachable. She was dealing with her own pain in her own bubble of silence. "You *can* talk to me," she said quietly.

"I will. Soon. But right now, I need you to trust me."

I grabbed my things, unzipped my duffel bag, and threw them inside. Flecks of ashy sage smudged against my fingertips. I couldn't stay in this house another moment.

"I do trust you, hija," Mom doubled-down, while Abuela continued to seethe, muttering under her breath about all the injustices I'd caused her by not being her paragon Catholic granddaughter.

"I still believe in God, I just...I don't want to be in the youth group anymore. I want to learn what else is out there, decide what I believe in, instead of being forced to follow your beliefs. Do you understand?"

Abuela crossed herself then paced in the hallway. In Spanish, she told my mother, "You need to put that girl back on the path. This is not our way. Our way is through God, Our Father, Jesus, his Holy Son. Take control of this situation, hija, before you lose her."

"Stop talking about me like I'm not here. I don't have to follow your lifestyle, Abuelo's lifestyle, or anybody's. I'm not even convinced that Mom believes in it anymore. Mom?"

"Lifestyle?" Abuela said. "No, my darling, God is not a *lifestyle*. He is the center of your universe. Never forget that."

"Of yours," I replied.

It was never my mother who insisted we go to Mass, it was Abuela. It wasn't Mom's insistence I do my sacrament of Confirmation last year (late, because we were dealing with Dad's departure)—it was my grandparents' after they moved in, as if forcing me to check off all the boxes would save me.

Abuela left for the kitchen.

My mother was staring at me, conflict all over her face. Would she ever stand up for herself? Would she ever stand up for *me*?

I didn't wait to hear whatever came next. I texted the only other sibling I had, my half-sister Macy. We'd learned about Macy when I was thirteen through 23 and Me. Five years older than me, Macy was the result of my parents' first separation, the second one happening right after we learned about her, during which time my dad's heart gave out while living alone.

At eighteen, Macy had decided to take the DNA test and found me and Dad living in Miami. She reached out. I would say the shitshow then began, but my parents' marriage had already been a shitshow for a while. Macy had kept in touch with me all these years through social media. She always asked when I would come visit. She never had a sister before, but I always held back—because of Mom.

No holding back now. I asked if I could come visit her, to which she immediately replied with an emphatic—*Yes! OMG!*

"I'm leaving." I grabbed my bag and shuffled past my mother.

"Where are you going?"

"To visit Macy in Yeehaw Springs."

"But that's six hours away," Mom said, as though it were the other side of the world.

"So? I can't stay here. You and Abuela need to hash it out. Macy has her own house and a job. I can stay with her while you decide who you're going to be loyal to."

My mother recoiled as though hit with a dart. "That's not fair, Vale."

"But it's true."

Mom's eyes filled with glossy tears. Abuela had wandered into the kitchen, moving around pots and dishes, while muttering to herself.

"Let me give you money," Mom said quietly.

I paused in the living room while she rummaged through her purse and opened her wallet. She gave me all the cash she had. "I'll transfer into your account, too. Tell..." She couldn't say Macy's name. "Tell your sister I'm grateful." And with that, she threw her arms around me and shuddered against my shoulder.

I rarely saw my mother cry. This probably felt similar to when she'd lost my father. I hated that, but still, I had to go. "I love you. It's just for a little while. I'll call you when I get there."

"Drive carefully, hija." She wept against my T-shirt, then pulled back and wiped her deep, soulful eyes. "Go before she notices."

I nodded.

Slipping out the front door, I turned back to give her a weak smile. She nodded. Abuela stepped out of the kitchen. She caught sight of me leaving, her mouth open, questions at the ready, the answers to which were no concern of hers.

What is going on?
Why is she leaving again?
How can you let her go?

I could hear the interrogation now. My mother bravely closed the door. As I threw my bag into the passenger seat and climbed behind the wheel, I heard my grandmother shouting at the top of her lungs.

My mother, done with restraining herself, screamed back, "ENOUGH!"

Four

My little starshine, sleep, oh, so tight
 My little moonshine, dream with the night
 When you awaken, Love you will be
My little sunshine Heaven gave me.

WHEN DAD PASSED AWAY, I started a habit of holding the little cross around my neck while I slept. Touching it made me think of him and the song he always sang before bedtime. When he was done, he'd kiss my forehead and "boop" my nose.

Now it was morning, and my dad's voice faded, as sunlight streamed through slatted blinds. Horizontal lines glowed across pale gray walls onto a colorful geometric tapestry. The bed squeaked lightly when I shifted.

It took me a moment to place myself in the small, simple room —Macy's house.

Last night, after the showdown with my grandmother and mother, I drove five-and-a-half hour north on the Turnpike. I'd never driven this far from home before, especially up a lonely, two-lane road. The whole time, I kept thinking how radical it felt to run away. In movies, it was normal for kids to go off on their own when they reached eighteen. Felt like real American life to me.

But as the only daughter in a religious, Cuban-American home, leaving had felt wrong, like I'd carried more than just a duffel bag into Macy's house at 1 o'clock in the morning. It felt like I'd lugged in a boatload of guilt and betrayal, too. Luckily, Macy had welcomed me with open arms, after which she'd quickly excused herself, saying she had an all-nighter to work on, but we'd talk today when I woke up. I'd appreciated the space right from the start.

Grabbing my phone off the nightstand, I checked the time—way past noon. No wonder my stomach was grumbling. I trudged across creaky old pine floors into the connecting bathroom. In the distance, summer thunder rumbled. I secretly hoped Macy had more work to do, so I could spend time alone. Thunderstorms plus solitude was a combo I didn't get often.

I headed downstairs, careful not to touch the handrail. Didn't want any intrusive thoughts at the moment, especially seeing this wasn't my house. Macy's home was cute, small, and quaint, with moving boxes in every room. Following the scent of fresh-brewed coffee, I found her in the kitchen standing against the counter, staring into her phone.

"Hey!" She looked up with a big smile.

In full daylight, I took her in. She was several shades darker than I was, which made me wonder what her mother looked like. Our dad was pretty fair with light eyes and hair. Hers was medium-brown and curly, up in a poofy ponytail. Her eyes were hazel green, which I knew because of her photos, not from the shy distance I was keeping.

"Hi, thanks for letting me stay. I don't know what I was thinking being so bold to ask you like that."

"What? No. Hey..." She put down her phone and walked up to me to hold my hands. I flinched but let her take them. Her warm, soft hands spoke of a nurturing spirit. Up close, it was like looking into Dad's eyes. "It's okay."

I swallowed a lump and politely took back my hands.

"Listen," she said. "I'm glad you asked. I've wanted to meet you for a long time. Okay?"

I bit my lip and nodded.

"Come on. You want coffee?"

"Sure."

From the cupboard, she pulled a mug that said *Failure is Not an Option* and poured coffee, setting it on the kitchen table. "Black? Creamer? Sugar? I haven't made breakfast yet. Didn't know if you were the bacon and eggs type, or the avocado on toast type, or..."

"Anything is fine. I know this was last minute. I'm so grateful. I have money for you—for food, bills, and whatever else." I felt like the few bucks in my wallet would never cover the kindness and generosity this girl I'd never met before in person had bestowed on me.

"Valentina..." She paused at the fridge door, looking at me with eyebrows raised. "Your money's no good here. Don't worry, I got you."

"Thank you." I took a seat at the table in the outdated kitchen and watched her pull out an assortment of yogurt, strawberries, coffee creamer, and sliced bread from the fridge. I bit back the urge to cry.

I had a sister—all this time.

Pouring creamer into the coffee, I pulled the mug close. My dad's bedtime song echoed through my head again. *My little starshine, sleep, oh, so tight...my little moonshine, dream with the night.* I sipped the coffee and basked in warm coziness.

"I won't ask you what happened." She sat opposite me with a knife and a tiny wooden cutting board to begin slicing up strawberries. "After seeing the look on your face when you arrived last night, I know better."

"That bad, huh?"

"Well, I recognize it. That's the thing. I've been there. Remember, I moved out when I was eighteen, too."

"I didn't move out. I'm just...taking a break."

"Right, that's what I meant." She passed me a small bowl of strawberries, along with a carton of yogurt. "What I'm saying is, we don't have to get to know each other all in a day. To be honest, I have a shit ton of work to finish for a project, but..." She pointed a spoon at me. "That doesn't mean I'm not here for you. Got that?"

"Yes." I smiled and peeled open my vanilla yogurt, dumping in some of the strawberries. "That means a lot to me."

"What? That I have a shit ton of work to do? Thanks a lot."

I laughed. "No, I mean that you're here for me, but not all over me all the time." I realized that sounded rude. "Sorry, what I mean is, I appreciate the space."

"I understood you. No worries. So, listen, I have to go finish a promo video I'm editing. But maybe we can have dinner together later? Sorry the place is a mess. You'd think I'd have my shit together after three months moved in, but...work's got me going twenty-four hours."

"What is it you're editing?" I asked.

"Videos for the state's Department of Tourism website."

"Sounds fun."

"I push buttons all day. It's a job."

"Oh."

"I'm trying to get a full-time position at an advertising firm in Orlando, so I can make commercials for theme parks, but...this is a good first step."

"That's cool. At least you have space all to yourself," I said, gesturing to the cozy little home, a place to call her own.

"Very true, Vale. Vah-le, right?"

"Yeah." I smiled. It sounded cute when she said it and a reminder that the other half of her heritage wasn't Cuban like both my parents'.

"I've actually gotten good with a little Spanish. Te gusta las fresas?" she asked, pointing to the strawberries.

"Sí, me encantan. Gracias," I replied.

"Yes, they enchant me?" She cocked her head.

"Means I love them. Sounds a little backwards, I know. So, to do around here..."

"Ah, yes." She straightened, using her spoon to emphasize an invisible list in the air. "Not much, sorry to say."

I laughed. It felt good to have an easygoing conversation with someone, especially one related to me. "Sounds perfect, if I'm honest."

"There's a bunch of Old Florida historic homes, an old theatre, an old state park, a dog park, the beach is about a forty-minute drive from here, lots of lakes and springs, but I guess you meant stuff where you can find other kids to hang out with."

"No, actually, isolation sounds great."

"I hear you. Oh, not far from here is a famous spiritualist camp called Cassadaga. Full of psychics. Also, there's Disney, if you want to drive ninety minutes."

"No, thanks. I just drove six. Besides, we do Disney all the time. I'll probably just hang out. Looks like you have a big yard." I peered out the window.

"Half an acre."

"I'm jealous. At home, our houses nearly touch side-by-side."

"Zero lot?"

"I guess that's what you call it."

She gazed out the window. "You'll love it out there. I haven't had a moment to enjoy it since I moved in. Now I feel like I have no life." Macy stared into her coffee.

"Hey, a job is a life," I said. "It's more than what I've got."

"Yeah, but we shouldn't live to work. We should work to live." She pondered her own words, dumped her garbage, and placed bowls in the sink. "Anyway, explore. Do what you want. I'll be in my office." She grabbed her mug and moved to the kitchen entrance. "Oh, and Vale?" She turned.

"Yeah?"

"I always wanted a little sister." Her smile filled a space in my heart I didn't even know existed.

FOR THE FIRST THREE DAYS, I did nothing. Just chilling in my room felt like vacation. Nobody to tell me to wake up, sweep the floor, help empty the dishwasher. Not that I was a slug either. I washed dishes, put away utensils in drawers, even tried cooking a few meals. It wasn't my mother's cooking, but it was enough to show Macy I appreciated her opening her door to me.

Being near her made me think of my dad more than usual. I wondered if it ever made Macy sad that she didn't get to experience the bedtime song, boops to her nose, or any of the dad jokes that would forever stay with me. I supposed she couldn't miss what she'd never experienced.

On the first night, we talked about her mother, how she'd had a falling out with her five years ago, but over time, they'd managed to reconnect. On the second night, we talked about my college plans, how I wasn't entirely sure, but I may want to major in business. My grandfather always said I wasn't aggressive enough to be in business—I should go into education, because teaching was a "great career for women." Whenever my father heard this, he'd mutter under his breath that I could do whatever I wanted.

On the third night, we discussed the differences in how we were raised. She was raised Baptist and went to church a lot, but over time, stopped and wasn't sure why. I suggested maybe religion wasn't fulfilling anymore, or that we'd outgrown the need for it. Maybe we were meant to find our own answers.

Macy said, "Or, nobody knows who to trust anymore."

She understood what was in my soul.

On the fourth night, she announced it was crunch time, gave me a hug that left me feeling appreciated, and disappeared into her "editing cave" to finish her commercial. I headed outside as I had every night after dinner.

I loved the quiet, the vibrant oranges and purples of the night sky past nine o'clock, the number of stars you couldn't see in Miami due to light pollution. Kicking off my flip-flops, I stepped onto grass still damp from the afternoon thunderstorm. A banyan tree loomed in the corner of her yard. Banyan trees always fascinated me with their hanging root systems that resembled damaged paintings dripping in the rain.

The waxing moon was out, bringing good things into the universe. I wondered if that was really true, if the phases of the moon could manifest wishes into existence or banish them. When it came to metaphysical stuff, my heart burned to know the truth of it, whether or not magic really existed, or whether, like I'd talked about with Macy, we just wanted to believe, since nothing else in the world seemed to be going right.

The night was perfect for going back inside, grabbing my tarot cards and palo santo, or hell, even my sage, since there was no one around to judge the smell of it, and sit under this perfect tree that was giving me life.

I was walking back to get them when I heard a sound coming from the other side of the tree. I listened. Not a loud sound, just a vague crunching of leaves.

"Hello?"

Macy had neighbors, but not for half an acre. A small house just over a knoll had its lights off, except for the glow of a TV inside. On the opposite side of the old house, there was nothing but an empty lot that looked like it'd been a playground at one point, judging from the circle of sand. Behind her property was a stretch of woods that looked denser the deeper it got.

I stood there, listening, heart pounding, the dark night alive with crickets and tree frogs, and a couple of cocuyos I was surprised to see this far north in Florida. The little lightning bugs with the glowing green eyes (actually phosphorescent dots on their backs) flitted underneath the banyan branches, flying in wide circles, searching for a good place to hide.

My mother always said they were good luck. My mother seemed to believe in magic at one point, long ago, before my grandparents came to live with us. I closed my eyes and absorbed the nighttime energies.

In Miami, I didn't spend a lot of time outdoors. It was too hot. But when I did, it was late at night when I thought nobody could see me. I liked to lie in the cool grass and sometimes hold my arms up to the sky. I wasn't sure what about that gesture felt right to me, but I always held back a bit, imagining someone like our nosy-ass neighbor, Alicia, spying on me, questioning what the frick I was doing.

Here, there was no one. Slowly, I lifted my arms to the sky. I hugged the expanse of the universe, the sliver of moon that looked like a smile, the banyan tree, and the little cocuyos for their light show. I felt thankful to God for this safe space. I never claimed to live a terrible life. I was privileged by most standards, but my decisions were rarely my own. Here I could make life however I wanted it to be.

Thank you for the breathing room, Universe.

I heard it—the crunching sound again.

When I focused my gaze into the trees, a black wolf was standing there.

Five

The quiet beast watched me.

Adrenaline kicked into high gear, as my hearing flooded with a soft ringing sound and the rush of blood. A wolf. Not on my ceiling but live in front of me. What were the chances?

I assumed it was a wolf. I suppose it could've been a large dog. Not a massive creature, on the skinny side, maybe a scavenger, definitely without a home to feed him. I assumed it was male, because it just looked like an alpha to me, but what did I know about wolves? Nothing.

It watched me from the shadows. Intently. Golden eyes studied me, nostrils flaring, sniffing the space between us, gauging danger. My brain scanned everything I knew about wild animals—

They're more afraid of you than you are of them.
Don't show fear.
Move slowly.

I had no clue if any of those were true.

"Hello." I reached out my hand, palm down. If wolves were anything like most animals I knew, they wanted to sniff you first. In all honesty, he didn't seem frightened. He didn't even want to sniff me. He simply took a couple of steps back, then sideways, then he faced the woods with his tail pointed at me. That seemed like a bold move for him, turning his back on an unfamiliar human.

What happened next, I can't be a thousand percent sure, but I swear on my mother's life this wolf turned its head back, as if to say, *Come*. And for some reason I couldn't explain, I knew in my heart it was okay.

Follow him.

First, the usual warnings dropped anchor—

Don't go.

You don't know what's out there.

Don't be stupid, you'll die.

Listen to your mother, your grandmother, God.

For the love of all that is holy, Valentina, LISTEN, for once.

I did listen. For the first time ever, actually.

The wolf waited, watched me. He would lead. I knew this in my soul to be true. I didn't care what any of the other voices said. This animal had something to show me if only I had the capacity to trust my instincts.

Screw it.

I dropped my flip-flops and slid my feet in, carefully stepping off the edge of the property, past the banyan, into the copse of trees. I wished I could say the woods became magical then, like a secret nighttime garden, but they were more like an entanglement of gloom, black and pewter dense canopies broken up in spots. Deeply purple sky peeked through the ceiling. Time fell away in a cocoon of decomposed leaves, dripping moss, and cricket shrieks. Smells of wood and damp foliage assaulted my senses. I'd been a Florida girl all my life but a city one. Walks underneath the cypress and live oaks at night in the middle of summer were new to me, and I lamented the fact. I'd gone biking through mangroves, kayaking in the Keys, splashing at every beach on both coasts, but Central Florida woods were entirely new.

Cocuyos darted into the peripheral, hiding behind trunks, as if clearing the way. Ahead, my lupine guide shifted side-to-side with a slow and steady gait, at times blending with the silhouettes of trees, so much that I had to blink often to make sure he was still there. I stepped over logs and ducked under low-hanging branches, scanning for amber eyes. Every so often, they appeared as if with a light of their own.

We went on this way for what could've been half an hour, though time seemed to cease existing. Eventually, we broke through the woods and came to a clearing where tall grass swayed in the summer wind, and a wide, open sky revealed the quarter moon. If it hadn't been for the wolf veering off to the left, I would've stepped right into what I quickly realized was a body of water, its gentle shoreline sneakily lapping in the dark. A lake about the size of two football fields together stretched before us.

"What is this place?" I asked aloud.

The wolf strode along the shore of the lake, pushing his way through the tall, razor-sharp grasses. Ahead of him, out of the gloom, emerged a structure so loomingly wide, towering and black against the night sky, I had to stop and squint to make out the wholeness of it. A building. An old building, decaying forgotten on the lakeshore. Most of its windowpanes were blown out like a carnival shooting gallery. Jutting out of the center was a tower of about ten floors with two wings of four stories each flanking either side. From its sagging veranda, I realized I was seeing the backside.

My instinct was to take out my phone and start snapping pics. I would risk my hiding place in the world to send Camila some shots, but I hadn't brought my phone out to moon-gaze in Macy's backyard. Besides, I hadn't driven all this way to stay connected with Cami. I quickly forgot about wanting to share and just enjoyed the moment.

My guide-wolf led me through the reeds and swampy ground. The closer we inched toward the building, the more threatening it became, the deeper my stomach dove. I raked my memory for the places in the area Macy had mentioned worth visiting—historic homes, a theatre, a dog park. Clearly, this was none of those. Whatever it was, it was larger than any of those and reminded me of the fancy Biltmore Hotel back home. If the fancy Biltmore Hotel were dead and gutted.

"Hey, uh...lobo, I don't want to get any closer," I told the wolf, as if wolves could understand either English or Spanish.

The wolf insisted I follow, still glancing over his back to make sure I was on his tail.

We were almost there. From a short distance, I could see a few details—cracks on the side walls, on the columns supporting the back veranda, around double wooden doors and the few windows still intact. Half the side walls were consumed by ivy and moss, the other half with graffiti. Breezes from the lake blew through the broken windows, creating a cooing sound. Whatever this place was, it'd been empty for a long time. Standing there, staring at it, I lost track of time. It could've been nine, eleven, or one in the morning. All I knew was that the quarter moon had arced in the sky since I left the house.

"Is this where you live?" I asked Lobo, deciding the name fit him. Maybe his pack was inside the building, smaller black wolves all huddled away from the summer elements.

Tearing my gaze off the structure, I looked for the wolf, but he'd moved. That was what I got for taking my eyes off him. What if his next move was to pounce on me from the darkness? What if this had all been a ruse to lure me away from human life in order to attack then ration my flesh to his wolfish family?

It'd been hard enough keeping track of him in the woods. Now, surrounded by knee-high grasses, he could've easily been hiding in the reeds. I waded through the sea of grass up to the building's back veranda where old wooden planks rotted in spots. I reached for a two-foot-long splintered piece of wood, twisting it off its frame to carry with me as a weapon. The black, rusted nail on the end looked like six tetanus shots to me.

The building had double entrance doors every fifteen or so feet, about six sets from what I could gather at a distance. A large open space in the middle opened to a courtyard closed off with huge walls of glass. Part of me wanted to touch the walls, run my fingers along the stucco, feel the solidity of everything in my dreamlike state. Should an intrusive thought enter my mind, I could always pull my hand off quickly.

When I tried yanking a door into the building open, it wouldn't budge. Above were cracks from the building's settling, which had caused the walls to put pressure on the framework.

No negative thoughts came to me, but visions flooded my mind.

Whatever this place had been, I could "see" the throngs of people it'd hosted over the years. They circulated through the doors and onto the veranda, greeting each other in vintage clothing, nodding their hellos, saying things like, "Good morning. Out for a bit of fresh air?" I imagined sets of silver being carried around, fresh orange juice, and rowboats along the lake. I imagined a whirlwind of bustling activity. At times, I saw nurses pushing sick people around in wooden wheelchairs.

It was lifeless now.

The third set of doors was open. I peeked inside and smelled the musty scent of humidity and decaying wood, not a terrible smell by any means, just old. When I stepped over the threshold, goosebumps broke out all over my arms, even in the summer heat. As my eyes adjusted to a new level of darkness, I could see the place was trashed. Light fixtures were dusty, walls broken, bricks exposed, and a fireplace I didn't understand (because Florida) was filled with dust and charred wood. Dirty papers rocked in the breeze. Cloth-covered couches sat, longingly awaiting guests. A black plastic binder lay on the floor, its pages glued together with humidity.

The room I was in opened to what appeared to be an even darker hallway, but I wasn't sure how far inside I wanted to explore. I'd seen enough. I should leave and come back another day while the sun was out. With Macy. On the other hand, there was nothing scary about an old building, I reminded myself. My father used to be fascinated by them, telling me stories of when the Biltmore Hotel in Coral Gables used to be abandoned in the early 1980s before its renovation. This building was just that—an empty shell. A place that time forgot. How often did I have a place *all to myself*?

I stepped in further.

The long, center hallway was like an artery, stretching across the entire width of the building, the spinal cord from where all the rooms branched out. Where I stood in the south wing, I could see clear across to the middle of the hotel, where vague light seeped in. The northern part of the hall disappeared into gloom. Standing here, holding my breath, my heart began a steady pound.

I sucked in a breath, told myself to chill out. Nothing was here, nothing but a wolf who wanted to play hide-and-seek. Wolves I could deal with. Wolves were already in wolf's clothing, so there was nothing to mistrust. Huge, empty buildings, on the other hand...so many secrets lurking.

Then came the sounds, like shuffling, from somewhere behind me. Maybe I was right, and this was Lobo's cave. Hopefully I'd find a family of black pups all wondering who this intruder was and not the secret home of the surreptitious skunk ape of Florida legend. I was about to turn around and leave the same way I came when I saw the glow. Way down the central nervous system hallway, soft beams of light split the darkness, erratically shifting in a way only human hands could command. The beams swayed back and forth, cutting through the dark.

People.

I stood rooted to the floor, my pulse inside my throat.

Why was I here again? What on God's green Earth had possessed me to walk this far from the house, not to mention drive so far from home, to venture into complete unknowingness, now faced with the possibility of running into other humans—humans that may or may not be harmless?

On the other hand, maybe they were exploring just like I was. God, I hated that place my mind immediately went to, where any light was a demon, and every noise was the bogeyman out to kill me. I had a whole community to thank for instilling anxiety into my soul.

But I hadn't come this far only to turn back like a wuss. Doing so would only confirm what I'd known all my life—that I was a coward.

I walked toward the glow in the gloom, careful not to trip on anything, using my feet and the piece of wood to guide me. I crossed what appeared to be the center lobby, what vaguely resembled a welcome counter to my left inside a grand entranceway, dark, broken, battered to shreds. Graffiti covered the inner walls, though I couldn't tell what anything said. It'd be worth another look during the day. In the corners of the lobby were Corinthian columns topped with marble fishtails and ocean waves, and the interior was quite possibly the most beautiful I'd ever seen, decay, vandalism, and all.

Behind me, something stood in silence so deafening, I had to turn around and face it. An enormous glass enclosure stretched into the tower above. An atrium, its broken glass bursting with leafy green plants invading through busted-out panels, foliage growing with no rhyme or reason. Statues of ocean life inside it were overtaken by vines and moss, and in the middle, a tall, dried-out fountain of a mermaid holding the sun in her hands, her hair flowing over her shoulders and stony breasts gave me a start.

Suspended in the center about twenty feet off the ground, stabilized by four cables, was a crystal chandelier. Turned off, of course. Electricity hadn't made its way here in ages. But somehow, that made the light fixture all the worse, hanging like a dark reminder of a heart that used to beat and a fountain that used to bleed.

I didn't know what it was about the room that gave me chills. I just knew I didn't like it. It almost seemed like someone was, watching me from the dense vegetation. I shuffled away as quickly as I could toward the light beams and my original purpose. I moved slowly, doing my best not to make any sudden noises, just in case I happened to stumble upon the hidden location of drug lords or an angry alien civilization. This was Florida, after all—anything could happen.

But as I got closer and listened, sounds became words, and words became conversations. "I didn't, did you?" someone said.

"No."

"Then, who did?"

"I'll go check..."

Someone had heard me. They would walk out and find me here, cowering in the hallway. I hurried to meet them head-on, so it wouldn't look like I was hiding. I peeked through the open doorway. First thing I spotted was a thick pillar candle glowing in the middle of the floor of what seemed to be a ballroom, judging from heavy green curtains, parquet floors, and more dark chandeliers. In every corner of the room were bags piled together made of modern polyester and drawstrings. Empty cans rolled around. An orange electrical cord snaked its way toward a generator, and books and notebooks sat splayed open.

Human things. Modern things. And the strong smell of burning herbs.

The only moving person was a tall guy in jeans, leaving through the side door, while others watched him from scattered, standing positions. In the pulsating light of the candle, three faces turned to me. Cautiously, I stepped into the room.

"Crow..." one of them said.

The guy leaving stopped and turned. They shifted to the center from different corners, stepping from behind walls and a busted piano into the candle's glow—light face, dark face, spiky hair, long hair in dreads, one of them hatted, all young, about my age, maybe older, a mixed bag. One of them, a beautiful genderless person with glowing bronze skin and half a shaved head, stepped forward.

"Hey," they said.

"Hey," I replied, my throat dry as pulverized bone.

"Who are you?"

"Vale."

"Vale," they repeated.

"Yes."

"I'm Mori. We've..." Mori calculated their companion's reactions regarding how much they should tell me. Seemed fine by everyone else. "We've been waiting for you."

"Me?" I said in disbelief.

"Yes." They smiled a beautiful, kin-hearted smile. "A long time."

Six

It was a dream—it had to be. I quickly reviewed everything that had happened tonight. Dinner, good talk with Macy, peaceful nighttime meditation outside, then a black wolf had led me here, to this abandoned place that wasn't so abandoned.

Sounded reasonable.

"There are no cars outside. I would've mentioned it," a girl said behind Mori. She was a pixie little thing with flowing strawberry blonde hair and a green skirt that swept the floor like an enchanted broom. Around her neck hung a string of colored beads.

"I didn't drive here," I explained.

They were trying to figure out what to make of me, whether I was here to blow the whistle on them, or what. Their faces, frozen in various states of blank expression, stared at me.

I turned to leave. "Anyway, sorry to bother you."

"Don't go," Mori said, rushing up.

"Who are you guys?" I stammered.

"We live here," Mori said.

"Mori," the tall guy who'd been leaving interjected.

I did a visual scan of them each to make sure there were no red flags I should be heeding. No knives, no guns, chainsaws...

There were four of them—the tall, White guy who was on his way out when I walked in. He had cropped purple hair, spiky on top, jeans and a Ramones T-shirt; the pale girl with the long blonde hair and hippie skirt; Mori with piercings on their nose, cheek, eyebrow, and outer lip; and a guy without a shirt lingering in the back who was Black and didn't know what to make of me either. None of them could be older than twenty-three or twenty-four. I was sure I was the youngest.

"What do you mean you've waited for me?" I asked, a nervous quaver in my voice. "I think you mean someone else. I didn't even know this place existed an hour ago."

"You didn't know you'd be here," said the tall guy with short purple hair.

"I don't understand."

"You, or someone, is supposed to be joining us soon."

"But I told you, I had no idea—"

"We did," the guy said, edging closer to me with his flashlight. As he approached, I saw he had impossibly blue eyes that seemed to glow with a light of their own. They narrowed.

"How?" I asked, taking a step back.

"Through a dream."

"I swear, I'm in a dream right now."

"Crow, let me." Mori came over. "So, it's complicated. We knew someone would show up tonight, and then you did. We're taking it as a sign. And...we're big into signs."

They all laughed softly, which helped put me at ease.

"Sorry if we're being rude," the girl with the long blondish hair stepped up, stopping two feet short of me. She was even more beautiful close up, with bright brown eyes and creamy, freckled skin. Her hair was actually in dreads. "I'm Fae. That's Wilky," she said about the guy in the back without a shirt. About the tall one, she said, "That's Crowley."

Crowley didn't warm up to me right away, but he looked

slightly less threatened now that Mori and Fae were handling things.

"I'm Valentina, Vale. I went for a walk and somehow ended up here. Sorry if I interrupted something."

"Just randomly ended up here?" Crow asked. He and Wilky exchanged looks.

"Yes," I said. "I was outside my sister's place. A wolf appeared. He started walking into the trees, and..." I realized I sounded crazy, following a wolf through the woods and ending up a mile or two away on the other side of reality. "You know what? I'm just gonna go."

"Valentina, Valentina," Fae sang, dancing up to me and taking my hand without warning. I cringed. Touching people made me nervous. She stared into my soul. Light brown eyes scanned the particles I was made of and made the assessment that I was no one to fear. "You said a wolf led you here?"

"Yes, you haven't seen one?"

They shook their heads.

"I lost track of where it went. I thought maybe it had a den in here. That's why I came in. I was looking for him. Do you...you do live here?" Were people allowed to camp out in empty buildings?

"Sort of. We're clairs," Fae replied, beaming with pride.

"Clairs?"

Fae reached out for Mori's hand and clasped fingers with them. "Never mind. We've known each other since we were kids. Crow invited us here after his dream."

"The dream again," I said.

"I'll explain later," Crow said. "We just want to make sure you're the right person. We have a goal we're trying to accomplish, so if you're not, we're going to have to ask you to leave."

"Dude," Mori said. "That is so rude."

He threw his arms out. "It's not. We don't know if she's a clair."

"Sorry," I said, "but...what are clairs?"

Fae twirled. "We see things, hear things. Take Mori—they feel things others can't."

"Clairsentience," Mori clarified.

Clairsentience. I'd heard about that in one of the thousand articles I'd skimmed over the last year.

"Wilky can hear things," Fae said, glancing at the guy in the back, who looked like he'd rather she shut up about his private abilities. "Sorry, but she needs to know."

"Clairaudience?" I asked.

"Yes!" Fae clapped her tiny hands together. "And Crow sees things...well, sort of."

"So, you're clairvoyant?" I asked Crow.

"Not to the level of some people," he replied, pointing his flashlight to a spot on a sleeping bag. "I can sense what's not physically there, but I need my tools."

He was aiming his flashlight at what looked to be a camera bag. I didn't want to pry. I turned to Fae. "And you?"

"Clairgustance and alience." She closed her eyes and took a long sniff. "I can taste and smell residual smells a place leaves behind. Doesn't always work, though. Want to see my garden?"

"Later, love," Mori said. "Don't overwhelm her."

I gave an uneasy laugh. A million questions roiled through my mind, even as the deep-rooted fearful part of me told me to go home, stay safe, and stick to the familiar.

"Our gifts only work part of the time," Mori clarified. "That's why we're here, honing and developing them. Getting better. What better place than this, right?"

I nodded.

"Crow came first. He dreamed that four other clairs would join him. So far, three have. We've been waiting for the fifth clair."

A fifth? I shook my head. "That can't be me. I don't have

special powers. I wish I did, but I don't," I said. I may have loved reading tarot cards, but that didn't make me a clair.

"Oh, but you do." Fae's whole countenance lit up with an inner light that felt magical and unnatural at the same time. "We all have it. Every single person on the planet. Some never develop it. Others have had it since birth. You've never had experiences that are hard to explain?"

I thought back to times in my life when having super senses would've gotten me out of situations. I never had a clear sense of being psychic, if that's what she meant. I only sometimes got weird thoughts whenever I touched objects or people.

This was a case of mistaken identity. "I think you're waiting for someone else. I'm nothing special."

Mori, Fae, Wilky, and Crowley all exchanged glances in the dim candlelight. Mori's chest shook with laughter. "That's what we all thought about ourselves at some point."

The only research I'd done into my ability pointed to OCD. Intrusive thoughts happened to a lot of people, but I wouldn't call thinking about my grandfather in his office when I touched Scary Mary a "power."

"What is this place?" I looked around the ballroom. "It's huge."

"You're not from around here, are you?" Crow pushed his back against the wall, allowing his weight to slide down until he was sitting on the floor.

"I'm not. I'm from Miami."

Fae pointed at Wilky. "So's he."

"Was, a long time ago," Wilky finally spoke in velvety tones, settling into a cross-legged position on his sleeping bag. "I haven't been since I was little. You're familiar with Little Haiti?"

"You're familiar with Little *Havana*?"

He smiled, a nice smile that brightened his entire aura.

Feeling calmer now, I walked in and began strolling around. "Was this a hotel once?"

"Depends on when you're talking," Mori said. "First, it was the Sunlake Springs Sanatorium from 1918 to 1943. After the advent of antibiotics, it became a psychiatric hospital for women until... 1960?" They looked at Crow.

"1958," Crow corrected. "After that, it was a WWII veteran's hospital until the summer of 1970. It was closed for about five years. Finally, from 1975 to 1979, it reopened as a new age wellness spa—the Sunlake Springs Resort. People have always believed this area to have healing powers."

"Because of the lake," Fae explained.

"The dirty cesspool?" I pointed to the algae-covered body of water I'd almost waded into while following the wolf. Everyone nodded. "Doesn't look very healing at all."

"There's a special energy here. We all feel it," Mori said, walking over to a blown-out window and staring out into the night. "That's why this area has attracted so many witches over the years."

"Mori," Crow snapped them off with a sharp tone.

"Uh, spiritualists," Mori corrected.

"It's okay. I know you mean healers, psychics, etc. I've been studying," I said.

"No, we mean *actual* witches," Mori said.

"Mori," Crow again reprimanded.

"So, you *are* a clair!" Fae smiled, tapping her fingertips together.

"I said I've been studying," I explained. Modern witches were simply anyone with the ability to heal through natural, holistic ways, not green cackling women who rode around on broomsticks. "Why was the building closed for five years?"

"Buildings get bought, sold, or transferred," Wilky said. "The county makes a decision on whether to destroy it for good or give it another chance. That's also why we're here, because Crow has a dream!" Wilky chortled.

"Shut up," Crow deadpanned.

"Let me guess. You'll tell me later?" I asked him.

"You know me so well already." Crow gave me a tight-lipped smile, as he uncapped his camera lens and proceeded to clean it with a soft cloth in the beam of his flashlight. "Anyway, you want to stay with us?"

"I..." His question threw me off-guard and presented me with brand new options for my visit to Yeehaw Springs.

"There's a portal here. An energy vortex," Fae said, her enthusiasm lighting up the dark. "You can feel it, if you tap in. We could combine forces. We could make ourselves stronger..." She reached out for my hands again.

"No, I..." I didn't want to hold hands with her or anyone. My hands told stories. They messed with my head. "I don't know, guys."

Crowley cocked his head. "Okay, look. We need a fifth spiritualist. We need your help opening the portal."

I stared at him, slack-jawed. I'd never as much as opened a can of black beans without someone's help, much less a portal of energy. The thought made me ashamed of how sheltered I'd grown up but also set my imagination alight.

"Didn't you say you were drawn here inexplicably?" Mori asked, moving in on me.

"Well, yes, but..."

"I was curious once." Mori raised their eyebrows and looked at Fae who giggled and twirled, showing off the sweeping circles of her skirt. "That's how it begins."

"It?"

"Growth." Mori smiled.

"Alright," Crow interrupted, procuring a lantern out of his

stash of belongings, lighting it with a lighter. "We can't use someone who doesn't want to be here. Just let her go."

I immediately felt relieved, but from the sly grin he was trying to hide, I realized it was a scheme to get me to stay. Wilky, Fae, and Mori all exchanged silent communications while I stood there, trying to figure out what I wanted.

On one hand, I wanted the safety and solitude of Macy's house where I could think without four people staring at me. I wanted the familiar. I liked knowing I could hop in my car and go back home if I chose to.

On the other, I liked these people, this assorted crew of weirdos. I wanted into their special club, regardless of who they were or whether or not I belonged. They were nothing like the friends I hung out with back home, nothing like each other. Four harmonious points on the cardinal compass.

"Valentina, we need you," Fae said.

"Tell me again why?" I asked.

"So we can better communicate with this place," Mori said.

"So we can find out what really happened here," Wilky added. The others nodded. "The records don't tell the whole truth. Things happened here that we can't prove."

Fae softly curled her hand around my shoulder. "We have fire." She pointed to Crow. "Water." She pointed to Mori. "Air." She looked at Wilky. "And earth. That's me." She pressed her palm into her chest. "Now we just need spirit to hold us together."

They were all staring at me hopefully.

Fae smiled. "That's you."

Seven

When I was thirteen, my father heard from Macy for the first time. At home, the yelling began, and my parents separated for the second time. The first time was before I was born, while they were still boyfriend and girlfriend, apparently when Macy was conceived.

But I wouldn't know about Macy for another year. After months of my parents trying to work things out, my mother asked my father to leave. On that day, he stood on the front porch, holding my hands. I could feel his sadness through his skin. Tears streaked down my face. The car engine was on.

"It's only for a little while. Until your mom and I figure out what we want to do," he'd said.

I threw my arms around him, reining him in tighter, smelling the woody scent of his neck. Maybe if I showed him I loved him more, he'd stay. "Papi..." I still called him Papi in those days. A year later, when I'd learned from my grandfather Cuco that my father had another daughter with another woman who was not my mom, it would become Dad.

"Vale, it's okay. I'll drive down every other weekend to see you, okay?"

No, it wasn't okay. I wanted my dad home with me. I didn't care if he and Mami were fighting. Fighting happened. Fighting was normal. It would soon go away. We could be happy again if we just tried. Why did he have to leave Miami?

I remember him trying to pry me off in the most loving way possible, but it still felt like my world was imploding. Watching him drive away. Waiting for him to come back to see me. Only seeing him once a month hurt—he hadn't kept his promise of every two weeks. Work kept him busy, he said. Seeing his closet empty with only hangers in it hurt, too. Seeing the stained-glass sun ornament he'd made as a kid missing from its spot by the window destroyed me.

I thought about this now, as I faced the clairs. I realized why— I was clutching the cross charm, the one he'd given me. I let it go. Maybe I did have an ability.

"Let me think about it," I told them. "I'll be back tomorrow."

THAT NIGHT, I dreamed of a wolf, dark pewter in the moonlight, leading me along, through the forest, around a lake until we reached a massive shell of a building that used to be somebody. In my dream, it'd been alive at one point, this human being of a building. Now it sat empty, a shriveled ghost of its former glory, whispering like the elderly when you lean in close to hear their innermost secrets, as death knocks on their door.

In my dream, the wolf lingered in the doorway between the real world and this other sanctum, a portal to the other side. It asked for my verdict. Was I in? Would I join the others? The wolf needed to know. It was personally invested in my decision. When I told Lobo no, I couldn't, I was too scared, he tipped back his chin and howled.

I awoke.

Macy's guest room again. Sunlight.

I sat up quick, remembering the entire night before. These clairs, this wolf, I had actually seen and met them. Last night. It hadn't been a dream. I'd told a group of people at the Sunlake Springs Resort that I would think about it—being part of their group—that I had to go for now. Then I did. I left in a hurry back the way I'd come around the lake, retracing my steps through the woods all the way to Macy's yard. By then, I'd expected my sister to be waiting for me, pissed and wondering where I'd been.

But she wasn't my mom or abuela about to unleash unfathomable guilt. She'd gone to bed, leaving me the light on. No note, no texts from her waiting on my phone. I'd felt trusted, old enough to make my own decisions. Nobody to give me a guilt trip felt oddly liberating.

Adrenaline rushed through my limbs. I dressed quickly and flew downstairs, eager to research The Sunlake on my phone, see what the hotel was all about, why it wasn't on Maps when I'd searched the area. Macy was in the kitchen, having brunch in her PJs and working. "Good morning! There's coffee."

"Thanks."

"Did you sleep okay?"

"Yeah. That bed is super cozy. Makes me want to sleep too long. Hey, can I ask you something?" I came to stand by the kitchen table where I could see outside, toward her yard and the banyan tree to make sure I hadn't imagined my nighttime frolic through the Central Florida landscape.

"Shoot."

"Last night, I went for a walk."

She nodded. "I wondered where you went. Find anything interesting? I'm sorry there's not much around here." She flipped through her iPad and wrote notes on a pad beside her.

"Well, that's the thing. I didn't mean to go as far as I did. Thought I'd just poke around, but then I ended up walking farther than I thought." I left out the part about how a wolf acted as my tour guide. "I stumbled into an old place a couple of miles from here. An abandoned building?"

"The Sunlake Springs?" she asked. "An old dinosaur swallowed by trees? Looks like it's drinking from a poisoned puddle?"

I laughed. "That's the one. What was it?"

"Oh. That's an old Florida ruin," she sighed. "Basically, a long time ago, Florida was nothing but swampland. It wasn't even considered part of the South, that's how uninhabitable it was." She laughed. "But when TB got really bad in the early 1900s, people flocked here in the hopes the warm weather could cure them."

"TB?"

"Tuberculosis. They believed the fresh lakes had healing powers. I told you about Cassadaga, the little town not too far from here, right? Founded by a medium whose own spirit guide told him to build a camp near the healing waters of Central Florida's lakes. Anyway, before you know it, sanatoriums for healing the sick began popping up all over. That place is one of them."

"Why did it close?"

She shrugged. "Dying breed? A relic of a bygone era?"

"But couldn't someone turn it into a new hotel or something? That's what they did with the Biltmore Hotel in Miami. It reopened after being closed for, like, twenty years."

"Not all hotels are so lucky," Macy said. "Some close when they lose relevance. Up here, people started flocking to Disney in the 70s. Nobody wanted to stay in an old resort on a lake too small for boating, especially a place with an identity crisis like that one. Sanatorium turned mental hospital, turned spa? The spiritualists at Cassadaga tried turning it into a new age resort for a short while, but by then, people were only interested in theme parks."

It saddened me that The Sunlake Springs couldn't recover from the theme park industry boom, and it was too far from the shore to be a beach resort, too. It was just smack in the middle of swampland.

"What do you consider a spiritualist?" I asked.

"Psychics, mediums, people who see dead people. Why?"

"Just curious." I thought of the clairs, how they were looking for a fifth spiritualist. If that meant someone who could see dead people, it was definitely not me. "Anyway, it was sad to see, a beautiful old hotel just rotting away in the dark."

I didn't mention the clairs. Didn't want her to alarm her. Even though Macy had given me carte blanche since I'd arrived, old habits died hard.

She looked up sadly from her iPad. "Will you be going back?" she asked. Concerned, but not judging.

"Not sure. Do you want to come along?" Though, somehow, I didn't think the clairs would approve of me bringing outside people. I grabbed coffee and a granola bar.

"I wish," she said. "But I'm slammed."

"It's okay. Truly."

"I feel like I've been ignoring you," she said.

"Honestly. I'm having more fun than I've had in years." I sounded sarcastic, but it was true.

At that, she raised her eyebrows. "Well, you know Yeehaw Springs is notorious for its hair-raisin' good times!" She laughed and collected her things, tousling my hair. "I have to get back to work, sis. See you in a bit."

"Okay." I watched her go and smiled from behind the rim of my mug.

She called me "sis."

IT WAS RAINING when I left the house. I remembered to bring my phone this time for taking pictures, and an umbrella, too. As late afternoon thunderheads rolled across the land, my car bumped along an overgrown path, which should've been my first sign that The Sunlake Springs didn't want visitors. When I came upon the metal gate leaning at an angle, it hit me why I'd come through the back way last time.

Where was my wolf when I needed him?

I leaned on my steering wheel, squinting through the semicircular path of the windshield wipers at the hotel's silhouette in the distance. The resort's central tower lined up symmetrically with the center of the gate, and when lightning struck nearby, I caught a glimpse of the building's façade. Even in decay, the old place was beautiful. If I stared at it long enough, I could see cars and ambulances pulling up, dropping off patients, hearses hauling away the dead.

I was thinking how to proceed, if I should get out here and hike the rest of the way, when a robust wind shook the car. Ahead of me, the massive iron gate swung open with a long creak.

"Um...okay."

I squeezed my car through the open space, hoping it'd fit, relieving me from having to get out and widen the gate by hand. My clunker fit fine, and I managed to drive the rest of the way to the front portico. Going around a circular stone path, I finally parked underneath a covered driveway next to a white truck with a pool company business logo.

For a minute, I sat there, too, waiting for the rain to die down, taking in the building's façade. It had definitely once been beautiful, but now needed major repairs. My father would've called this "a Tuesday night special," as he named any badly decrepit building he had the pleasure to inspect. The front doors featured a great, big bronze sun rising out of a body of water and eels or giant fishtails splashing the surface.

I stepped out and ran over to the doors, realizing, once I got there, that they were chained together. "Shit."

I checked every door and window. Locked. Locked again. Spiny droplets pelted my face and body, as I battled with each door stuck to its frame. Eventually, I found an unlocked one that gave way when I tugged at it. I entered what seemed to be the area behind a front reservation desk. It faced a two-story lobby, and I realized that ahead were the columns decorated with fishtails and ocean waves I'd seen the night before. Two huge gilded birdcages sat empty on their metal stands. I hadn't seen those in the dark.

Outside, thunder cracked. I shook off the rain from my shoulder-length mop of hair and stupidly tried using a curtain to dry my arms. Rookie mistake. The layer of dust was so thick, it left dark streaks of grime on my wet skin. Whatever, I was in. And thanks to storm-filtered sunlight coming in through arched windows, I could see. The place had some furniture—old wooden chairs, velvet sofas turned on their sides, a few dead lamps. Walls, columns, and floors served as canvases for graffiti. On one wall, someone had practically sprayed an essay:

The lady lives!
You should go. And...
Punk ass bitch

...were a few of the lovely epithets scrawled in neon colors across peeling wallpaper. The whole place seemed to wallow under a heavy blanket of regret that made an ache throb deep in my chest. Roaming through the lobby, I got a better look at the two birdcages. I loved the ones at the old Biltmore and knew most of the glamorous buildings of the time had them. It must've been a beautiful sight back in the day, filled with finches, parakeets, and cockatiels.

I coiled my fingers around one of the bars to see inside better. A grinding sensation, like the giant propeller of an ocean liner starting up, awoke inside me. My stomach felt like it'd suddenly developed a tumor that pulsed as it grew. I pushed back on the bar and skittered, gaping at the cage.

Note to self: do not touch anything.

I hurried from the room, crossed the hallway, and stood at the entrance to the grand atrium to catch my breath. Once my elevated pulse subsided, I stared at the beautiful glass enclosure rising several floors into the sky. Rivers of rain ran down the sides of the glass, pooling onto the Mediterranean-tiled floor through broken panes. Enormous palm fronds and wild palmettos thrashed wherever the wind crept in. The large fountain's mermaid, hoisting her sun globe, gazed up hopefully. The center chandelier swayed back and forth like a chained monster, fighting its restraints.

I stood there, unable to think of anything but the sense that someone inside the atrium was watching me. But that was ridiculous; no one was there. Once, then twice, I checked behind me to make sure I didn't have a straggler. *It's nothing,* I told myself. While watching a ghost-hunting show one time, the investigator explained how high levels of electromagnetic fields could make a person feel like they were being watched. I wondered if the storm had anything to do with it, though I'd felt the same last night without a storm.

Standing in the hallway between the birdcages and the atrium felt like I was on the fence between worlds. And I supposed I was, in a way. Everything about this last year had that sense about it—I wasn't a child, but I wasn't a full-fledged adult either. I wasn't Catholic at heart, but I wasn't another religion either. I wasn't fully comfortable with the in-between and knew I had to start making choices soon, or suffer a sort of itinerant loneliness.

I strode into the atrium, all the way up to the mermaid fountain, and placed my hand on the stone bowl. If I had special powers, let it be known. Closing my eyes, I waited for visions to enter my mind, but all I could think about was a little boy. I had no idea what he looked like in my mind's eye, but I knew he was fascinated by this mermaid. In fact, the whole atrium had once been his magical playground.

My hand quivered on the stone. I tried to see the boy better, but the vision had gone, which was just as well, because suddenly, movement in my peripheral vision caught my attention. A swirling green mass hovered in the air, expanding and contracting like a school of silverfish being chased by a barracuda, shifting and ducking, and...*breathing?*

I sucked in a gasp and fell onto broken cobblestones. The sharp edge of one cut into the flesh of my palm without breaking skin. Biting my lip, I hugged my injured hand and glanced up at the swimming, swirling mass again that had looked so much like a sea creature for a split second. Upon closer inspection, it was nothing more than Spanish moss hanging off a tree, blowing violently in the wind.

Holy shit, that looked alive.
I held onto my cross.

My little starshine, sleep, oh, so tight
My little moonshine, dream with the night

I HAD to get out of here fast. If I explored the rooms again, I'd do it with one of the clairs by my side. Rushing into the hallway, I hurried towards the ballroom with mental blinders on, feeling like a total idiot. *Way to scare yourself, dumb ass.* I willed my heartbeat to slow, my lungs to draw deep, rehabilitating breaths.

"Hello?" I called.

If they were psychic, wouldn't they know I was here? And if *I* were psychic, I'd have avoided so many things. Touching that birdcage or that fountain, for example. Antoni last summer, for another. I'd have dodged that bullet a mile away.

"Mori, Fae?"

Wind whistled through cracked panes. Though it was summer with temperatures in the nineties, I hugged myself against a chill in the hallway. The resort did sit on the edge of a lake, a body of water, where breezes were bound to blow, I reminded myself. I was also damp from the rain.

When I reached the ballroom, I stepped inside. Mori, Fae, Crow, and Wilky weren't in. The carpet and wallpaper were a Victorian-era assault on my eyeballs. Bundles of bags and pillows lay scattered around the room. An electric burner, still ticking from recent use, was unplugged from the generator. I hovered over a pile of discarded lunch boxes. A handwritten note was still taped to one—

Hope you're hungry! – C.

Something on the dance floor caught my eye. Four white pillar candles set like a square, or a diamond, depending on how you looked at it. In the center of the diamond was a round, black iron receptacle. I would say cauldron, except it was more like a metal dish with a low lip. Inside was a grungy mix of ashes, shell fragments, sand, and an unburned corner of paper.

I crouched to pluck out the paper. In pen, someone had written: *Goddess Moon of fertile June, complete the circle and...* The rest was burned. I tossed it back in the dish and wiped my fingers on my shorts, squatting for a minute. In the light of day, it was easier to pick up on the building's desolation. A once-majestic hospital was now reduced to a shelter for squatters who burned bonfires inside her walls to try and rouse her secrets.

Crossing the room, I headed for the nearest window, parted the curtains, and peered outside. The rain was just barely beginning to let up slightly. A beautiful small herb garden glistened with fresh rain.

Behind me, someone spoke. "Do you see them?"

Eight

I whirled, catching fragments of light sweeping across the floor, sparking like electricity. Crowley stood in the doorway leading from the central hall, his tall form a darkened silhouette in the illuminated space. His hand, curled around the strap of the camera slung across his body, was tense.

"Sorry, didn't mean to scare you."

"Don't worry, I've scared myself enough already." I swallowed the lump in my throat. The sparkles of light were gone. "Do I see who?"

"The ghosts." He strolled through the room with ease, raising his hand in a twirling motion. "Spinning on the dance floor. Waltzing, having a great time."

"No," I said. "Why, do you?"

He stopped six feet from me. "Only in photos." He looked into the old-style camera he was holding and turned it around to show me. A swirly ectoplasmic mist hovered above the ballroom floor. "See?"

"Pretty cool," I replied.

"If I'm lucky, conditions are right. I have a great shot of this one mist, two, actually, standing right here. And I swear, if you look carefully, you'll see two people dancing."

I contemplated telling him all the visions I'd had in the ten minutes alone since I'd arrived but ultimately kept them to myself. I wasn't fully comfortable with Crow and kept scanning the outside veranda for the others.

"Where is everyone?"

He shrugged. "Scattered. We each have our favorite spots during the day. At night, we hang out more together." Crow's blue eyes really were beautiful; they were just so luminous, it was unsettling, especially when he stared at me as though testing how nervous he could make me.

I cleared my throat. "Why's there a ballroom in a tuberculosis hospital?" I asked.

"Lots of old buildings have grand halls where they'd line up patient beds for fresh air. This was back before there was A/C. They'd open windows; the lake breezes would blow through. It didn't become a ballroom until later."

"Because veterans wanted to dance?" I smiled, looking away. "Or because psychiatric patients needed to let off a little steam?"

Crow fixed a setting on his camera. He aimed the lens at me. I looked away, embarrassed by his attention. "They entertained guests. Some families could only celebrate special events here. They weren't allowed to take their sick loved ones off campus. It made sense to have a space for that. This was a new age resort, too. Maybe my mists are disco-dancing hippies."

"My grandparents used to hate hippies," I said.

"How could anyone hate hippies? They're full of love and peace, man," he said in a Californian drifter accent.

"I don't know, it's just what my mother said. Her whole side of the family has always been very strict. She grew up with law and order, religion, and yeah...I guess it made sense that they hated 'free spirits.'"

"Hate's a strong word." His eyes fell on the cross around my neck.

"I'm saying they did. I don't hate anyone."

"No one?" Crow moved around me like a shark, his eyes taking in everything about me. It took me a moment to realize he was framing his next shot.

Who I hated or didn't hate was none of his business. Besides, I didn't. Everyone deserved forgiveness, especially family. I wanted my father to know this so bad during the time he was away. I wanted to visit him, wherever he was living, to prove I wasn't mad that he had another daughter. That I still loved him, even though he hurt me.

"You don't talk much," Crow said. "You don't trust anyone with your secrets."

"I don't have secrets." But right away, I knew it was a lie. Memories I didn't want to share with a stranger weren't really secrets, just thoughts I preferred to forget.

"I'm glad you're here, Valentina. So, to be clear, last night, Fae made it sound like we have superpowers. We don't. That's why we want to open the portal," Crow said, moving to my left. "Don't move." He took a shot and then another.

"Why?" I asked.

He snapped another photo of me. I held up my hand, and he stopped. "Don't you ever want confirmation that the stuff you experience is real? For just once, I'd like to see ghosts actually dancing in front of me instead of just catching glimpses of them there."

"Maybe there are none," I said.

Crow shook his head. "They're there. Fae gets woken by the smell of blood. Isn't that nice? Mori can feel people's pain like it's their own. Wilky hears screams."

"Screams?" I clutched my cross.

My little starshine, sleep, oh, so tight...

Crow stepped up to me, and for a moment, a shudder slid through me. "Screams. Of five thousand patients who died here during the sanatorium and hospital years. Of war veterans with ghost pains. Of God-knows-what. So many things happened here over the years, and not all of them during the open years either."

"What happened while it was closed?"

"We don't know," Crow replied. "That's part of why we want to tune in. Opening a portal can help us find answers."

"Maybe the building doesn't want to give up its secrets."

He gave me a tilt of his head. "Why were you in here?"

I tried not to let his proximity or the cloud of weed smell clinging to him bother me. I didn't want him to think he made me anxious. "I was looking for you guys."

"Gotcha," he said.

"Look, I don't care that you're living here. I'm not going to inform anyone, if that's what you're worried about."

He stared another few seconds, then blinked, as the corner of his thin lips turned into a grin. "I *was* wondering, actually. What do think about this place?"

I sighed. "It holds a sad energy."

"What else? Of the building itself?"

I studied the decaying surroundings. "It's in bad shape. It's sad the way it's just rotting out here. Definitely beautiful, though."

His eyes narrowed. "Why'd you come back?" Crow pressed his hand against the wall next to my head, close enough for me to sense his warm breath. He could've been handsome by all typical standards—nice nose, strong chin, sturdy build with a hint of a colorful tattoo poking out of his sleeve—but there was something disingenuous about him that set off my internal alarm.

I stepped aside and jangled the keys in my hand. "It wasn't to snoop."

"But you *were* snooping. We're not drug addicts, or a cult, you know."

"I was just curious. I'm trying to understand why you say you need me. Seems like you have it all under control."

"We need the right person. Are you that person?"

I pulled out of his visual grasp. "I already told you I didn't think so, but you seem to think I am."

He looked at my fingers, dabbing at my cross. "Why do you touch that so much?"

I didn't even realize I'd been touching it again. "My father gave it to me."

"Do you see him when you touch it?"

"No. Do you? You're the clairvoyant one." It was a cheeky reply, but I didn't like the way he was drilling me, as if I owed him anything.

"You're being snide."

"You're getting personal."

He stared at me for the longest time. I wanted so badly to tear my gaze away, but I held it. It was a matter of control and showing him he didn't hold sway over me. "The others told me I had Spirit. What does that mean?"

Crow was distracted by something in the reflection of the mirrored wall. He turned and fired off a round of photos. "Spirit is all-encompassing. It's the general sphere that holds earth, air, water, and fire together. Spirit's job is to keep us from killing each other."

So, spirit was a little bit of everybody. "Like a mediator."

"Yes."

I could mediate. If I was good at anything in life so far, it was making sure everyone was happy. Make Mom happy, make Dad happy, make my grandfather happy, make the church happy, make Camila happy. Hell, I could've started my own United Nations with my mediating skills. It was my own happiness I knew nothing about.

The others arrived then, wandering in like dripping puppies

from the rain, in various stages of undress, holding their clothes in the crooks of their arms, shaking water from their hair.

"Heyyyy, she's back," Wilky said with a crooked grin. "Told you she would be."

I was surprised to see his mostly naked body, as he strolled toward his bundle of belongings on the floor and lifted a towel to wrap around his boxers. He may as well have been a sculpture escaped from a museum.

Fae's long blondish-reddish hair coiled down her fair shoulders like rat snakes, covering her small, bare breasts. She smiled at me, but I looked away at Mori who was half-naked as well. Two lateral scars across their chest told me Mori might've once had breasts in a former life but now was perfectly happy in their new shape.

"Are you in, Va-len-ti-na?" Fae enunciated my name carefully, correctly, then strutted toward her stuff, dripping on her way to grab a green towel. "The amplification is next week. During the full moon. We kind of need to know."

"Amplification?" I asked.

"Opening of the portal," Mori added, throwing on jeans and a T-shirt. "It's going to be an eclipse, too. Makes for a powerful cocktail."

"Right, so if you don't join us, we have to wait 'til next full moon and eclipse. Pretty rare combination. That's what the Lady of the Lake said anyway." Fae slipped into a brown dress that reached the dusty floor.

"Who?" I asked.

"I'm shocked Crow didn't tell you in the time you were alone with him. It's all he talks about," Fae laughed. Crow shook his head and walked to the windows to look out. She stage-whispered, "It's a ghost."

"A spirit guide," Crow said. "Not a ghost."

"Sorry, a *spirit guide*," Fae corrected, still stage-whispering. "She's a tuberculosis patient. She jumped from the bell tower the first year this place was open, crashed right where the atrium is now, where it used to be just a garden. Splat!"

"Fae, be sensitive," Mori scolded.

"Sorry. Now she roams the resort, asking Crow for favors."

"That's not..." Crow shook his head, then looked at me. "That's not how it is. She comes to me in my dreams. I have conversations with her. Sometimes, I think I see her roaming the hotel."

"Is that why you take photos? To try and capture her image?"

"Yeppers," Fae replied.

"I can talk for myself," Crow shot at her. "Yes," he said to me.

"What does she say to you?" I asked.

"She predicts the future. She said Fae and Mori would join me, and they did. She said another would show up, a man seeking truth, and that was Wilky."

Wilky raised his hand in silent confirmation.

"She also says she sees the building coming back to life as a grand resort, filled with people, enjoying a new era."

"She wants Crow to take the best photos he can," Fae said. "So the historical society can—"

"Okay, okay," Crow interrupted. "She doesn't need to know everything. Not if she's not committed to helping us. What if she goes and tells the county everything we just told her? Then what?" Crow slung his camera onto his back. Disgusted, he walked out of the ballroom.

Fae's shoulders slumped.

Mori shook their head at their girlfriend. "Valentina, it's really simple. We all have something we want from this place. Crow wants to meet his Lady of the Lake, I have my reasons, Fae has her reasons, Wilky, too. Haven't you ever wanted answers?"

I understood wanting answers. "Yes, for sure."

"Right. So, if you help us, we get to see better, hear better, feel better. What little abilities we have would become stronger, and maybe we'll finally be fully psychic, and in being fully psychic, we'll find answers. Get it?"

If their abilities were vague, then mine were even vaguer.

Would I still be here next week? I thought about my mother at home, doing her best to give me space but texting once a day to see how I was faring without her. She wanted me home. I wasn't sure I was ready. Macy said I could stay as long as I wanted. But would Macy be okay with me spending more time here than with her? It wasn't like she had much time for me anyway.

"Is that all? No other urgency?" I asked.

Mori, Fae, and Wilky exchanged glances. Wilky came clean. "The Sunlake might be demolished soon."

From the other room, Crowley groaned. "Dude."

"Bro, it's not like I'm telling her a fucking secret," Wilky shot back.

"Are you sure?" I asked.

"Mori's aunt in Cassadaga overheard people from DeLand talking about it," Wilky explained. "And, I mean, just look at the place. It's entirely possible."

"And if it's true, there's a lot we need to know before they tear it down," Mori said, running a hand through their half-shaved hair, flumping back against cushiony bags.

"I'm sure you can find answers with the county's historical society. Researchers, historians..." I suggested. "What do you need to know?"

"I have a great granddad who was a rum runner." Fae twirled in her dress, dancing with an invisible partner. "My grandmother kept his journal. He says he hid money here in the 1920s. That was before the hospital was built, when the Coast Guard was after him, but his name is in absolutely zero of the historical society's documents."

"Fae doesn't care about her grandfather. She's just a gold digger," Crow laughed.

Fae shot Crow a middle finger. "Have you noticed it's always rich people who talk like money doesn't matter?"

"Everyone to you is rich."

"Anyway." She looked at me. "I want to find the stash. Because money, sure, but also so my family can know the truth. Wilky isn't as greedy as I am."

Wilky didn't deny it. He didn't explain his reasons either.

Fae did a squat then launched into a scissor-like leap. The girl never stopped moving. "Mori wants to help the souls trapped here move on."

"They're in pain," Mori explained. "I can't stand to feel what they went through. We all deserve to move on into light and peace. I would want someone to do it for me."

"I get that." Once, Camila called me an empath. She said I picked up on the thoughts and emotions of whoever I was around, but I'd never tuned into the pain of the departed before. "What does Crow get from the amplification?"

"I get to be right," he called from the other room. "When the portal doesn't open, and the ritual doesn't work, you'll know it was because we invited the wrong person to help us."

Wait. I was the wrong person?

What had changed between last night and today?

"You don't know that, Crow," Mori muttered. "She knew where to find us."

Apparently, they'd talked after I left. Apparently, now he wasn't sure of me.

"You don't think it's me?" I asked. No wonder he was drilling me before the others came in.

"Him, not us," Fae said. "He thinks you're full of shit. He thinks a different clair will show up by next week."

I found myself seething at how much I wanted to prove Crow wrong. What if I did have a clair ability? What if it simply hadn't developed, but with training, I could make it work? I did find them, after all.

"What does he really get?" I whispered.

Fae dropped to the floor in a heap, arms raised over her head like a ballerina. "The Lady of the Lake will show herself to him in person. That's what she told him, so that's what he wants."

"To see his spirit guide," I said.

"He's a little obsessed with her," Mori said.

"Right?" Fae giggled. She turned into a zombie, eyes bugged out, arms straight out. "I...am...the lady of...the laaaaake."

Crow returned, throwing his lens cap into his heap of belongings. "You've both told her enough. There's such a thing as being too empathetic, Mori."

"Oh, yes, too much kindness and inclusion. I can see how that might be a problem in today's world."

"When you lose your ability to take on criticism, or the cruelness of the world, or knowing where a limit is, yeah—it is. How about you and Fae shut up already?"

"How about you bite me?" Mori scoffed.

"That's enough," Wilky spat. I was beginning to see what their dynamics were. Clearly, Wilky didn't care much for Crow, and clearly, Crow thought himself this group's leader.

"Yeah, Crowley, enough." Mori waved him away and walked out, muttering, "Fucker."

I felt bad for Mori. I may not have known them that well, but the stuff Crow said sounded uncalled for. "What do I get from helping you?" I asked.

"That's for you to decide." Fae took me into her arms before I could protest. She twirled me, and I politely stepped out of her generous hold. In her hands, I felt sadness, a life without much to go on, hunger. "Aww, nobody wants to dance with me." She pouted.

"Isn't there anything you want?" Wilky asked.

I wasn't about to tell them I wished I could have a real life, a reason to wake up every day, numbness gone from my life, my own decisions to make, my dad around to talk to...

"Whatever it is...opening the portal can help you find it," Wilky added. "It's like a kundalini awakening for a location's soul instead of a person's."

I didn't know what a kundalini awakening was, but I knew I would search it up the moment I got back.

My brain screamed at me to get back to Macy's. Go home. Go to church. Get back on the straight and narrow path my family had laid out for me. Stop hanging with strangers who dabble with the spirit world. If I accidentally invited something dangerous into my life, I'd never be able to put it back. Opening an energy vortex inside a haunted hotel sounded like a pretty terrible idea.

Suddenly, from the far reaches of the resort, someone screamed.

Everyone burst into action. The four of them hightailed it into the hallway, turning on their flashlights. I followed, not about to be left inside the ballroom by myself. Mori led the way, seeming to know where it was coming from.

I heard the sound again, only this time as a cry for help, a whimper.

Mori entered a room on the first floor where mobiles of stars and planets hung in the windows. On the wall, a tapestry featuring a seated human silhouette with seven colorful chakras lighting a vertical path along the spine hung askew. In the corner was a seated Buddha covered in graffiti mustache and beard.

"I've sensed her before," Mori said, gasping in the center of the room. Dirty, musty cushions lay scattered everywhere.

"I've heard her, too," Wilky added. "But on the third floor."

I didn't see anyone. And I was pretty damn sure we'd see a person here. That was how clear the scream had sounded. "Who is it?" I asked.

"We don't know." Fae sniffed the wall closest to her.

Crow began taking photos, shot after shot after shot, every corner of the room in quick succession like it would all evaporate if he didn't move fast enough. He took great care to frame the shots, adjust the camera's levels, then shoot again.

We waited for the sound to come again. My adrenaline had shot through the roof, my vision adjusted to new light levels. The rain was dying. Whoever had screamed was not anymore, and after a few minutes, the group collectively sighed and began trudging back to the ballroom, discussing the highlight of their day.

But I was rattled.

I saw what the clairs meant about their abilities being vague at best. I would've wanted answers, too. If a spirit was scared for some reason, I would want to help them. I was always grateful, in a way, that if my father had to go, he'd gone by heart attack. Quickly, with little to cause him pain. I would've hated knowing he was stuck on the other side. With nothing I could do to help him.

I walked into the house, set my keys by the door, and climbed upstairs. In my mind-numbing state of stress after hearing the disembodied scream, I forgot my no-touching rule and brushed the staircase railing with the palms of my hands. I heard another woman crying, but this one was begging.

I stilled to listen. The crying fizzled away.

"Macy?" I started up the stairs.

I found my sister throwing clothes into a small suitcase inside her room. She smiled and caught her breath. "Holy crap, you scared me. Okay, there you are. I was just texting you. Ignore my last message."

"Were you just crying?"

She looked at me blankly. I checked for redness in her hazel eyes. "No. Why?"

"I swear I just heard crying coming from upstairs." I glanced into the dark hallway.

"Maybe you heard my video? People screaming on a roller coaster? Yay, Florida?"

"I don't think so," I said. It had sounded like begging, pleading not to go. I rubbed my eyes. The hotel, and whoever had screamed, was still on my mind. "What were you texting me about?"

"Ah, so listen. They're having a meeting tomorrow in Orlando about a new project that came up. I'd rather drive tonight than get up early in the morning. Just wanted you to know in case you got back and found the house empty."

"How long will you be gone?"

She searched her drawers for shirts. "No idea. Just keep an eye on the house, garbage goes out Tuesday and Thursday nights, and lock all the doors if you go anywhere."

"I will. Remember I'm from the city."

"Yeah, well here in the middle of nowhere, most people don't. Did you have a good day?"

"I did. I took pictures of that hotel I told you about." Actually, I hadn't taken a single one and chastised myself for lying to Macy. I didn't need to do that anymore and hated the fact I'd been conditioned to.

"Well, be careful if you go urban exploring. Police are handing out hefty fines to trespassers, and that's one thing I can't bail you out of. Not until they give me a raise."

"Don't worry, I won't." It didn't feel right assuring her of something I didn't know for sure wouldn't happen. "Can I ask you something before I hit the shower?"

"Always."

"The other day you mentioned an energy vortex in this area, how people have been coming here for years in the hopes of feeling it."

"It's amazing what people will do to connect with the other side, isn't it?"

"Do you believe? In another side?"

She smirked, folding a white shirt. "I think so? I want to believe. But I honestly don't know. What about you?" She looked at me.

Slowly, I nodded. "I always have. I mean, the Father, the Son, and the Holy Spirit is all I ever heard growing up. My whole religion is about ghosts."

She laughed. "Isn't that funny? So true."

"But besides that, I don't think millions of people around the world would lie about their experiences. You know what I mean?"

"That's true, too. You're wise for your age, Vale."

"Thanks." I sat on the edge of her bed, remembering the times I tried to do the same with my mother but inevitably, our talks would descend into arguments over something. I loved that Macy and I could talk about anything. "If you had the chance to open a portal into the spirit world, what would you use it for?" I was nervous asking. Any moment now, Macy would ask what I was up to.

"Use the chance for?"

"Yeah."

She sat on her bed, running her fingers along the texture of her comforter. She looked up at me, and for a split second, I saw my father's smile in hers. I was elated to see him again, if only for a nanosecond. "I'd talk to our dad. Wouldn't you?"

NINE

Tarot cards in hand, I sat outside in the late evening after Macy had left. No matter which question I asked, I got a Major Arcana card which indicated major events in a person's life journey.

Should I stay home alone? THE HERMIT.
Am I on the right path? JUDGMENT.
Which path should I follow? THE STAR.

Answers were up for interpretation, sure, but I tried to go with my instinct. I'd hoped sitting under the moonlight would help, but nothing clear came to me. I needed guidance now more than ever. The Moon knew it all. Even dark, she was claircognizant. That was her most powerful time when she brimmed with pure potential. Tonight, she was halfway through waxing, bright enough to lead anyone through obscurity.

"What do I do?" I asked straight up, toes nestled in the cool grass.

I held my deck against my chest. A few cocuyos flitted from blade to blade, then chased each other into the canopy of the banyan. I kept my eyes out for my wolf, assuming I hadn't hallucinated him that night.

"Do I stay out of trouble, or go back?" I asked the moon.

I could hear Father Willie, Camila, and the rest of the gang telling me the answers lay with God. Just search my soul. They weren't wrong. But God was everywhere. Why did I have to find him in a church? God was just as much in the tepid outdoors of muggy swampland as He was anywhere else.

"Anyone?"

Talking to the universe—that was one thing about me that hadn't changed in the last year. Whether God was a He, a She, a They, or a collection of countless souls didn't matter. I knew that every moment of the day, someone could hear me. The spirit world was probably the only part of life I truly believed in. What kind of person would I be if I ignored its call?

But the Sunlake Springs scared the hell out of me. That atrium gave me nightmares. Could I hang with the clairs and not get caught up in my own fears? Could I handle screams in the middle of the night? Would it be any different at Macy's? I'd heard screams here just the same. At least at the Sunlake I wouldn't be alone.

"They can help me," I reasoned. "If they're really clairs, they can help me communicate with Dad. Right?"

I hugged my knees and gazed at the moon. "You're not helping at all. It was a simple question. A sign for yes. Silence for no. I'll accept whatever you say." I watched the sky for any streaks of light that might shoot across the cosmos.

Nothing.

Sighing, I turned toward the house. I was halfway across the yard when I heard it—a long, clear howl in the distance. I smiled. "I'll take that as a yes."

I ARRIVED PAST MIDNIGHT, duffel bag slung over my shoulder, hair wet from a shower, probably my last for a while. I brought all my stuff, including my fear, open-mindedness, sense of adventure, and cross around my neck. Just in case.

I heard them before I reached the auxiliary door through which I'd entered last time. They were laughing, shrieking, screaming in the empty corridors. Pausing outside the loose door, I listened. If I heard any Satanic singing, I'd get back in the car and drive home. I didn't believe in Satan in the sense of a horned, red demon with a long tail and trident, but I believed in evil like I believed in love, and I wouldn't mess with either.

The longer I listened, the more they sounded like people my age having a good time. I pulled the door handle and slipped into the front desk office, letting the door close softly behind me. I measured my way through the lobby, picking up shapes sitting in darkness—covered sofas, the old birdcages again, the columns with the fishtails. The interior was murky, filled with shadows that had me moving fast.

Again, I stopped in front of the atrium.

Again, I stared at it, despite the knot that formed in my stomach every time.

What was it about this room? By all accounts, it should've felt lighter, energetically. After all, there were plants, glass, and soft moonlight filtering into it. Even the mermaid sitting atop her fountain, holding up the sun was beautiful with the fine, rounded features of a cherub. Shadows here shifted, and yes, the Spanish moss freaked me out yesterday, but there was something else. Something I couldn't pinpoint. It was as if the atrium hated me.

That was utterly stupid. How could a place hate me? But that's how it felt, like the room itself was pissed that I was here. Like I was going to alert authorities that it, along with the rest of the building, was more than ready for demolishing. It didn't take an expert to see that.

Down the hall, the ballroom was pitch dark, its entrance hard to make out. I had to hold onto the walls for support and follow the sounds of laughter. When I did, I sensed immense sadness and pain. Isolation, desolation, worry that my family wouldn't come visit. They weren't my thoughts—they were somebody else's. I let go of the walls and the intrusive thoughts went away.

The floor felt unsteady. More than once, I tripped over something. A wave of discombobulation overcame me. I grabbed a column to keep from falling and immediately let go. Floor tiles were fissured and sunken, creating valleys in the hall. Finally, I saw the pulsating glow of candles come into focus.

"Bring her to me, bring her to me, bring her to me, three times three!" Fae was singing, her melodious voice echoing from an unknown location. I watched her emerge from the depths of hallway, sweeping down the corridor in her panties, strawberry blonde hair flailing out behind her. "Oh!" She stopped short when she saw me, skidding to a halt, honey eyes wide and startled. "I guess it worked."

I waved. "Sorry, I should've made a noise or something."

"She's here!" Fae cried. She did a sweeping pirouette and rushed over to me, the smell of burning sandalwood preceding her, as the others came out of the woodwork into the hall like ghosts permeating walls.

"You're back!" Mori, fully dressed, gave a triumphant clap. They glanced at Wilky, as though he'd had some sort of personal investment in my return. I suppose they all did, if having a fifth clair would help their causes.

I was glad to help. And now, I had a cause, too.

I couldn't wait to tell them.

Crow stood a good distance behind them all, watching me with that mistrustful gaze of his. I hated that he'd gone from happy I was here on the first night to not trusting me anymore. I felt almost personally responsible for his discomfort. He wore jeans without a shirt, showing off the tattoos I couldn't see before. Over his right pec was a skull intertwined with a moth. On the other was a beautiful nude woman, long hair sinking into a pool of water.

"Valentina, welcome back," he said, kicking aside the extension cord.

"Thanks." I patted my duffel bag. "I guess I'm here, if you need me."

Fae's fists tapped together. "You'll help us? You'll be the fifth?"

"I have nothing to lose," I said, letting my arms fall against my sides. I entered the ballroom, looking for a good space to call my own. It wasn't entirely true (having nothing to lose). I could easily get lost in their world, lose my soul, get arrested for trespassing, come home with a terrible reputation. But they would be mistakes of my own, and I was good for it.

Mori, Wilky, and Fae came charging at me, blurs of beautiful skin shades. They wrapped their naked, admittedly not-so-fresh-smelling arms around me, and I felt a deep sense of belonging. I'd come home to strangers and couldn't be happier with my decision. I was all too aware of Crow brooding in the shadows, but I wouldn't let it bother me. It was within his right not to trust an outsider.

"Let me make something clear," he said. The others quieted. "This place wants to live again. You'll feel its sense of survival in no time, Vale. But if I find out you're here to expose us, observe living conditions, record the number of cracks, or file paperwork for the county—"

"I'm not from the country, I told you that," I said.

"We've been here a year. You've been here a day. If you're going to help us, like you say you are, you have to swear that you don't have ulterior motives. We've seen them."

The others nodded.

"They come with their clipboards, hard hats, they take notes... They want this place torn down, and we've managed to delay them every time. The project I'm working on has bought us some time."

"Unity spell!" Fae ran off to grab a few things from her stash.

"The Sunlake is not just a place we love," Mori said to me. "Our future's here."

"Our past is here," Wilky added.

Crow walked up to me. "We'd do anything to see this place live again. So, if you stay, you're sworn to a vow of silence."

They looked at me, four beautiful beings vibrating at different frequencies. I imagined their auras in my mind. Fae's was green, Wilky's yellow, Mori's blue, and Crow's either red or orange.

"I'm only going to say this once...I just want to learn from you all. I want to help. And maybe you can help me, too. I think I figured out my why."

"Your why?" Fae asked.

"My reason. I lost my father a few years back. I want to communicate with him. I miss him," I said with some difficulty.

Crow stared through me one last second. "Then we have a week. Your training starts tomorrow." He collected the clairs into a hug and brought the bunch to me.

Everyone threw their arms around me, Fae plucked a strand of my hair, "for our unity jar," and someone thanked the goddess Hecate for my arrival. In their group hug, I felt a mixture of hope, excitement, but also apprehension. It was hard to tell if it was Crow's or mine.

Ten

I slept on my duffel bag using my rolled-up clothes for a pillow. Each clair slept in their own corner of the ballroom—Mori in the west, Fae in the north, Wilky in the east, and Crow in the south. That didn't leave me a corner, so I occupied an alcove along the east wall that opened to the back veranda. I might've been "Spirit" to them, but I couldn't be everywhere at once.

I spent most of the night staring at the ceiling, listening to frogs sing out by the lake. Shadows of moving foliage shifted in the dark. Once, I fell asleep only to be awakened by the sense of falling (hate that).

Another time, I dreamed I was in this building, following the sound of water dripping. I stood in the long, center hallway, staring at a soft green light at the end of the hall. Floating toward it, I ended up in a men's bathroom, and though I couldn't see him, was lucidly aware that somebody lurked there. When I turned to leave, an invisible force held me in place. I fought the force so hard, I woke up in a heavy sweat.

Eventually, I gave up on sleep altogether and headed out to watch the sunrise. Wide swaths of royal violet sky were pierced by yellow stick rays. Egrets and herons pecked through lakeside grass.

The lake's misty surface broke with jumping fish or snapping turtles. There had to be gators out there, too, but gators didn't scare me.

Barefoot, my feet picked up flecks of wet grass from yesterday's rain. From the corner of my eye, I saw a figure. It was Wilky, sketching in his sketchpad by the lake. He looked so serene, I didn't want to bother him, so I found a spot out in the wilderness to do my business. That gave me a different view of the Sunlake Springs Resort, all lit up as it faced east. What a sad, lonely, disheveled place it was. The north side even looked lower than the south.

As I headed back, I took a shadier path than the one I'd taken out. Most of the trees in the area, aside from the woods I'd walked through with Lobo, were bare and gnarly. Many leaned in the same direction, windswept and shaped by a past hurricane. One tree in particular was taller than the rest, thicker, twisted, like juniper trees of the West. It didn't look like a Florida tree at all.

I sat in the grass staring at it for a long time. A need for sleep overwhelmed me. My eyelids kept dropping, so I gave in to meditation. After a while, I heard voices—men whispering, giving each other orders. People were here. A survey crew? Hunters?

My eyes flew open, my legs ready to spring.

Plumes of orange light moved in a line just ten feet in front of me, bobbing up and down as they headed north. The voices disappeared, replaced by a sickly feeling in my stomach. More disembodied sights and sounds. My heart pounded against my rib cage. This place really was a hotbed of energy. I'd never been more receptive to anything in my life. I hadn't even touched anything!

Scrambling to my feet, I walked past the twisted tree, fighting the urge to stop and stare at it. I didn't want to witness creepy lights again, nor hear voices. I hurried back to the hotel. Wilky was gone. The others were slowly emerging from their sleep, Mori being the last to get up. Everyone got dressed quietly for the day, while I sat there contemplating what was happening to me.

If I was this receptive now, what would happen once we performed the ritual?

WE HEADED OUT ON I-4. Hot summer wind whipped through our hair, as we drove southeast toward Cassadaga in the back of Crow's truck. I'd never been to Cassadaga before. I'd never even heard of it, actually. Somehow a town full of occult people with occult abilities had managed to exist all my life, a whole municipality with its own magickal City Hall, and I'd managed to reach the age of eighteen having never known about it. If that didn't represent the bubble I'd been living in, nothing did.

Being surrounded by pool cleaning materials reminded me that when the clairs weren't busy being clairs, they led normal lives. "I never see Crow leaving," I shouted at Mori next to me.

"What?" they shouted over the wind.

"Crow. I never see him leave the hotel for work." I gestured to the pool supplies.

Mori shook their head. "It's his uncle's business. The man rents his extra trucks out sometimes. Cheaper for Crow than renting a car, I guess."

I nodded. Other people's lives were so different from mine. I couldn't imagine my own family charging me to use their extra car.

We arrived in Cassadaga to little fanfare. In fact, I didn't even realize we were there until I saw a sign. The sleepy town was one, maybe two cross streets, a lake, a big cemetery, a fairy garden trail, enough houses to constitute a neighborhood, a hotel, and a "downtown" area. Coming from a city with the 3rd tallest skyline in the country, I was underwhelmed.

Crow pulled into a space outside a duplex where both units had signs displaying mediumship services. Citana Rose lived on the left side painted light green with garden gnomes all around, while Barkley Nichols lived on the right painted yellow where angel statues poked out of the grass and cherub chimes dangled off porch eaves. Evenly distributed between both houses were several welcome-cats.

An all-pewter gray kitty without a tail mewed a hello before honoring me with his fallen body at my feet.

"Hey, Bob Meowly," Mori said.

I crouched to scratch under Bob's Meowly's chin, as a feeling of intense déja-vu overcame me. This house, the Sunlake Resort...I felt like I'd been here before when there was no way I ever had. Mori stepped up to the screen door, as Fae and Wilky sat on the porch swing looking through his drawings. Crow took a walk down a gravelly path. The door opened and a tall woman with tanned skin and a gray, shoulder-length blunt cut stood there with her arms out.

"My Mori!" she cried.

"You just saw me last week, Tata." Mori chuckled. "Meet my new friend, Vale. Vale, this is my auntie, Citana. She's exaggerating. We visit her all the time."

"No. They don't visit me. They pick up dinners I make them. Not the same." As Mori rolled their eyes, the woman with the crinkly skin reached out to give me a hug. "Nice to meet you."

"Nice to meet you, too." I was happy to receive a hug from a welcoming older woman. Guilt bombs went off inside of me for feeling this was how a grandmother-type should be, and for ignoring Abuela's texts over the last week.

Citana gave Fae and Wilky big hugs, as well. "And Crow?"

"Went for a walk." Wilky smirked.

Citana shook her head. "That boy. I bet he's tried to bully you, hasn't he? Don't let him bully you," she said to me.

I had no idea what to say to that. "I love your house." I stepped into the foyer. Wilky waved goodbye from the front porch. Guess this was between just us.

The house was filled with houseplants, stained glass birds, cushions on the floor, and a wide assortment of Seminole palmetto dolls. The wallpaper was flowery, and the small space smelled of copal and sandalwood incense. A plume of smoke rising from the east window confirmed it.

"Thank you," she said. "Would you like coffee?"

"After, Tata, after," Mori suggested, taking a seat on a couch that looked like something from the era of my mother's childhood pics. "Let's do the...thing first."

"Oh, right," Citana replied. "The thing."

Not sure what that was about. Maybe whatever we were about to do required that we keep empty stomachs. She led me to a small round table by the incense window where a deck of Tarot cards awaited us.

"You read cards?" Citana Rose's brown eyes searched mine.

I wasn't sure if she was asking or if she already knew. I decided to go with truth. "A little. I just started. I don't really know that much, honestly."

"I'm not supposed to read them either, but my mother is long gone." She smiled at the cross around my neck and tapped the chair. "Have a seat. Let me look at you."

I sank into a wooden chair fitted with a flowery cushion and tried to act comfortable. I'd never been to a psychic medium before. Growing up, all my otherworldly messages had come via the flamboyantly fabulous Walter Mercado on my abuela's Spanish channels. Funny how she had no problem with him, but tarot cards were off the path.

"This is informal, Valentina," Citana said, taking a seat. "But we'll get you protected in a jiffy."

I sat mesmerized, fairly sure that Mori had said my name was Vale, not Valentina. I was also in awe that other people spoke the same lifestyle language I did without freaking out about it. First, she burned loose herbs in a dish, then she wafted it into the space between us. Citana shuffled her fraying deck of cards, muttering a prayer in a language I didn't understand.

She smiled at me with a kind expression for a long time. I felt totally at ease with her reading me. Finally, she lay down four cards facing each other like a compass rose. They were all pages, one of wands, one of swords, one of cups, one of pentacles. All young people studying their craft, but the one in the middle was the High Priestess.

She looked at me. "You are gifted?"

"Uhh...sorry?"

"You don't know your gifts. Of course, that's why you're here." She said something else in her language, and Mori replied. Now I knew how gringos felt when we talked about them in line at Sedano's back home.

Citana threw down another card—the King of Cups, reversed, followed by the three of swords piercing the big red heart. "Your father was a troubled man?"

Was. "I don't know how to answer that," I said. "He was separated from my mother when he passed away. My father held a lot in, especially around my mom's family. He never quite fit in."

She nodded through a sad smile.

"He's with you. He's always with you," she said. It felt gratuitous, like something she would say to anyone with a loved one who'd passed.

"Do you see him?" My insides quivered at the thought.

She squinched her eyes. "I get impressions of a man around you, protecting you. He says he's sorry for the way he passed."

My eyes welled up. Dying hadn't been his fault. He took care of himself as best as he could; he monitored his health. Bad luck happened even to healthy people. I wiped my eyes with a finger.

"He died of a heart attack," I sniffed. "Not exactly something to be sorry for."

She gave me a tilt of the head. Next, she threw down the Moon card. "You're drawn to the moon." She pointed to the High Priestess she'd pulled and now this one. In my deck, it was symbolized by Hecate, Crone Goddess.

"Yes. Definitely."

"Keep doing everything you're doing." She looked over at Mori with a nod. They smiled, lips smashed together. "There is a lunar eclipse next week, though we won't see it in this hemisphere."

"I heard."

"The hidden comes to light."

I knew that much about eclipses.

"Your magical self is emerging," she said.

"Is it?" I doubted I had magic in me. I was interested, that was all. It was nice to hear I wasn't a horrible little devil, though, hell bent on making my family's life difficult. I almost cried at this more than her words about my dad.

Citana pulled out a smudge bundle and held it over the open flame of her candle, wafting the smoke over me with a feather while reciting an incantation. She told me to envision a purple light falling over me from head to toe, repelling negativity as it went. She told me to ask my spirit guides for help, or my father, or any of my ancestors, and they would be happy to assist.

I had a hard time imagining a spirit guide, only because I'd never seen one. It was hard to imagine what one couldn't see, but if I could do it for Jesus, God, and love, I could do it for a spirit guide.

"You're wise, Vale." Citana reached for my hands when she was done.

"I am?" I would've laughed if I hadn't felt her deepest sincerity. Reluctantly, I gave her my hands.

"Yes. You'll develop skills in no time. Nothing to worry about."

"Thank you so much," I said. Her hands were warm, a little dry, and the image of a child with long, braided hair laughing as she ran through sawgrass flitted through my mind. "Do you see them?"

"Who? Your spirit guides?"

I nodded. I loved how she knew what I'd meant.

Folding her hands in her lap, she successfully evaded my question. "Tell me, Valentina, how do you like Yeehaw Springs?"

"It's quiet. A lot quieter than where I come from. Weird name, too—Yeehaw Springs." I laughed a little.

"It's Creek."

"Oh." Now I felt bad for calling it weird. "I thought it was yeehaw, like what a cowboy says."

"Everyone thinks that, but it's not. It's a bastardization of the Creek word 'eyahah,' meaning wolf."

My ears perked up at the mention of the word wolf. "Is that because there's lots of wolves around here?" I asked.

"Oh, no." Citana shook her head, little rose earrings dangling off her ears. "There are no wolves in Florida. Not anymore. Last species was the black wolf years and years ago. Went extinct in the 1920s, I believe."

"But..." I'd seen one. I'd heard it howling, too. I wanted to dispute, but I doubted that Citana Rose would be wrong about her Florida history. "I didn't know that either."

"Now, you do." She smiled, her eyes disappearing into her sunny face. "And knowing is half the battle."

"What's the other half?" I asked jokingly.

She smiled. "Being protected. Which, now you are."

. . .

For the rest of the day, I went around in a dreamlike fog, wondering if spirit guides were with me. Wondering if I'd seen someone's emaciated German Shepherd instead of a wolf. Wondering if I'd be able to talk to my father after the full moon "amplification."

After receiving Citana's protection spell, Mori explained that they took me to see her "just to be safe." I felt empowered and legit, ready to tackle anything. And I'd finally gotten Citana's coffee along with amazing gingersnap cookies. Bonus! We meditated at a nearby lake in Cassadaga that was rumored to have healing powers. Mori meditated longer than we did, engrossed by the water's surface. I wondered if they were scrying, gazing at the water as a means of divination. Fae said they were hoping to hear answers.

To which questions? I wondered.

In early evening, strips of bright orange sunlight slashed across the hotel's cracked walls, highlighting its intense physical damage. I stood by the atrium, staring at the mermaid fountain, thinking of the hundreds of thousands of people who'd died here. I had no doubt that a certain sadness permeated this particular room, putting me on the verge of tears. I left after a minute.

On the veranda, Fae made a delicious dinner of roasted eggplant and summer squash on the camping grill they kept plugged into the generator. For dessert, we ate a few more of Citana's cookies. When the moon was high, the clairs plucked strands of hair off their heads and threw them, together with mine, into a mason jar filled with essential oils, water, and...

"Spit," Fae ordered, holding out the jar.

They each spit into the glass. I hesitated, questioning the process. Then I remembered that using hair and spit had been part of Roman Catholic rituals, too, a practice dating back to ancient times. Bodily secretions, skin, hair, and nails enhanced the power of any spell.

"Complete the circle, together we grow, powers combine, secrets flow," Fae chanted, holding the jar up to the moon. She dug a hole in the grass using her hands and pressed the jar into it. Then, they all stripped to their underwear again and dove into the lake, while I sat on the shore mesmerized by it all—their sheer lack of inhibition and the sense of family.

"Aren't you coming in?" Fae called when she came up for air.

"Nah, I'm good."

"Are you scared of being naked?"

Mori and Wilky both shushed her.

"Maybe," I called back.

"It's good for energy flow," she said. "Gets that sacral chakra lit up, so chi can flow all the way through you. Oo!" She shook as though having an energetic orgasm that made Wilky and Mori laugh.

Crow watched on, quietly seething. I felt his disapproval of me growing. I wanted to tell him how unlikely it was that anyone else would come along to complete his circle besides me. I was the best he was going to get.

"Come on, Vale! We've all seen boobs before!" Fae shouted.

"No, thanks." I smiled. "Algae's not my favorite."

"It's not that bad," she replied.

Getting naked would feel too much like a departure from my puritan upbringing. It was fascinating to see their bodies, though, so different, all colors, shapes, and styles, young and beautiful, cavorting in the lake. The clairs raised enormous amounts of positive energy that reminded me of little kids who simply didn't give a shit. I'd be lying if I said I didn't try to catch glimpses of the boys occasionally, but I managed to avert my eyes for the most part.

I'd always been shy.

Antoni hadn't helped that aspect of me either. The way he'd

taken my hand, forced me to touch him, when it would've been just as easy to *ask* if I wanted to. The more I thought back, the more I was convinced he'd used me. To get off *and* to explore his sexuality. I'd had fleeting visions when I touched him, and I was pretty sure Antoni had been under pressure to be "normal," to be straight.

He'd used me as his experiment.

I'd told Cami a dozen times I was fine. I was over it.

Then why did the incident still haunt me?

I wished I could discard anger like a jacket when it got too hot. I wanted to get naked and play with the clairs underneath the moon, feel what it's like to not give a shit what others think, not be judged all the time. I'd never be free, though. Every CCD class and lecture about modesty I'd ever been given made sure of that.

On the northeast side of the lake was that odd tree again—the gnarly, mangled, twisted one I'd seen earlier that looked like it'd lost a fight with a Category 5 hurricane. If a tree could look like it wanted to hurt you, wrap its branches around your neck and strangle you until you choked and sputtered, it'd be that tree.

Just then, I felt a pulsating throb in my ears followed by a pain so sharp, I sat up, dropped my face between my hands, and rocked to try and make it stop. No accompanying sound or ringing, just a radiating pain in my brain.

"Are you okay?" Wilky called from way out in the water. He was already dripping next to me on the grass by the time I looked up. "Vale..."

"My head." The burning sensation spread from my neck all the way down my spine. I couldn't focus. The pain stole every ounce of my attention. I felt distant from my body, as if I'd gone into someone else's. For a moment, I saw the glowing orbs of fire bobbing up and down in the woods again east of the lake.

"Where does it hurt?" Wilky's hands, cold from the lake, cradled my face.

"Here." I pointed to my ears, my neck, my whole forehead. "This whole area is hot. But it's going...it's gone." And then, that was it. I labored to catch my breath, craning my chin up to take gulps full of air.

Mori had scrambled onto the shore. "What happened?"

"Pain. Is this normal for you?" Wilky took my hands.

I immediately slipped mine out. I couldn't handle any more pain that wasn't my own. I shook my head. "I've never felt that. Not even a migraine."

Mori patted my upper back. "Know what? You've had a long day. My aunt opened you up energetically. I was wondering if you'd feel alright."

"Wasn't she supposed to protect me?" I asked. I used their hands to stand. I needed to get inside and off to bed, start over tomorrow.

"She did, but it's the vortex. You could be highly susceptible. More than us."

"Great," I muttered.

"What were you thinking of when the pain started?" Wilky asked.

"I was looking at that tree over there, the twisted one with the big roots."

Wilky and Mori followed my stare then exchanged glances. Abruptly, Wilky stood and walked off, placing his hands on the back of his neck, as he paced along the lakeside.

"Did I say something?"

"The Devil's Tree," Mori said.

"What about it?" Whatever it was, I didn't care for it.

Fae waded out of the water, breathless, sniffing the air like a dog. She gagged and winced. "Ugh, do you smell that? It's like something burning. Like...flesh."

Eleven

I tried catching whiffs of whatever she was smelling, but nothing even remotely resembling burning flesh came to me. Only the slightly putrid smell of the stagnant lake. "I don't smell anything. I'm sorry."

"I don't either, love," Mori said, their hand on Fae's back, as they tried to get on Fae's same level of sensory perception.

This was Fae's clairalience, I was pretty certain. She gagged, folded over, and threw up into a sandy patch. "It's gone...it's going..."

Wilky cast a solemn glance at us huddled around Fae, then went back to staring at the Devil's Tree, hands on hips. That boy lived as much in his own world as Crow or even me, for that matter.

We stayed with Fae until her moment had passed, then I stepped onto the veranda and caught my breath. What the hell had I experienced out there? I'd picked up on the resort's sadness, and I'd seen weird things, but I'd never felt actual pain until now.

I rubbed my neck and prayed for God to protect me, feeling like a hypocrite for both abandoning and asking Him to assist at the same time. Mori headed up the hilly slope, holding Fae's narrow shoulders.

"Are you okay?" I asked when they came up to stand where I was. She nodded weakly. It was weird to see Fae like that without her usual high energy.

"I think we're opening up," Mori said. "There's five of us now."

"And that's without the full moon ritual. Maybe..." I thought about my words carefully. "Maybe we shouldn't do it?"

Fae and Mori both looked at me, wheels in their brain cranking away. "We just have to get used to it. It'll be fine." Mori waved to Wilky and Crow to let them know they were taking Fae inside.

Enough for one day. An ice-cold drink was what I needed, but we had no ice. Instead, I chugged down a bottle full of warm water and headed off to bed, my head spinning. The ballroom felt heavier than usual, but that made sense given what we'd just gone through.

I WAS IN A BATHROOM—A public bathroom—surrounded by urinals.

The tile was light green. There were cracks in some of them. The ceiling had a wide, ugly amber stain. Drops of water dripped through the stain, and I realized it was pouring outside. For some reason, as often happened in dreams, I couldn't leave. I was stuck; my feet didn't work.

I texted Camila to come get me, but Camila wouldn't answer. She was mad because I'd left the retreat. It took minutes to press each letter on my keyboard. I'd mess up and have to start over again. Frustration mounted. Tears slipped from my eyes into the corners of my frown. I looked up from the phone and saw I wasn't alone. Antoni was there. Good ol' fresh-shaven, clean-cut Antoni, leaning against the sinks with his hands pressed on the edge of one.

You should be honored, he told me. Other girls would've done anything to spend that time with him. I got lucky. Couldn't I see that?

I told him to shut up and go away, I was trying to work my phone, to get us out of here before the campground closed and we'd be forced to stay overnight.

Nothing happened, he said. He'd been polite. By doing his business at the sink, he'd left me out of it. He'd spared me. He hadn't "used" me. He'd done the correct thing. Other guys wouldn't have been as thoughtful. I needed to stop acting as though he'd done something wrong, because he hadn't. I was making a mountain out of a molehill.

He went on. He wouldn't shut his mouth. I certainly hadn't brought it up, so why did he insist on talking about it? I rarely thought about him during my waking life—yes, my waking life, because I was dreaming, I knew it. So, why wouldn't he stop talking about it?

My phone refused to work. I had to start the text all over again. Men had needs, he went on. All he'd done was act on impulse. He hadn't hurt me. He'd respected me.

Shut up, Antoni. Shut the hell up.

A strong hand curled around my arm. I stared at his fingers, digging into my flesh. He had the balls to touch me? To lay his hands on *my* arm? I yanked it out of his grasp. *Touch me again,* I warned.

Behind him, something bubbled in the sink. Something thick, gurgling up from the drainpipe. I didn't want to look, though he wanted me to. He wanted me to see what was in the sink, what my hand had made him do. He was proud of the outcome, proud of how he'd handled the situation. Would I rather he'd done it there or inside of me? he asked.

He hadn't hurt me. And I needed to know that, he insisted.

I don't care anymore. Just fucking stop, I told him.

My eyes opened to a nearly lightless ballroom. A few ribbons of moonlight filtered in, illuminating dust vortices closest to the windows. The rest of the vast space sat in obscurity. The ballroom felt like it had a pulse, or was that my heart? The dream had felt so real, I half-expected Antoni to be here.

I let out a slow breath. Our conversation still lingered in my mind. I was shaking. From the dream, but also because the stupid incident wouldn't leave me alone. It was still in my psyche despite my insistence that it wasn't. This asshole was still in my subconscious, a demon who needed exorcising.

"Shit..." I sat up.

Rubbing my face, I stood and moved to the window to peer out at the filthy veranda overgrown with weeds, the grassy slope to the lake and Fae's garden. Far in the distance, the gnarly, twisted tree hid in the shadows of the quarter moon high in the clear, still sky.

I looked away.

Last thing I needed was another memory invasion. The burning and tugging sensation had not been my own—I knew that. Staring out the dusty glass, I watched the stagnant lake shimmer with a glow of its own. In this half-wake, half-sleep state, I knew in my bones that we were not alone.

The clairs were asleep—I counted three bulky lumps (Mori and Fae slept together tonight). Someone stood a few feet away, invisible, scrutinizing eyes watching me from the darkness.

Judging.

But I hadn't done anything wrong.

I imagined my eyes widening like a cat's, irises adjusting to take in as much light as possible. I tried to make sense of the hotel's scattered, discarded objects. What might've been a bar or fallen stools could've been a dead man lying in his own filth next to a piano. Gossamer cobwebs hanging from curved archways, dancing in the draft, could've been a woman dangling from her neck. The one column just outside the ballroom in the central hallway, lined up with the entrance arch could've been a person watching me.

The feeling of displaced air intensified.

Why are you here?

It sounded like a woman's voice.

Another woman replied, *Leave her.*

The ballroom felt alive, simmering and waiting.

I needed to use the bathroom, but hell if I was walking past the Devil's Tree again, and hell if I was going anywhere near a bathroom in the dark. I was haunted enough as is. I forced myself back to bed. It wasn't until the soft rays of sunrise lit up the room's faded red wallpaper that I was able to finally sleep, even if it was half-baked. By then, my feelings over the dream had subsided, but resentment ate away at me like tapeworms devouring the lining of my stomach.

Twelve

I awoke to a viciously hangry stomach, but Wilky saw my head pop up and immediately brought me a plate of sausage and eggs balanced on his sketchpad. "I kept it warm for you." He pushed the plate into my hands, along with a fork.

"Thank you." I stared at his hands. He had nice hands, clean nails. "I barely slept last night," I said, digging into the food.

"You've missed half the day. Did the Sunlake keep you awake?" He sat cross-legged, sketching a drawing of what looked like a landscape with lots of trees.

"The Sunlake, or my own brain, one of the two," I said between bites.

"I had wild dreams. But I always have wild dreams." His Haitian accent reminded me of home.

"What did you dream about?" I scarfed down the last of the eggs, working in a glance or two at his inquisitive brown eyes. "If you don't mind my asking."

Wilky saw I was done and handed me his cup of orange juice. "You can have the rest."

"Thanks."

"I always dream about people...shadows...torches."

I stared at him over the rim of the cup. I thought about the glowing orbs in the trees I'd seen last night, the bright blobs of light I'd seen yesterday morning, too, how much they reminded me of people carrying torches. "They move like a line of people walking?"

"Yes. Like this." He turned around his sketchbook. His drawing was of the trees behind the lake, with the Devil's tree in the background. Walking toward it was a line of shadow people holding what could've been perceived as torches.

"I think I saw them last night."

He stared at me. "By the lake?"

"I think so. It was hard to tell, my head started hurting so bad, but I'm sure it was torches. That would make sense since Fae smelled burning, right?" But she hadn't smelled torches—she'd smelled cooked flesh.

Wilky looked like he had at least a half million things he wanted to say. His gaze was focused on Crow taking photos in the hallway. "I think it's more likely that Fae was smelling the fire."

"Fire?"

He looked at me again. "The one that closed this place down when it was a resort. A kitchen fire in the late seventies. Lots of spiritualists died."

"Oh." I put down my plate.

"Haven't you seen the burnt kitchen?"

I shook my head.

He sketched for a minute. "What I experience is something else. I hear screams, I see torches, and it always, always feels like I'm there."

"Like you're in someone else's body," I guessed.

"Yes." He stared at me. "Like, I'm experiencing someone else's memory."

Exactly what I'd experienced last night by the Devil's Tree—someone else's memory. "Do you wake up right away?"

"Not always. I usually get to the part where they reach the tree, but I don't know what happens after that. I wake up sweaty. But uh, you don't want to hear about this. Finish your breakfast. Mori and Fae will show you around when you're done." He stood with his sketchbook.

He didn't wait for my reply, that I *did* want to hear about his dreams. I wanted to know who was carrying the torches, who did the screaming. I wanted to share my crazy-ass nightmare about Antoni, explore why he was still on my mind. He took off, though.

My phone vibrated—a text from Cami, asking how I was doing, and could I call her. *No, not now.* My mind was far away in another world.

After a short walk, I was throwing my hair into a ponytail, thinking about Wilky and watching Crow move through the halls with his camera, trying to capture his spirit guide lady when Mori and Fae approached me, hands clasped together.

"You were up last night," Mori said. "We could see you standing by the window. Ghosts keeping you up?"

"Ghosts inside my head," I replied.

Fae reached out, and I flinched. She was only trying to run her fingers through my hair to detangle and drape it over my shoulder. "The worst kind."

"True," I said.

"When we got here a year ago, we couldn't sleep either," Mori said. "We thought we needed getting used to the hotel, but it turned out the hotel needed getting used to us."

I never thought of it that way before, a building needing adjustment to new inhabitants. "I'm fairly sure The Sunlake Springs doesn't want me here," I said.

"Why do you say that?" Fae asked.

I shrugged and checked my phone absently. Five new texts from my mom, three from Abuela, and a couple more from Camila. Shutting off the screen, I slid it into my shorts' pocket. "I don't know. It's just the feeling I get. How long do you plan on staying?" I asked, changing the subject. "A year seems like a long time."

"I have no other place to be." Mori looked at Fae.

Fae was now behind me, braiding my hair. "Me neither. As long as it takes to find what we all want. It's not like anybody's missing us. My mother thinks I live in Atlanta with my rich boyfriend."

"Seriously?" I laughed.

"Yeah. I'll tell her the truth one day. Right now, she doesn't need stress. Better to make her think I'm fine." Fae tapped Mori's chin then bottom lip. "Which I am."

Mori smiled, but I could see they probably felt bad about Fae living a lie. I understood. We lied when we were afraid of hurting people. We lied when our loved ones couldn't accept us. I longed for a day I could be completely honest about who I was.

"Nobody cares about us, Vale. We're totally okay with that."

"I care," I said.

Fae swung around my side and stared into my soul. "That means a lot. It really, really does. Thank you." She popped a kiss on my cheek and went back to braiding my hair.

Mori reached out to take Fae's hand again, or to make her stop touching me, one or the other. "Come on, let's take a walk." Mori led us out the ballroom and down the hall. At first, I thought we were headed toward the atrium, and I was glad I wouldn't be alone inside it, but then they turned and faced the lobby with an upward sweep of the hand. "Voilà. Zees ees ze grand lobby. Bee-oo-tee-full, right?" they said in a bad French accent.

"It is. Every time I pass by it, it blows my mind," I said.

In the full sunlight, the old rusted bird cages glinted with flecks of gold paint. I remembered the odd feeling in my stomach when I'd touched one the other night.

"It's one of my favorite parts of the hotel." Fae did a grand jetté across the floor, landing, then another leap in a different direction. "What room are you in, ma'am? May I help you with your bags?" She giggled.

I admired the hippie child in Fae. I wasn't sure I could dance the same way knowing my family didn't care about me.

Mori pointed to a spot near me. "Right here is where Crow took a photo of a white figure that looks like a mermaid. You can even see her tail. It's pretty cool."

"But why would a mermaid be walking in a hotel?" I asked.

"Why would a hotel by a lake have paintings of mermaids?" Mori asked rhetorically, gesturing to a large painting high up on the wall. I had, in fact, not noticed the enormous work of art featuring a gorgeous siren coming out of, not the ocean or beach, but a lake's surface. The trees behind it and the rowboats were the giveaway. "There's siren symbolism everywhere. Check out the columns."

"Those I've seen," I said. "They're beautiful."

"We're not that far from the ocean," Mori said, "and Florida is nearly an island anyway, so it's not a surprise they're a big part of The Sunlake's Art Deco history."

"Some people say the Lady of the Lake *is* a species of mermaid," Fae said.

"More like a water spirit," Mori told her. "Trust me, I know my water spirits."

"True, but I like to think of her as a mermaid. So, there. Anyway, Crow took another photo over there." She pointed to the chained and locked double door entrance. "Of someone pushing a woman in a wheelchair out the doors."

I imagined people from long ago moving through this space, like escapees of Crow's photos. I saw multiple layers of time overlapping each other, playing on 1.5x speed—doctors, nurses, patients, orderlies, veterans, hippies, all criss-crossing in time and space. I even saw the little boy from the atrium, cutting through the lobby with a toy in his hand.

A toy—or a craft of some kind.

"Where is he anyway?" I almost missed his grumbling about the clairs agreeing to let me stay. "Crow?"

"He's in the north wing today."

"What's in the north wing?"

"The north wing was used for veterans, the south for women's psychiatric ward," Mori explained, taking us past the atrium. I stared at the mermaid perched on the fountain, holding up her sun. She watched me intently, as we walked past.

"That's not an accident, by the way," Mori said. "North was considered higher, closer to God, war heroes deserving of Heaven. And south...well, closer to Hell."

"Yay! Women are the root of all evil!" Fae said sarcastically.

"Same reasoning behind blue for boys, pink for girls," I said. That was another thing my wonderful patriarchal religion had taught me—that, as a woman, I was the cause of everybody's misery.

Fae's eyes widened. "I never knew that, Vale. You just taught me something."

"I'm a treasure trove of useless information," I replied. "What's Crow's photography project about?"

"Preservation." Mori took us down the central, dividing hallway. Above were Moroccan-style lanterns hanging from the ceiling, the glass tiles of which were pretty intact. "He's trying to convince the county to restore the hotel. I think the place is beyond saving, but I don't tell him that. He hates hearing it."

Suddenly, my foot sank into a depression in the tile floors, and I twisted my ankle. "Ow, damn it..."

Mori and Fae hung onto my arm. "Whoa. You okay?"

I winced. My ankle hurt like hell. Walking through the Sunlake was like stepping through a fun house at the fair. Floors were wonky; walls strained under the weight of the tall ceilings. Crow's wish to see this place restored would make for a breathtaking sight, but it shouldn't happen. They'd have to raze the place to the ground and start all over to make sure it was all to code. My father had seen less damaged buildings demolished for more minor offenses.

"So, we're headed to Hell now?" I chuckled, hobbling into the south wing.

"We never left," Mori made a mock eerie voice.

We stepped through a double doorway to a vast room with rusted metal counters and carts knocked onto their sides. Brick walls were charred black, while other black circles of soot radiated throughout the floor. The low ceiling's wooden beams were also charred and broken up in spots where water leaked in and dripped down the moldy walls.

"Here's the kitchen," Mori said. "A fire killed twenty people here in 1979. They never opened again. Through there is the dining room, which you'll see has beautiful floor to ceiling windows."

Mori and Fae stepped over puddles of water toward the dining room, but I stayed behind. Through the double doors stood a woman, watching me. She was perfectly still, arms by her sides with straight brown hair that hung below her waist on one side. The other side of her hair was gone. Her scalp was a bloody, singed mess. The skin of her face was missing, exposing ligaments and an eyeball about to fall out.

She lifted a hand in greeting.

I nearly threw up my breakfast.

"If it's early enough in the morning, I can smell cooking in here," Fae said from far away.

The woman lowered her hand, dusted it off on her apron, and vanished. I couldn't speak or move. She wasn't a vision like the others. She was a person right in front of me, a solid human for a whole minute until she disappeared, and neither Fae nor Mori had seen her.

"Vale?" Mori called.

"Yeah, I..." I hurried off toward the dining room, unable to put what I'd just seen into words.

Mori had caught on to something wrong with me, but Fae was going on, running her delicate hand along wooden tables devoid of tablecloths. "Sometimes I get the taste of coffee in my mouth. Sometimes I smell cigars over in the smoking room. Wilky hears the clink of silverware in here. Isn't that cool?"

That woman had seen me. She'd looked right at me. She'd said hello, happy that someone had finally noticed her. But I couldn't get over the burns covering her body. That was a ghost, wasn't it?

"Vale, you okay?" Fae asked.

"Yeah." I decided I would wait before letting on that I could see them—I could see the ghosts of the Sunlake Springs Resort. The clairs hadn't, but I had. "Speaking of Wilky," I said. "What happened to him last night? After I felt that pain in my head?"

"Oh." Fae's expression fell flat.

"Wilky's got his own shit he's dealing with," Mori said, showing me through the dining room. It really was gorgeous with soaring, floor-to-ceiling windows, half of which were cracked or had holes in them. "He deals with it in his own way. Don't take it personally. It's not you."

"I won't. Did something happen to him here?"

"Not to him, but family members, yes. There's no evidence of it, of course. The state does a fantastic job of keeping stuff like that out of the public eye. But Wilky hopes to find proof. I don't think it'll change anything. It's more of a peace of mind thing."

"What happened to his family?"

Mori and Fae looked at each other. "I'm sure he'll tell you in time."

So, unspeakable things happened to people Wilky knew, and

he was here trying to make sense of it before the hotel got torn down. I hoped he'd find it and that I could help somehow.

Fae stretched my hand out to look at. "You have pretty nails. Mine are horrible." I tried to leave my hand in hers. I was never going to form relationships with people if I kept being afraid of what my hands would see. For the brief instant she held it, I saw a world of sadness heavy enough to fill a chasm. It made me admire her positivity that much more.

"Yours are great, Fae. Everything about you is." I had to tell her that. Something about Fae struck me as needing lots of love, like maybe she hadn't gotten enough as a kid. "All of you is great. I'm in awe of your abilities."

"Awww, Vale. We're so glad you're here!" Fae clung to my arm. I let her.

We headed down a set of steps, sinking into cooler air compared with the rest of the hotel. "Vale, we're all born with them, but the older we get, the more we lose that innocence needed to wield magick. We lose ourselves in tech and tune out energies. Gut instincts come from your solar plexus, by the way." Mori pointed to my stomach. "Part of developing your senses is learning to get out of your own way. Trust those instincts."

They were so right. Being away from home, here in this place, with no other distractions had helped me tune into the world around me. I wondered how strong I'd become if I stayed long enough.

"Yay, now comes *my* favorite room." Fae tapped her fingers together with delicious anticipation. "Welcome to the basement."

Mori gestured to a horrible underground made of all brick walls. The thinnest slivers of light filtered in from two windows near the ceiling. The north wall boasted a tall, wide set of metal doors, one of which was open and tilted sadly on its hinge.

"I thought Florida didn't have basements because of limestone," I said.

"Some buildings do. I don't know...this one does." Mori leaned against a wall and watched me. If I didn't know better, I would've said they were waiting to see what I felt in here.

My initial impression of the basement was that I immediately wanted to leave.

Fae twirled and danced across the filthy floor. "Don't you love it? Do you smell the mustiness? I can't get enough of that smell!"

I didn't care for it. It was more like mold. And I didn't care for how far underneath the ground the room was either. Felt totally wrong for a state where the subterranean levels were mostly water. "Why is this your favorite?" I asked Fae.

She floated over to the metal hatch and jumped into the open doorway, posing with her legs up against the wall and a hand in the air. She reminded me of a forest nymph flitting from flower to flower. "Because this is the treasure roooooom," she cooed.

"Well..." Mori rolled her eyes. "Nobody knows that."

"This is where we think my great-grandfather's money is buried. In his journal, he wrote how they shoveled fifty yards west of the south end of the lake just before they started building the hotel. He never reclaimed it after he got out of prison."

"You're sure it's still here?" I asked.

She flipped her palms up. "No. For all we know, a construction worker found it and kept it for himself. I know it's stupid to think it might still be here, but wouldn't it be sublime if it were? Mori thinks I'm insane, but I can almost smell it!" she cried. "Right here, behind this wall!"

"You smell dead bodies, love," Mori said. "And we don't say insane."

"If only I had a sledgehammer!" Fae pretended to smash the wall with a mighty mallet.

I stared at them both.

Mori raised an eyebrow. "This chute is where dead tuberculosis patients were dumped. Bodies rolled down the tunnel and came out by the north side where the elevation is lower. Trucks came every morning to haul them away."

"Sounds...lovely," I said.

"It's not," Mori said flatly. "Sometimes I do trance writing in these rooms, and I feel them crying. They want to go, but they can't."

"Want to look inside?" Fae gestured to the black hole in the wall.

"Tempting, but no." I backed away. A watery sound was coming from the wall. A thin, steady stream dripped out of the brick and trickled in a mini river onto the floor where it drained into a hole in the corner of the basement.

For a moment, we stood in quiet reverence. There were no words for this. Centuries slid on past, while walls held secrets. It was up to us to discover the events that took place using all the clues at our disposal. Energies changed. Mori seemed worried about the trickling water, same as I was, while Fae's dreams of finding gold spun through her head like cotton candy around a paper core.

Crow would have a hard time convincing anyone to restore this hotel. I was no architect or engineer, but there was just too much structural damage. "Let's find Wilky. He'll show us the rooms," Mori broke the silence.

I couldn't get out of the basement fast enough.

IN THE EVENING, we did more group meditation, carefully smudging ourselves with sage and asking our deities and spirit guides to envelop us in protective light against negative energies. I envisioned the purple light that Citana Rose taught me to envision, sweeping over my body like cascading paint, from head to toe, creating a cocoon of impenetrable strength.

At first, I found it hard to concentrate, but eventually, by the end of the hour-long session, I felt like our breaths were in synch. So were our hearts. It wasn't all that different from that part in Mass when we all take communion then recite the Our Father, then face each other to shake hands.

Community. Love. Brotherhood.

I didn't see a scowl on Crow's face. For the first time, he shook my hand and gave me a playful side-eye. "Valentina," was all he said.

"Crowley."

They headed inside for food Mori had picked up from Citana, while I stayed on the veranda, studying my tarot cards, staring out over the still lake. It was peaceful but I wasn't at peace. I was experiencing too much at once, and I couldn't help the feeling that the hotel hated me and wanted me out. That was ridiculous, though—how could it? *Why* would it?

Something moved on the south side of the lake. Nervous energy, flitting. I saw the pair of golden eyes before I could make out the rest of the shape. The wolf, or German Shepherd, or coyote, whatever he was, paced back and forth along the shoreline.

"Hey, Lobo." I waved. "Nice to see you again."

Lobo's tongue lolled. He scanned the resort from right to left, lowered his head in that way dogs do when they don't know how to get around an obstacle, and watched me. He seemed panicky out there in the tall sawgrass. I called to him to come. I wanted to see him up close, make sure he was real, that I wasn't imagining a black wolf, even though they were supposedly extinct.

Maybe he was one of the last, hanging on like a final soldier, hiding out like Sasquatch from mankind, his sworn enemy. But Lobo didn't want to come around, or maybe he couldn't. The lake itself presented a challenge, as though he'd forgotten how to circumvent it. I watched him for a while, until he finally gave up and receded into the shadows.

. . .

On my duffel bag, I found a flower. A pink, five-petaled bloom similar to the hibiscus that grew in my backyard. I twirled it in my fingers, looking around amusedly to see who might've given it to me. Whoever didn't matter. What mattered was that, through this flower, I was a member of a new family. Welcomed and appreciated, which was more than I was at home.

Mori smiled. "It wasn't me. I'm not the one with a love of swamp rosemallows," they laughed, lifting their chin to Wilky sitting on his bed, drawing on his sketchpad.

"What?" He had the worst fake-innocent look on his face I'd ever seen. "It wasn't me."

"Sure, it wasn't." I laughed, slipping the bloom into my hair over my ear.

He broke into a lovely smile that made my stomach knot up. "Welcome to the Sunlake Springs Resort, moon child," Wilky drawled. He turned his sketch around. It was of me with the very same swamp rosemallow over my ear. He'd perfectly captured my stance, my body, my long hair over my shoulder...the curve of my calves.

Behind me were four silhouettes. Stringy and bony, long-haired Fae, stocky, bold, and strong-armed Mori, tall and lanky Crow with his spiky hair, and muscular Wilky with his signature boxer stance. Rising behind us, bright and bold in a dark background, was the fullest, largest of all moons, watching over us.

"I love it. Thank you so much," I said, my heart full of gratitude. I'd found friends with which to hang, after all.

Thirteen

I sat on the floor of the old meditation room, staring at Buddha. Despite having new friends, I felt unsettled. I'd seen a ghost yesterday when no one else had, and that was cause enough for worry, but I couldn't figure out why else I felt this way.

Ignoring every message my family had sent me in the last few days was making me feel too rebellious. Maybe I was too far gone. I'd also traded Camila for a coven of witches. Who was I anymore?

The amplification ritual was in two days, and the clairs seemed excited. I, however, was beginning to think it wasn't a good idea. The Sunlake Springs didn't need help getting its message across. In twenty-four hours, I'd seen odd things in the atrium, the kitchen, the Devil's Tree, and felt an odd sensation of dread in the basement. I'd seen the spirit of a burned woman. I shuddered to think what else I'd experience *after* the amplification.

Macy texted from Orlando to see how I was doing. I'd said fine, and when she asked if I could find something in her office that she needed for one of her meetings, I had to admit I wasn't home. Nor would I be for a bit. At least I didn't lie. To her credit, she responded with a simple "okay," which blew my mind. I felt proud for telling the truth, but it made me feel out of my body, like I was living someone else's life.

Mori and Fae wanted family to love and accept them. I had family that loved me but didn't understand me. My family went so far as to isolate my dad's few relatives, all because they weren't religious. I never got to know them. My grandmother died long before I was born, so my mom's family was all I had.

It made me sad, and I spent a good twenty minutes crying by myself. I hadn't lived a terrible existence in my eighteen years, but I hadn't really *lived* either. Fear of God had made sure of that. I'd been a prisoner all this time, a finch inside a golden cage of lies. A week at Yeehaw Springs and four days at the Sunlake, and now look at me—a veritable wild child.

I cried so hard, I had a coughing fit and spent the next several minutes breathing deeply to calm my sobs.

CITANA ROSE HAD SAID Crow could be a bully, that I shouldn't let him intimidate me. So, my first order of business today, aside from further cultivating my "gifts" was to meet him head-on. His disappointment was still palpable, and giving a shit what people thought of me was a special skill ingrained in me since birth by the women in my family.

I found Crow in the south wing, taking photos of what looked like patient rooms. His camera made soft clicking sounds, as he captured image after image of the peeling paint, outdated dressers, and bed frames. I stood inside the doorway, watching him. He had passion for his art, that much was true.

"It's weird, isn't it?"

He spun around startled. He saw it was only me and went back to peering through his viewfinder. "What is?"

"This whole wing, the way they never refurbished it, not even when it was a wellness resort."

"Only the north wing was used as the resort. The owners were hoping to make enough money to refurbish the rest of the building, but then the fire happened."

In my mind, the charred ghost woman waved in greeting.

Crow aimed and shot some more, each time looking at his viewfinder to see if he caught something worth keeping. "Besides, it belongs here. It's part of the hotel. You can't remove it."

Click, click, click...

"I guess you're right. I mean, it's over forty years sitting here." I waded into the room. "What are the photos for again?"

Crow ran a hand through his spiky, purple hair. I was sure I heard the most imperceptible sigh, then he moved closer to the window to frame a shot of the broken glass. "I'm putting together a proposal to present at the county next month. Hopefully, the historical society will vote to give this place another shot. There's too much beauty here to just leave for dead."

"No doubt." I walked around the room, skimming the walls with my fingertips. I saw patients lying in their beds, nurses serving them trays of food, and a few who wouldn't eat. They simply stared. When I blinked, it was a debris-filled room again. "Do you think it'll work? There's so much damage."

He cocked his head, then righted it for another photo.

I remembered Mori mentioning how Crow didn't like to talk about the possibility of it being torn down forever. "I'm asking because my dad was a code enforcer for Miami-Dade, and I know for a fact he would've—"

"Your dad's not here," Crow snapped.

I recoiled. "No, but..." I stared at him. Mori was right. "Why do you want it restored so badly?"

He put the camera down. "Can you...not?"

I held firm. "It's just...if I'm going to be helping you during the ritual, I need to understand what you're getting from this. I know

Mori, Fae, and Wilky, but I know nothing about you." *You haven't made it easy.*

He sighed, went back to framing his shot. "What do you want to know?"

"Why are you so obsessed with the Sunlake?" I asked. "You've lived here a year, roped your friends into your project. I just want to know what's so worth saving. Seems to me like all that ever happened here was death."

"You mean besides historical and groundbreaking architectural significance?"

"Well, sure, but…"

Crow faced me. "I was asked to do this. I don't expect you to understand. You just got here."

"I can try," I said.

He dropped to his knees, sank onto his back, and aimed his camera at the ceiling to capture the cool molded designs rotting away that no one would ever see again.

"The Lady of the Lake," I guessed.

He sighed. "She wants the place revived, and yes, I fight for her, for what's left of this building. If they knock it to the ground, an entire century of history will be gone. She…" *Snap, snap, snap.* "Will be gone."

"So, you're scared if that happens, you'll never see her again," I wondered aloud. "And if you don't see her anymore, you won't feel special anymore. I can understand."

"No, Valentina. Like I said, it would take you a year to understand."

Fair enough. "Can I ask you something else, then?"

He held his breath, shot a vibrant blue-eyed glare at me, then stood to his feet, brushing dust off his jeans. "If you feel so compelled."

"Why do you feel like you have to help her? What's so special about the Lady of the Lake?"

"You're saying this isn't worth my time."

"I'm only asking. We're all obsessed with something. I just want to understand."

He moved to the doorway. He was done with this room, or maybe done with me. "When I was a kid, we went to church. A lot. My father taught Sunday school; my mother played the organ. In third grade, I checked out a book from the school library. It was called *Religions of the World*. Near the back were photos of skulls and candles, of voodoo priests covered in feathers, of chickens bleeding from their hands, and caskets being carried in the streets."

"That must've been a shock," I said.

"A delicious shock, fuck yeah. Soon little baby Crow was asking the pastor about the underworld and telling him that witchcraft was real and the occult was my main interest."

I chuckled. "I'm sure that went super well."

"It didn't," he replied, not getting my sarcasm. "They kicked me out."

"For asking a question?"

"For being inquisitive. I studied it well into my teen years, in secret, and that's when it got dangerous. For them, not for me. The pastor found out and was so sure I had the Devil in me, he threatened my parents to kick them all out of the congregation and make our lives impossible. I don't know where you come from, but where I come from, that causes major dishonor."

"Wow, Crow. I had no idea."

He picked something out of his teeth. "We had to move. Gulf Coast to East. I got put in a private Baptist school where the libraries don't have books with photos about chickens and voodoo priests."

"Where the books only show you one perspective," I ventured.

"They put blinders on me."

He nodded, and in that moment, I understood. He wasn't a dick who randomly spat rude things. He was angry.

"We're not so different," I said. "My family's religious."

"I knew that." His gaze flitted irritably to my cross. Only when Crow did that did I ever realize I was touching it. "But unless you've been told you're going straight to Hell by everyone, including your parents, you don't know what I've been through."

"That happened?" I flinched. "Jesus."

"They chose God over me." His eyes cut through my heart. "Kicked me out. At sixteen. They chose the Church over their own kid. According to them, I'd bring evil into their home. So they got rid of me."

"Oh...I am so, so sorry."

For once, he didn't have a quip. His contemplation melted the intensity in his facial muscles. "Don't be. It was around then that I started dreaming about the Lady every other night. She said there was a way for me to bring her back. I could meet her in person. Once I followed her instructions, she would answer any questions I had about the spirit world."

"Meet her in person?" I asked. "You mean, you'd be able to see her ghost."

"Meaning I wouldn't have to take ten zillion photos to try and see her. I'd see her just like I'm seeing you right now. I wouldn't need this." He held up the camera.

I was starting to understand. He was envious of the clairs. Of me. He could "see" ghosts but only by capturing anomalies on camera. He couldn't see them with his sixth sense, third eye, or whatever. "But why is that so important to you?"

I got the thinnest of smiles in return. "She'll answer my question."

"What question?"

"If there's really a Hell. And if there is..." A muscle in his jaw tensed. "Will I end up there?"

"Oh, Crow."

I strolled up and gave him a hug. I hadn't held anyone this long in a while, and through my hands, I saw a bitter, scared kid wishing his parents would love him enough to defend him, a boy wondering how and why he'd been forsaken, and to what end?

Crow was a lot like me, more than he'd ever know.

Which was probably why he hated me.

DURING THE DAY, the Sunlake Springs was beautiful in a sad, longing way. She was an aging movie star who'd once been glamorous but now had no leading roles and only five cats in her audience. At night, the hotel's walls grew taller, its shadows stretching from floor to ceiling. A desperation took over, bound and gagged whispers longing for release. It was all fun and games during the day, but when the sun went down, I didn't want to be caught alone in certain areas.

I explored the halls while there was still sunlight.

In the upper desolate halls, I found no less than eight or nine paintings of the Lady of the Lake hanging askew on the walls. Some depicted a beautiful nude white woman with long blond hair, like Botticelli's Venus on her shell, emerging from the sea. Others depicted her wearing a flowing nightgown, stepping out of the water under the moonlight as lake grass artfully clung to her curvy form. In my favorite, she appeared with a long scaly fish tail, a mythical mermaid, only Cypress trees and sawgrass filled the background instead of the ocean.

Her legend was the mythos and soul of this place, but to Crow, she represented love. Maybe hope. She was the object of his affection and attention. Did she really want to come alive? Like the Sunlake Springs, the Lady of the Lake also seemed like an old actress begging for one last curtain call, while Crow was the lone janitor in the front row, applauding her performance, tossing red roses of adoration onto the stage.

Wandering in and out of rooms, I wondered if the Lady was

real, or if Crow's PTSD-suffering teen brain had made her up to replace his parents and community. It'd be no different than someone's relationship with Jesus during a time of loneliness.

The sun's rays filtered through the west windows at lower angles, bending light into orange and reddish tones. In the third-floor hallway, I approached the grand atrium's glass walls which penetrated the hospital vertically and reflected the glow. From each floor, one could peer into the atrium from above and see a world of vegetation, the mermaid fountain, and the chained chandelier below.

In my mind, I heard a scream, but I knew it wasn't real-time—it was a memory of two days ago, when we'd all heard a shout echoing through the building. We never figured out who it was. That was how the Sunlake operated—in bits and pieces, a 5,000-piece jigsaw puzzle.

I paused a few feet away, my heartbeat pounding.

I hadn't visited this very spot yet. This wasn't where I'd panicked before, but seeing the glass structure sent a spike of anxiety through me just the same. A discarded wheelchair sat in the middle of a cloud of suspended, illuminated dust particles, next to a rusted old gurney blocking the passage. Someone, a long time ago, had sat in that chair. Someone had lain on that gurney. Carefully, I stepped up and wheeled the gurney out of the way, letting go of its cold metal quickly.

Even so, I couldn't pass.

My little starshine, sleep, oh, so tight
   My little moonshine, dream with the night
   When you awaken, Love you will be
   My little sunshine Heaven gave me...

. . .

A WOMAN FLOATED into the hallway. Her hair was soiled and sweaty, her skin a sallow gray. She wore an oversized hospital gown. I hadn't seen her a moment ago, but there she was, standing with feet apart, shivering with something in her hands. Down her legs, rivers of bright red blood streamed and blended with the sweat on her legs, thinning the rivulets, splintering them into more rivers that leaked onto the floor. In her hands, she held a roundish, dark garnet fleshy...*thing*...with ligaments hanging off the sides. Droplets of blood dripped from the ligaments.

Miss, please...

...please help...

She could see me. I froze, my body draining of reason, and breath. She could see me. I could see her, just like the woman in the kitchen. I clenched my eyes shut and clung to my little cross.

My little starshine, sleep, oh, so tight...

MISS! The woman—the spirit—called me. *Miss, please.*

"What..." I could barely utter a word. *What do you want me to do?* I tried asking, but the words got lodged in my throat.

She held the blob of flesh toward me, her lined expression pained and full of regret. *They took it. They took it out of me...*

"Out?" I stared at the bloody mass. It might've been a stillborn, or a...or...I couldn't think, couldn't reason in any way that might help her.

The woman gave a painful cry, clutched her belly with one hand, the other still holding the blob, cringing as her insides squeezed out a gush of blood containing heavy clots from between her calves. The clotted fluid slid down the insides of her legs, pooling around her feet.

They took it!

"What did they...?" I managed to whisper.

I may have been imagining this, the building's history playing tricks on me. I couldn't tell what was real, what wasn't. All I knew was it was twilight, the woman cast no shadow.

My womb. They took it.
They took your womb??
She nodded. *Without asking.*

Then, drawing the hemorrhaging mass of flesh toward her possessively, the woman projected it forward, hurled her bleeding, extracted uterus at me. It caught the edge of my arm with a wet slap. I felt its heat, its thud against my skin, the slickness of membranes and skin cells gone to waste. I screamed without sound, covered my eyes with trembling hands.

"Go away, go away...go away," I chanted in time to my ragged breaths.

When I finally gathered enough courage to peek through my slatted fingers, nothing was there. The hallway was empty, only an old gurney and wheelchair blocking the path.

I pushed past both, bolting past the atrium with eyes closed again, heading for any room that didn't feel oppressed. In the northwest corner, I ducked into a random junk-filled guest room to catch my breath. Something moved, a shadow that skittered along the wall. Logic told me it was the silhouette of a bird flying past the window, but after what I'd just been through, I couldn't be sure.

I sank to the floor and sat there, holding my head with my hands, waiting for my body to stop trembling. I felt that sense of air displacement again, like an invisible body standing near me, sound waves and energy rushing around it. A moment later, it was gone. Was she following me? The bleeding woman in the hallway? As much as she needed help, there was nothing I could do for her.

Who the hell was she, and why would anyone take her *womb?*

I was about to sprint downstairs to rejoin the others when something in the adjacent room made a sound. A human sound. A metal drawer closing. Footsteps. Sneakers. "Hello?" I called.

A familiar voice replied, "Mori?"

From the rich baritone, it had to be Wilky. I pressed a hand to my chest to still my heart. I couldn't do this again, this wandering-around-by-myself thing. I wasn't used to it.

"It's Valentina." I made my way into the room.

Wilky seemed shaken but relieved. He was holding onto a metal file cabinet. "Oh, hey."

"Are you okay?" I asked.

"No." He pulled a file from a rusted old drawer and took a seat on a stool that tipped slightly when he put his weight on it. "I hate doing this."

"Looking through files?" I was happy to have normal conversation to distract me, though I couldn't get the woman out of my mind.

He nodded, riffled through papers and tossed a file on the floor. "What were you doing up here?"

"Stupidly exploring," I replied.

He looked at me with sad, tired eyes, like he could tell I'd seen something. If he did, he said nothing.

"Sorry for intruding," I said. "I didn't know you were here. You want me to leave?"

"Of course not." He forced a new expression, happy for the distraction, it seemed. A sigh escaped him. "I get inside my head too much. I thought it'd be a good idea to come up here and check records *again*, but..."

"But what?"

"It's pointless."

"How?"

"I never find anything. I come up here every few days. I'm obsessed with these..." He kicked a file cabinet with his shoe. "Garbage. Tons of records that amount to shit. I can't prove anything, but I know this place was something else at one point. I can't prove it. It's fucking maddening." He kicked a rusted wire trash can, too. It bounced off the wall and rolled away.

I felt his fury and sense of responsibility to provide his family with answers. "You're frustrated. I'm so sorry."

"It's fine." He shook his head. "I have to accept that I'll never know the truth. I'll just have to take my family's word for it. If history was erased, it was erased. Fuck the victors."

"I don't..." I had no idea what he meant.

"The victors," he explained. "History is written by the winners, the oppressors."

"Ah," I replied. "What else do you think this building was used for?"

"Not think, know. I *know* it was used for evil."

I bristled at his word choice.

"The sanatorium was meant to heal people, but nobody healed, Vale. Ninety percent of patients were sent here to die. The veteran's hospital didn't go well either. One association's records show a staggering eight-five percent death rate for any patient unlucky enough to have been registered here after World War II."

"Holy shit."

"Women sent here weren't treated well either."

The vision of the woman holding her own uterus, claiming that they'd taken it without her permission would haunt me for the rest of my life. If I could see my own father and talk to him with the same clarity as I'd done with her, however, I would get over my fear in a heartbeat.

"Then, of course, the kitchen fire during the resort years was the nail in the coffin. It pretty much failed immediately. Something about this place..." I could see his hands shaking. "They say it's an energy vortex, but it's more than that. Why do so many terrible things happen here?" he asked without waiting for an answer, not that I had one. "Nothing healed here. Nothing. Only pain succeeded."

His anger was so thick, I felt responsible for it. "What else do you think happened here? You said history was erased."

He paced around the file cabinet, stood at the window, looking out at the sunset. "When it was closed to the public, sometime between the mental hospital and the wellness resort, this hotel was a meeting place. A secret meeting place," he stressed. "I know because my mother's family has lived in this area going back as far as a hundred years. They know."

"A meeting place for who?" I had a feeling for whom, but I needed to hear it from him.

"The Brotherhood of Klans," he breathed.

I stared at him, holding my breath, until he looked at me.

He did, and in that moment, I wanted to apologize for the sins of the world as though they all belonged to me, as though I'd caused them myself.

"And that tree you found by the lake?" An odd expression that looked like a smile morphed into a wistful smirk, full of pain. "Was where they lynched people who looked like me."

Fourteen

The memory of two nights ago slipped into my mind, when I'd sat by the lake staring at that twisted tree. I was so sure I'd been in someone else's body. My throat, the tugging, burning, and torches.

"Who did you lose?" I asked.

Wilky had never directly told me he'd lost anyone, but I knew his determination to find paperwork was personal. "My great uncle," he said. "He went missing in 1969. Went out for a pack of cigarettes and never came home. A case was opened with Volusia County, but we know how useful police investigations turn out for Black people."

"I'm sorry."

He nodded and returned to peruse the files. If I could find evidence of Wilky's uncle's disappearance just to lift that heaviness off him, restore a bit of his smile, I would. Against my better judgment, I held his arm.

He paused his paper shuffling.

I listened, through my fingertips.

The room shifted, knocking me off balance. Vertigo caught hold, the walls tilted. I grabbed onto the file cabinet to keep from keeling over. When the room righted itself, I blinked and focused on his face until two Wilkys became one.

"What happened?" he asked.

I let go of his arm. I hadn't told anyone about my ability. Until recently, I hadn't even realized what it was. "I saw someone in the hallway before I found you."

"Who?"

"A woman. A patient. She..."

Wilky listened to my every word.

"I think you're right about terrible things happening here. She didn't seem happy with the things they did to her."

"Was she in the south wing?"

"Yes. She said they took her womb." It sounded crazy uttering that out loud.

Wilky searched the floor. He picked up a short stack of files and thumbed through them.

"What are you looking for?"

"I've read all these files over the course of a year, Vale. Not one says anything about hysterectomies."

"That's what I thought. It was a psychiatric hospital, not a medical one."

"Right." Wilky opened a file, pointed to a doctor's scrawling. "But I always wondered what this meant. Patient suffers from schizophrenia. Mentally unstable. A harm to herself and others. *Sterilization recommended*."

I stared at the file as he held it out. "So, because a woman suffered from mental illness, they prevented her from reproducing? Is that even legal?" Horror at the thought rippled through me. The woman had held out her uterus—her *uterus*.

"Were lynchings legal?" Wilky countered. "That's my point. This shit isn't in the books. We'll never find it here. Doesn't mean it didn't happen." He slapped the file closed.

"That is insane." I gawked at him. "Why isn't anyone talking about this? I've never heard of such a thing."

"There's a *lot* nobody talks about."

I was back to feeling sick to my stomach. People needed to learn about the history here. We couldn't just let it fade into obscurity. The truth would mar the Sunlake's reputation. It would block Crow's attempts to highlight the building's beauty, would sabotage his efforts to bring this place back to life, but it'd be the truth.

Wilky's eyes snapped toward the east wall. "Hear that?"

The air felt alive with a buzzing vitality, like molecules bouncing off each other, making the atmosphere itself seem to quake. I did hear something faint. "What is that?"

Wilky took my hand. "Let's go. We need to shake this off. They're starting."

"Starting what?"

"The mock ritual."

It felt nice to have his hand hold mine, and because he wasn't thinking about anything negative anymore, I didn't "see" anything negative in his touch. Wilky tugged me out the door, down the hall, to the stairwell. We dropped down in a frenetic rush of twists and turns.

The closer we got to the ballroom, the louder the drums beat, until we were on the veranda, looking toward the lake where Crow sat cross-legged, beating on a small leathery hand drum embossed with a mandala design. Mori and Fae cavorted around a bonfire, holding hands. All three had shed their clothes again, shades of light and medium tanned skin moving in the fading sun. Wilky did not hesitate to strip down to his dark butt and join them.

I averted my eyes at first, then snuck a look.

"Come on." He reached out his hand.

I'd spent a few days with them in various states of undress, but not like this. Not the full monty. It shouldn't have been a big deal, but to my Catholic sensibilities, it was. I needed to unfuck that immediately.

Fae was breathtakingly gorgeous with little wildflowers in her long, matted hair; Mori wore a woven crown of sawgrass on their head; both pranced like dancers in a Matisse painting against the violet sky, and Crow swayed back and forth on the ground.

Wilky raised an eyebrow. "You coming, moon child?"

On the horizon, the nearly full moon was rising—a luminous ball of rust. It called to me, challenged me to cast my fears into the fire. My shyness, my modesty. Shed the old Vale and become a new one, or risk turning into stone.

Crow beat on his drum, purple hair flipping with each pound of his hand or small mallet against the taut surface. Primitive rhythms snuck into my bones, navigated my limbs. The bonfire beckoned. The clairs wouldn't be complete until I joined them.

"It's okay," Wilky said. "I promise."

Without another moment's hesitation, I kicked off my flip-flops, crossed my arms, and held fast onto the edge of my shirt. Lifting it over my head, I heard the pearl-clutching gasps of everyone I'd ever grown up with ring through my mind.

I ignored them—*Get it. Get that freedom.*

Their hisses were replaced by four happy cheers of my coven mates. Unhooking my bra, I tossed it, followed by my shorts and underwear, onto the veranda. And for the first time ever, I truly danced.

It's the way we were meant to be.

Humans dancing naked since the beginning of time.

I fell into an easy rhythmic circle. I had no clue what I was doing, but it didn't matter. I just danced. Side-stepped with each beat, lifted my arms to the stars, and twirled with Mori and Fae. Wilky gave me his hand. In it, I saw his ancestors dancing, too, white head scarves, white dresses, beads flying, raising energy,

Yoruba chanted into the mountainside and palm trees, all in joyous harmony.

I got no hate stares from Crow either. He watched me the same way he glanced at everyone else. Nobody leered at my body. Nobody was "checking me out." Nudity had felt shameful because people *made* it shameful. I'd learned that in CCD classes, that God punished Adam and Eve in the Garden of Eden by making them carry shame forever and ever. We were born of sin.

What a shitty thing to tell a child.

What a shitty thing to tell girls, that they were to blame for the sins of the world, for every terrible thing that had ever befallen man, had thrown him off the righteous path.

But worst of all, what a shitty thing for boys to hear, that they were absolved of all fault.

Sinful, tempting Eve. Now good men will suffer because of you. Perfect, law-abiding Adam failed because of YOU. Wicked little witch.

I danced out my anger, flailing, knocking imaginary people out of my circle—CCD teachers, Cuco, Abuela, my family for trying to suppress me, my father for leaving me when I needed him most, the people who wrote cautionary tales to keep children in line, Hansel and Gretel for not listening to the warnings, for making it harder on us kids, the Little Mermaid for dying all because she wanted a life outside her realm. Because of them, I was taught to—

Fear everything.

God forbid we should stray from the rules.

God forbid we should *make* our own rules.

I danced.

And when the clairs lifted their arms and called to the spirits of air, I called to the spirits of air. And when they called to the spirits of water, I called to the spirits of water. To the spirits of earth. To the spirits of fire. Four of them knelt while I remained standing.

"Encircle us," Mori instructed. "Bring us together."

I painted an outer circle with twirls and jumps. I was Spirit, the all-encompassing force, the glue that made them all One. The opposite of shame and guilt. I was power, important power, good power. I never felt more beautiful, more needed, inspired and emboldened than I did now. This *was* God's will for me. One thing my religious education got right—we *were* created in God's image.

We were powerful, like Him.

We were creators, like Him.

In the distance, on the edge of the woods between the copse of trees and the muddy blended edges of swamp, Lobo sat on his haunches, watching the raising of unified energy with worried determination in his fiery eyes. He howled, and we howled with him.

VIVID, wild dreams of flying around the hotel came to me that night, my arms out wide, soaring over the lake like an eagle. I was untethered, free to go where I pleased. When I awoke in the morning, I was disappointed to find I was a mere mortal once again, but at least I had no nightmares. Next to my head I found a pouch of mugwort, an herb to amplify dreams.

Fae caught my eye and winked.

The full moon ritual was tonight. We spent most of the day writing our intentions, sketching, or visualizing in some way. I did three tarot card spreads to see how things would go. Each presented the Tower—a brick, castle-like structure on fire, lightning zapping from the sky behind it. The Tower represented destruction and chaos. Most people were scared of the card just like they were scared of the Death card, though both were more symbolic of change than anything.

In the late afternoon, we performed the mock ritual again, only Crow invoked the Lady of the Lake using aquamarine, rose-mary, and a Queen of Cups tarot card. To summon her, he recited an incantation, followed by a rapid-fire photo session to see if he'd captured her, but she didn't appear in any of the pics. None of us seemed to see or sense her either. If I was able to see the kitchen ghost and the hallway ghost so vividly, wouldn't I have also been able to see the Lady?

I felt bad for him.

At the end of the bonfire, the clairs gave me a progress report. I was tuning in, they said, opening up nicely. In just a few days, they'd seen drastic changes in me. I was no longer a timid newcomer and they seemed to agree I was nearly on the same vibration as they were. To help accelerate things, they suggested I take a hit of their weed. Though I'd never smoked pot before—cannabis, marijuana, ganja, hash, whatever you want to call it—I was all in.

If we were going to bond, let's bond.

"Don't hold it in your mouth," Mori said.

"Breath it into your lungs," Fae said.

"Finish the whole thing, or it doesn't count," Crow said.

Wilky rolled his eyes. "How about we leave her alone."

I tried to make them all happy, but mostly, I listened to my gut instinct and only inhaled about 50%. That was enough for me, and I coughed—loudly—to everyone's delight. Suddenly, quiet, little me was talking. I told them about my upbringing, my church life, my grandfather being my school principal. I told them about Cami and felt intense guilt for ignoring her texts. I told them about my encounter with the hysterectomy patient and the kitchen ghost. They were amazed I'd seen the hotel's spirits as clearly as I had. Especially Crow—with envy in his eyes.

Had I seen anyone else? They wanted to know. *Not yet.*

Mori was concerned that both women couldn't move into the light, that fear kept them tied in this dimension, doomed to relive harrowing experiences over and over for all eternity. They said both spirits might benefit from Mori's trance writing exercises, so as the sun began to set, we set out to search for the bereaved ghost on the third floor.

We set up in the hallway where I'd seen her, said a prayer for protection then summoned her, but she didn't manifest. Mori did sense another woman, beautiful and radiant, drawn to me who lovingly stroked my hair, but I didn't feel or "see" anyone.

"I want to try something else," Mori said, heading to the south stairwell, as Wilky and Crow fell out, and only Fae and I followed.

"What do you want to try?" I asked.

"An experiment. Where do you feel the most heaviness?"

"In the whole building?" I asked. "The atrium, without a doubt."

"Really." Mori clucked their tongue, and before we knew it, that's where we were headed, notebook tucked under their arm. They seemed determined to make contact tonight, come hell or high water. I wondered why we didn't just wait until after the amplification ritual. "Why the atrium?"

"I can't say for sure. It's almost as though the room hates me."

"Hates you?"

"It's irrational, I know." We arrived at the entrance to the atrium, where I looked up at the chandelier. "I don't like that thing," I said, tilting my chin up at the broken light fixture swinging softly between its chains.

Mori glanced at the chandelier full of crystals refracting sunlight through the broken windowpanes.

"I don't like the moss hanging from that tree either. The first night I saw it, I thought it was an entity swimming in the air."

"An entity," Mori repeated, fascinated. They handed me the notebook and pen. "Sit here."

"By the fountain?"

"Anywhere underneath. Don't worry, I'm with you."

"No offense, but that doesn't help," I said.

"You get used to it after a while, Vale." Mori pulled out a sage bundle and lighter from their pocket, proceeded to set it ablaze, then wafted the smoke over me. "Imagine the violet light. It comes from above and covers you like a warm, loving blanket."

Sighing, wishing thoughts would come to me that way and not like an army of red ants blanketing my frozen, panicked body, I closed my eyes and imagined the light I'd been taught to imagine. I envisioned a cocoon of love surrounding me, protecting me from all harm. Inch by inch, my nervous muscles loosened, I began to relax.

"Set aside all thoughts that don't belong in this moment. Yesterday is gone, there is no tomorrow. There's only now, this moment." Mori's voice was a warm honey embrace. "Be grateful... in the moment."

I felt their fingers slip into mine. In their touch, I sensed a deep longing for love and acceptance that made me well up with sadness. I sensed a painful past and rejection no child should ever bear. Their soft voice lulled me into a weightless slumber. It was quiet in the atrium, except for birds chirping in the distance. A breeze whistled through the cracked glass panes. The heat felt like a doorway to an underworld.

ALL I HAVE IS NOW...
My little starshine, sleep, oh, so tight
My little moonshine, dream with the night

AT FIRST, nothing happened. Then, I rested my hands on the warm cobblestones and breathed deeply.

A male doctor stood next to another male patient lying on a bed. The doctor waited until the old man couldn't talk anymore, then he unsheathed an injection. The patient had two missing legs, the stumps of which had healed long ago. He was old, with long white hair, long crusty nails, and he wore an eye patch. He'd been there a long time.

This doctor connected the man's arm to an IV and plunged down on medication. It entered the man's bloodstream. The old-timer slumped. The doctor turned to me. *It's better this way.*

"Go," I said.

"Go?" Mori asked. "Who should go?"

I had no answer.

Mori wanted to know what else I could "see."

A nurse in a white dress, like the old-timey Halloween costume. Her hair was ragged, and her eyes almost bled from lack of sleep. *They're dying, they're all dying...*she cried. She flitted from one dead patient to the other, crying about none of the treatments working. They would all die.

None of this was happening in the atrium, but in the floors above it. I wanted to snap out of the vision, but it kept ahold of me.

I heard glass break. A woman's body smashed through the atrium, landing in the plants with a sickening thud. Nurses abandoned wheelchair-ridden patients to see what had happened, finding the bloody pulp of a body broken in the landscaping. I saw her jaw broken in half, contents of her skull spilling into the pond, coy fish feasting on the chunks.

I suppressed a gag. "I see her."

"Who?"

I clutched the pencil in my hand so hard, I felt my nails digging into my palms. "She jumped. From the tower."

"Is it the Lady?"

"No." Not the Lady—a young, beautiful woman whose spirit would remain at this property for the next hundred years. And yet, she might've been the lady in the paintings. I couldn't be sure.

Another body, a man's, well-built, dropped into my view from above. His neck bent in an awful, sharp angle to the rest of his frame. His eyes bulged grotesquely. His throat turned a sickly blue hue. His legs kicked wildly a moment before petering out. He wore modern jeans and T-shirt, not a hospital shift, and he swung from a rope dangling from the chandelier.

And a smell. A horrible, decaying smell filled my nostrils, as the man's body decayed in fast-forward time lapse. His mouth fell open to speak, but I couldn't hear his words—I was screaming too loud.

Mori gripped my forearms and shook me. "Shh, Vale! It's okay, it's okay."

He was horrible to look at, hanging there from the chandelier, swinging like meat on a butcher's hook.

"What is it?"

I fell into Mori's shoulder and wept. "I can't. I can't do this..."

"Vale, they can't hurt you."

"Like hell they can't." Emotional trauma classified as "hurt," damn it.

"Who did you see this time?"

I pointed without looking. My whole body trembled. "A man. He's dead. He said something, but I..." I couldn't put the words together. Of all the things I'd seen so far, this was, by far, the worst. I watched a man *die*.

"'Tell them I love them?'" Mori asked.

"Huh?" I sobbed.

"You said, 'Tell them I love them.'"

"I did?"

"Yes."

Now that Mori said the words, I heard them in my mind, uttered from a broken neck or another layer of time. *Tell them I love them.*

Pulling away, I glanced down at the pad of paper in my lap. I hadn't written a damn thing. The pencil fell from my fingers. I stood, sucking in lungs full of air, and staggered to the entryway. I would never come back to this room, not willingly, not if I could help it.

I stumbled into the hall, relieved to be back in the present when a very normal, very welcomed text came in. *Where are you?* Macy.

With friends. It wasn't a lie.

You might want to come back.

Why? Everything OK?

The gray ellipses of composition wiggled a few seconds. She was writing an essay. Was she mad that I was out? But she'd assured me I had the freedom to do as I pleased. Maybe I'd gone too far. When her reply finally appeared, it made no sense. I had to read the words three times, each time reeling me back harder, like a marlin losing its fight and getting dragged into a boat.

Camila is here.

Fifteen

By the time I pulled into Macy's driveway and spotted Cami's car sitting there, my stomach was ready to purge. In the ten minutes since I'd left the Sunlake Springs, I'd gone through every single possible reason I might give Cami as to why she couldn't stay. None of them would go over well. She would fight me. I knew this.

I stepped out of the car and hopped up the steps to the house. No matter what happened, I would convince Cami it'd be best if she got back in her car and drove six hours back to Miami. Tonight. After she'd driven six hours to get here.

Okay, sure.

I opened the screen door and strolled in like I'd just gone out for a quick Frappuccino. Macy's rolling bag stood in the foyer. She must've just gotten home when Cami arrived. I jingled my keys to signal I was home.

Macy and Cami stood talking in the kitchen at the small island. Macy saw me before Camila did. She had that look in her eye when someone has been holding down the fort for you while you're away doing bad things. I threw on my best fake enthusiasm.

"Oh, wow..." I faked surprise.

Cami's face whipped my way. She gave me a bright smile, as though she were the best gift I could possibly receive.

"You're here? No way!" I floated into her orbit, as she reined me in with her gravitational pull.

"Surprise!" I was swooped into the Cami hug, and I'd be lying if I said it wasn't like coming back to Earth after visiting Saturn.

Macy's expression was mixed worry, relief, and admiration. Right before I pulled away, Cami got a whiff of my sweaty-ass, weed-stinky body and gave me an odd look.

"Yeah, sorry. Need a shower."

"Good Lord, girl, where've you been? Dumpster diving?"

"He, he, funny." Immediately, there was tension. The old me would never smell like baked armpit.

Macy pulled out a stool and sat to watch the show. "Cami was just saying how it rained the whole way on 95 until she got here, then the sun came out."

Cami beamed. "Yep. It was a sign. I was getting closer to you. My sweet sis." She swung her arm around my shoulder. Something was off. I could read Cami like a book. She'd come all this way as an ambassador from Youths for Jesus, possibly even my family.

After a few pleasant exchanges, I invited Cami upstairs so we could talk in private in my room while Macy shook her head quietly and popped open a bottle of wine. *Thank you,* I mouthed over my shoulder at her.

She nodded.

As we headed upstairs, Cami made small talk about the cars that had cut her off, how hard it was to see through the driving rain, and Praise Be to Jesus she'd made it in one piece.

All I could think about were the ghosts of the Sunlake Springs and how I could see them.

"I take it you asked my mom where I was?" Because I sure as

hell hadn't told her. Getting away literally meant getting away, in my book.

She nodded. "She gave me your sister's address, told me you'd enjoy having a visitor. Hope it was okay that I surprised you."

It wasn't.

And I'd be having a word with my mother at some point in the next few days.

"Yes, so happy to see you." *Too bad I'm going to have to kick you out soon.* "How was the retreat?"

We entered the room. I closed the door behind us. There was nothing of mine there to even nervously fiddle with, so I threw myself on the bed and hugged a pillow, pretending I was really tired. Outside, the sun was lowering in the west, creating tangerine stripes across the wall.

Cami threw her packed bag that looked like it had enough stuff for a week's stay into the desk chair. "Ay, the retreat," she said, voice loaded with resentment. "The one you left me at by myself."

"I guess we're going to talk about that."

"Shouldn't we?" She sank onto the edge of the bed. She looked different, though it was probably me who'd changed.

"There's nothing to talk about."

"Are you sure?"

"Yes. I've been thinking about it for a while, Cami. Believe it or not, you're the first person I said anything to. I haven't been into the whole Youths for Jesus scene for a while now. Even before Antoni, so don't think that's why," I added before she could mention it.

"I was going to ask you that."

"Of course, you were."

She watched me a moment then glanced at her nails. "I thought your grandfather's death also might've had something to do with it. Didn't it affect you? I thought it was weird how you didn't mourn him that much."

How could I explain to Cami that Cuco hadn't meant to me what he'd meant to the whole Ministerio Rey Jesus family. To me, he was my strict grandfather whose sole way was the highway. To them, he was a pillar of the community, a treasure. "I miss him, but that's not why I ditched the retreat."

She shrugged. "Thought maybe you left because he wasn't around anymore to watch over you. I know you felt pressured by him."

"I did. But Abuela is the same way, and so is my mom, to a certain extent. All our friends are. So is school. I mean, MRJ has been our whole life since we were little, our entire worldview. There hasn't been a moment I haven't been immersed in it, you know?"

"It's a good community."

"It's not everything."

"It's a good, safe place, Vale, filled with good people. I know we're not all perfect, but that doesn't mean we should be discarded."

"I never discarded anyone, Cam. I just needed to get away. You understand that, don't you? Everyone needs a vacation. Mental health is a top priority."

She sucked in a breath. "So, you wanted to see what it was like outside the church walls."

"Basically."

"I guess I can't blame you for wanting to visit your half-sister."

"It's just sister, Cami. We don't call ourselves 'half-sister.' We don't purposely quantify the fifty percent, you know? Besides, we've gotten close like full sisters." I felt a bit guilty saying that. I'd spent so much time away from the house.

A minute went by where we didn't say anything. The full moon ritual was set for tonight, 10:05 PM, and I could not, under any circumstances, miss it. I wracked my brain trying to figure out how to get back to the resort without Cami. I would have to make an excuse, another lie. Two steps in the right direction, two steps back again.

"Were they surprised I left?" I asked.

A puff of air escaped her lips. "Um, yes. Father Willie wanted to call you and talk to you, Sister Agatha called your mom, and everybody kept saying how rude it was the way you left."

"Rude? I quietly slipped out. I bothered literally no one."

"But you know they don't see it that way."

"See, that's my point. Now you understand why I don't want to be a part of it anymore. Did anyone consider maybe I was having a crisis? Did anyone give me the benefit of the doubt? This is my point, Cami. The church is supposed to be about acceptance, tolerance, love, understanding, yet when people don't act perfectly, everyone gets judgy."

"No one got judgy."

"You just *said* they were saying how rude I was! That's judgy. Look," I pressed my fingers against my eyes, "I don't want to discuss it. I came here to refresh. You're the one who decided not to warn me that you were coming, and the first thing you talk about is the retreat."

She crossed her arms. "You asked how it went. I told you."

"Fine."

"All I'm saying is it's okay to try something different, but ultimately, we all go home, Vale." *To God, to the Lord.* She didn't have to spell it out for me to understand what she meant.

"What if we don't?" I asked. "What if we find happiness elsewhere?"

"Are you saying you're happy here?"

"I might be. I don't know. I've only been here two weeks."

"Then find a church near you, wherever you are. That's the important thing."

I gawked at her. I hadn't wanted to open this can of worms

here and now, but if we were going there, may as well. "Why is that 'the important thing?'"

Cami blinked a few times. She scanned the room for a reasonable answer. Like most people I knew, she couldn't begin to fathom a life without religion. "Because it is. Because you need God in your life, Vale."

"Who says I don't have God in my life, Camila?" I was nearly shouting. In thirteen years of friendship, I'd never shouted at her.

She stared at me.

I never said I was done with God, no matter how feverishly I'd danced buck-naked under the moonlight with strangers. Thinking of them felt at such odds with Cami's presence. This had all been easier without her here. Now that she was, I felt disoriented and lost.

For a moment, I considered giving in to the safety of my former life. Maybe the clairs *were* leading me astray. Maybe Cami was here to save me.

"Where's your stuff?" She glanced around.

I looked at her. "Like what?"

"Your clothes, your bag...there's nothing here but a bed and a desk. Where were you before I got here? Your sister texted you, then you arrived fifteen minutes later. Just tell me."

"I was out." I was my old self again, defending my actions with partial truths.

"Where? Tell me, Valentina, for fuck's sake, just talk to me!" She huffed and walked over to the window. "You're different. I can tell."

"I am different, Camila. That's what two weeks away from home will do to you."

We were two canoes in a swiftly moving river, each traveling at a different rate, at times moving near each other, at times drifting far apart. My heart hurt to think I'd decided our friendship would be on pause long before she got here, before the retreat, maybe during our senior year, and I hadn't bothered to tell her.

She had a right to be angry.

Staring at the neighbor's yard, she clucked her tongue. "Is it a guy? Someone you met online?"

"What? No. Camila, it's not always about a *guy*." I stood and paced the room. There was no changing her. I couldn't bring her along where I was headed either.

Outside, the sky grew deeper purple. The clairs were probably going batshit wondering where I was. I owed them nothing, yet I didn't want to let them down. For once, I was exactly where I wanted to be. *My* choice. I wanted part of the full moon ritual. I liked the new possibilities, the new friendships, the exploration of this new spiritual side, even if, at times, it was scary as balls.

"Look, I know you came all this way just to see me, and I promise I will explain everything to you. I'll come clean, but for now I have to go." I moved to the door, hoping she'd leave of her own accord.

"You said that last time right before you left the retreat."

"And if you're my friend, you'll trust me."

"I drove six hours. I'm not going back tonight. It's dangerous to be on the road late by myself. I don't think you want that for me, do you?"

"Then stay here. Macy has everything you need. She's a great hostess."

"I don't want to hang with Macy, Valentina. I want to be with you. Whatever it is, I can handle it. I want to be a part of your life, no matter what it is."

I stared at her. "You don't want this. Trust me."

"Trust *me*, Valentina."

We'd been friends since the age of five. I was pretty damn sure she couldn't handle it, but who knew? She might prove me wrong.

I didn't want to be a hypocrite like the others. I wanted to give her the benefit of the doubt.

"Fine," I huffed. "Come along, or stay here. I don't care. Just don't say I didn't warn you."

"Don't be so dramatic."

"Suit yourself."

I left in a hurry. If Camila wanted to join me on this journey I'd started without her, I was no one to stop her.

Sixteen

Letting Cami come had seemed like the right choice, but now I had a devout Catholic in the car who also happened to be a Youths for Jesus leader, from Ministerio Rey Jesus, which *also* happened to be one of the city's biggest mega churches, and we were en route—where else?—to meet a coven of witches.

I'd stormed downstairs where Macy had picked up on my fuming vibes. She'd pulled me into the kitchen and stared deep into my eyes with absolute sincerity. "Do you need me to keep her here?"

"No. I've inconvenienced you enough."

"I don't mind."

"I appreciate it, but I need to deal with her myself. Stupid of me for thinking I could have a summer of peace and quiet."

"I'm sorry, Vale."

I sighed. "I'll be back soon."

She grasped my arm—our eyes connected. "And you'll tell me what's going on then?" She knew something was up.

"Yes. Promise."

She'd touched my chin and let me go without another word.

Truth was the least I could give Macy Edwins.

Now, pulling into the long, cracked driveway of the Sunlake Springs Resort, it seemed like such a stupid choice to bring Cami. I should've insisted she stay behind until I could complete my obligations.

"Where're you taking me?" Her wide gaze absorbed the dark surroundings. We ventured further away from the main road deeper into darkness.

"To your death."

She stared ahead without a word.

"I'm kidding." I stopped the car and got out to pull the iron gate as far open as it would go. Shuffling back to the car, I drove through the gates. "Just a head's up, you're going to have a *lot* of questions. Save them to the end."

"You're scaring me."

"There's nothing to be scared of. I've met some people, that's all, and we're doing a prayer tonight."

"That doesn't sound so bad."

"Not the kind of prayer you're used to."

I could see the cogs in her head chugging at a furious pace to keep up. "I don't understand."

"I told you to stay, Cami." I drove down the darkened path of shrubbery that had, from all the rain, grown considerably in the last few days. The ground beneath was uneven, as we bumped along. Branches reached out to scratch the sides of the car. Up ahead, the old Sunlake came into view.

"What the...?" Her gaze had fallen on its silhouette bathed in moonlight. It looked ominous with its dark and forbidden central tower and most its windows blown out. "What is this?"

"An old hotel. A hospital. It's called the Sunlake Springs. Remember, no questions." I pulled up to the building, parked in my usual spot, and got out, rehearsing how I was going to explain this to the clairs. I considered asking Cami to stay behind, though from the looks of it, she didn't want to get out of the car anyway.

"You're going in?" she asked incredulously.

"Yes. You can stay or follow." I didn't wait for her reply and left to locate the unlocked auxiliary door behind the registration counter. She decided to leave the car and follow me in.

I squeezed through the gap in the doorway. A feeling of coming home to a place I barely knew overcame me. Tonight, the lobby was extra dark, particularly disheveled, and I felt Cami's trepidation like nervous rats around my ankles.

"I don't like this." Her voice was out-of-place in the dusty stillness.

Without my flashlight, I scanned for shadows and listened for voices so I could confront anyone before they saw her. "Wait here."

"Vale." She panic-whispered. "Don't leave me."

"I said, wait here." I walked away.

Inky darkness greeted me, a gloom that deepened with each stretch into the expanse. I passed the bird cages and came face-to-face with the dreaded atrium. After all I'd seen today, I covered my eyes and hurried past it.

"Don't come out. Do not..." I warned the spirits.

"Valentinaaaa," Cami whispered.

I ignored her. "Hello?"

The hallway felt cold.

A crack snapped behind me, Cami tiptoeing into the hallway. "Are we allowed to be here? Why on Earth are we here? Oh, my God, oh, my God..."

Doubt at having brought her continued to seep in. My stomach clenched into itself. I knew I'd face questions. Crow would go back to mistrusting me. From where I stood, I heard the low thrum, the heartbeat, his drumming in the distance. A peek at my phone told me it was still early—8:30 PM—still the clairs had already begun raising energy just like we had with the mock run.

"This way." I led her through the ballroom, where the heaps of bags, clothes, and personal belongings tipped Cami off that we weren't alone.

"People live here?"

"Just temporarily," I said, to ease her fears.

I was so used to making things palatable for Cami and others who would disapprove. Why I worried so much about other people's reactions, feelings, or fears, more than mine, would always be a mystery to me.

"What's that noise?"

I led her through the room, hoping I wouldn't "see" whatever curious spirit was there. My heart jumped into my throat when I heard a voice from the alcove to my left.

"I knew it," someone groaned.

Cami let out a squeal. "Oh, sweet Jesus."

"Crow." I pressed a hand to my chest. He wore his jeans without a shirt, kept his arms crossed over his skull-moth and nude, long-haired woman tattoos. "Why are you lurking in the dark? Aren't you supposed to be outside?"

"Don't tell me where I should or shouldn't be, Vale. Who is this?"

I stepped aside to reveal Cami hiding behind me. "This is my friend, Camila. She surprised me with a visit. That's why I left earlier, because my sister called me. Don't worry, she's not going to bother us."

"She is bothering us. Why did you bring her?"

"I didn't have a choice." I glared at him. Surely, he understood that sometimes shit just happened. "You know I have a family. They worry about me."

As soon as I said it, I felt bad for insinuating that I had a family who cared, and Crow didn't. That wasn't what I meant.

"That's not my problem. You know what's involved. Soon we'll have cops here asking us to leave."

"She's not going to do that," I said.

"Who is this guy, and why is he talking to you like this?" Cami was charging up, ready to defend, something she did when she wanted to appear tougher than she was.

I turned a glare on her. "Can you please?"

"We can't have her here," Crow said. "Get her out."

"Cami, just...take my car and go back. I'll explain later. I promise it's nothing."

"It's nothing? You brought me to a place that looks like Halloween Horror Nights and some random guy comes out of nowhere and starts telling you what to do? What's going on?"

"There's something I have to do." I wrestled with offering an explanation, but we didn't have that kind of time. "See my things over there? Sit for a while. Don't go anywhere until I come back. Believe me, you don't want to be caught alone in this place."

"Is this urban exploring, what you're doing? I can't believe this," she mumbled, doing what I asked and plopping beside my duffel bag, drawing her knees to her chest. "You owe me, huge."

Crow stepped out of the alcove and took me by the elbow, but I yanked it out of his grasp. We walked out the back doors onto the veranda. When we were far enough away, he turned his scrutinizing gaze on me. "What were you thinking bringing a friend here when you know what we're doing tonight?"

"I told you, I didn't have a choice! She blindsided me."

"You always have a choice, Vale."

Fae flew up the slope, wearing her flowing skirt on the bottom half but nothing on the top. Her hair was covered in wildflowers. She looked glowingly beautiful, as always, but now, instead of appreciating her, I cringed inside, thinking of what Cami would say about her.

Mori waltzed up the walk to the veranda, a little more modest wearing an open-sided tank top. "What's happening?" they asked.

"Valentina brought a friend," Crow hissed.

Mori gave me a confused expression. I didn't care anymore if Crow got upset with me, but seeing Mori's questioning face suggesting possible betrayal to the group hurt.

"I had no choice. She drove a long way to see me. When I said I had something to do, she insisted on coming along. I'm sorry, guys. We can still do this. She's not going to bother us."

"Her being here is already a disruption," Crow said.

"I can't say I disagree," Mori said.

"One I can't do anything about," I insisted.

Crow clenched his jaw. "If she reports us, you're going to hear it from me." He jabbed a finger in my direction.

I slapped his fingers away.

"Crow, stop," Mori said. "We can't do that, not tonight. Negativity will throw off everything we've worked hard for."

"Whose fault is that?" he spat. "I knew she'd do something like this. Even if the girl doesn't interfere, now Vale's not in the frame of mind. We can consider this botched."

"It's not botched, Crow," I said. "I'm fine."

"That better be the case." He walked down the slope to the lake.

"Is everything alright?" Fae asked, coming up to me and holding my face in her hands.

"Yes, you can count on me. Let's do this." I didn't know why it was so important to me that they trust me when I said everything would be okay, but it was.

I had to forget about Cami for a while. She was my past, my childhood. She stood for everything that had led me to this point, whereas the clairs represented the new. Not the future—I wasn't sure how long I would live with them, but they were definitely my present. My now, the only moment we really had.

I had committed to helping them. I had to give them that.

The moon above shone brighter than anything I'd ever seen. Beautiful and just as ready for this as we were, wearing her crown of brilliant rays. I'd prayed we wouldn't have rain, and the universe had provided. Wilky, drumming by the lake, wore a white wrap around his hips. In his state of half-awareness, he looked in the zone.

I gave one last look at the veranda to see if Cami was there, if she was watching, and then, like a dandelion in the wind, I let the problem of her being here go. She wouldn't interrupt. I would commit 200% to this moment.

My clothes came off.

Fae spread black salt and flowers in a wide circle around us, while Mori poured bowls of lake water along the same arc. Crow worked on lighting the fire inside our metal fire pit, tossing wood in to make it roar and spit, as Wilky pounded beats to match the ones inside my chest. Fae set handmade flower crowns atop everyone's heads, little daisies from the fields.

Mori poured water over our shoulders. *"Goddess Moon, we see you tonight. Goddess Moon, lend us your light,"* they sang with Fae.

Crow smudged us with sage that burned my nostrils and filled my lungs, an earthy aroma I was beginning to love. Mori started chanting in the same language I'd heard them use back in Cassadaga with Citana Rose. I felt each word in my soul like I'd heard them a thousand times before. Fae's twirling both dizzied and drew me in, as she grasped my hands, and together we frolicked around the fire to Wilky's beats and Mori's song.

Every time I held Fae's hands, I saw a sad little girl wishing she had more than a dirt floor to sleep on. I wanted her to have it all, to be successful, to have the confidence of ten thousand goddesses.

It was a beautiful night for a full moon ritual—my first with other people. And despite my best friend sitting alone in a hotel full of questionable energy, waiting for me to come back to her, back into the fold where all was safe and familiar, I was ready to move into the unknown. Ready to dance freely. Ready to open this portal.

"Let's do this." I smiled at the moon.

And the moon smiled back.

Seventeen

"Goddess Hecate, we invoke thee to join our celebration, awakening, and amplification." When Mori spoke, something inside of me rejoiced. Their voice had a reverent tone to it, as though they'd been born for this moment. "Come out of the shadows."

Fae joined in, her musical voice lighter than gossamer. "Come to us, Goddess. Lend us your fullest, most loving potential, your highest light and most awesome powers of manifestation." Her arms swooped toward the heavens. She was a golden angel, thin-boned with blonde dreads dripping over slender shoulders down to her waist.

"We are complete, Goddess." Wilky pounded the drum. "We have our fifth element of Spirit." Hearing Wilky speak and watching his normally quiet self blossom, put a smile on my face.

This was it.

We were doing this.

I was dancing with witches under a full moon.

The irony of it made me laugh.

I couldn't believe that for once, I had a purpose in life besides going to school or church, feeling alienated from my family, hiding my passions. There was *so much* out there to learn. My worries seeped out from underneath my bare toes, soaking into the ground.

As the element of fire, it was Crow's turn to speak. "We invoke thee, Lady of the Lake, to come forth and be with us. Show us your face, your fierce determination, your love for this space, this land, fire, and water." His voice had a solemn determination to it.

Why was he talking about the Lady of the Lake? None of the others had asked for personal spirits to come through. We hadn't included that bit in our rehearsal yesterday.

I caught a quick exchange between Mori and Fae, but the flicker was offset by a shadow in the distance, near the south edge of the lake. Lobo paced back and forth with an uneasy gait, dipping his head, tipping it back to let out a lonely howl.

What's wrong, buddy?

The clairs reached out to each other and held hands, but Mori gestured for me to step outside the circle, which I did. "Take the walk, Valentina. Join us," Mori instructed.

I did as I'd done during rehearsal, creating an outer perimeter with my path, imagining the clairs as one unit. I raised my arms and pretended I was painting a dome of energy around them. In the flares of firelight, I almost saw the vibrant dome go up, a semi-spherical aura surrounding the clairs. They lifted their hands to the moon then lowered their bodies to the ground and knelt before their offerings. Yesterday, I had felt left out. They were the four elements, and I was something else. But my job was just as important, so I danced around them, imagining their strengths combining as one power.

As air, Wilky went first, because the sun rose in the East. "Guardians of the East watchtower, keepers of Air, we welcome you to this sacred space," he intoned with that lovely tinge of

Creole in his voice, beating the drum and lifting it high. "Please lend us your ideas, intelligence, justice and truth. We humbly accept your guidance."

There was a pause while we stilled to feel the power of Air joining us, and sure as anything, a gust of warm wind swept over the circle, flickering the flames, tickling my skin, whipping my hair. Wilky beamed.

It could've been a rogue breeze, though I chose to believe the ritual was working. We were powerful beings, capable of creating change.

"Guardians of the South watchtower, keepers of Fire," Crow went next, "we welcome you to this sacred space. Please lend us your passion, your drive to successfully open the portal. We humbly accept your guidance." He lifted his arms to the full moon.

To successfully open the portal. I suppose that was the goal, but where Wilky had asked for positive attributes, Crow had asked for direct results. I brushed it off. We all had different styles. I closed my eyes, focusing on the words coming to fruition, on the elements lending us their individual properties.

Behind closed eyelids, I saw her emerge from the lake.

A peculiar woman.

The same one I'd seen falling through the air during the trance writing. The woman who'd broken upon impact in the atrium. It was hard to tell—she'd fallen so fast—but it looked like her. Only now, her brittle hair had turned to seaweed. Her facial skin moved and reshaped itself like oil worked by an artist.

One moment, she was beautiful. The next, grotesque.

Trying to stay focused, I danced, watching the woman, in my mind's eye. She waded out of the lake into the center of the circle toward the fire. For a moment, I was afraid she'd walk right into it and burn. My eyes flew open to warn her, but there was no woman, only the flames of the fire spiking high in a tall column, sending a radial burst of heat in every direction. I shielded my face. When I looked again, the female spirit had disappeared.

Fae and Mori shrieked gleefully, Wilky's drumming skipped a beat, and Crow's face held a smug smile. *What just happened?* And why would the lake woman respond to a call for the element of fire to join us when she lived in water? It didn't make sense.

I danced the circular path.

Bring them together, make them as one...

My curiosity shifted between the bonfire, to see if the lady would emerge again, to Lobo on the horizon, pacing back and forth, watching the ritual with worry. I also kept checking the veranda, in case Cami should come out and see me participating in a pagan ritual. I wanted nothing more than to concentrate, to relive the magic of last night's beautiful dance, but it wasn't the same.

The air grew colder, though it was midsummer, though a fire blazed in front of us and hot, muggy swampland surrounded us. Mori raised their arms and sang to the moon. "Guardians of the West watchtower, keepers of Water, we welcome you to this sacred space. Please lend us your emotion, your fluidity, adaptability. We humbly accept your guidance." They lifted the bowl of water to the sky, and within seconds, it started to rain.

Not the famous torrential rain of summertime Florida, but a light drizzly patter out of nowhere. No thunderheads in the sky, no massive rain clouds, no power deluges to put the fire out. The sky was clear and beautiful. A smile spread across Mori's face. Our attention was drawn to the lake, which apparently had something to say, too.

The surface of the water rippled with waves about a foot to two feet high. There was a sudden surge, as water rose and spilled onto the shore, across the grass soaking our feet. When its squelchy fingers reached the iron cauldron, the outer shell sizzled and let out plumes of steam.

I'd never seen water behave that way. I clutched my cross and tried to stay focused.

My little starshine, sleep, oh, so tight
My little moonshine, dream with the night

FAE LOOKED at Mori with unease, then raised her arms. She lifted flowers to the sky and called her quarter. "Guardians of the North watchtower, keepers of Earth, we welcome you to this sacred space. Please lend us your nurturing love, your wisdom and eternal strength. We humbly accept your guidance!"

At her words, the ground itself shook, a strong tremble. We shrieked. "What's going on?" I called in the middle of my orbital path, but the clairs did not respond. It felt like an earthquake, though earthquakes rarely happened in Florida.

Energy.

Magic; now I understood it.

We were forcing change, invoking powers I'd only dreamed of having. Five intuitive people, stronger than one. The ground stopped rattling, a good thing because my heart almost couldn't take anymore. I thought of my father, wondering if that was how he'd felt on the night of his fateful passing.

The four clairs spoke at once, an incongruous, unsettling melody that covered my arms in goosebumps. "We invoke thee, Spirit! Keep us together, keep us potent in our Goddess's name. Make us whole. Make us powerful. Make us one and the same!"

They chanted their words to the beat, over and over, each time getting faster, their arms to the stars. I moved with the rhythm, accentuated by Wilky's drumming. I wished I'd been here as long as a year so I could grasp the whole of it all.

Lobo howled his sad song, though I couldn't see him anymore. The hotel loomed large, sad, desolate against the illuminated sky. The lake, forlorn and unkempt, looked like a swamp. I did my best to maintain the circle, the spirit, and dome.

"I am spirit. Bind us. We are one, we are one," I said over and over.

"Make us whole, make us powerful...one and the same!" they chanted.

We were in unison, one heart with all its separate parts, working together to pump blood, life essence, and potential into this hallowed ground. Something was happening. It was as if Earth, Wind, Water, and Fire were all finally speaking to each other, molecules in synch, as though they hadn't seen each other in ages and were now raucously chumming it up. The ritual was their wild party.

Suddenly, the wind, lake, ground, grasses, fire, branches, loose leaves, and all of nature's splendor around us all spasmed at once.

Lobo howled again.

The clairs made room for me in the circle, we held hands and danced faster and faster in tune with nature's song. It should've felt magickal, congruous, but for the first time since we started, I was scared. Not unsettled or creeped out, but deeply nervous about what would happen next. The atmosphere buzzed with electricity. I could reach out and touch it, positive and negative ions shooting through me, our steps growing faster, energy surrounding us, silvery and vibrant.

It wasn't in my mind anymore. It was real.

I COULD SEE IT.

And then, the summer sky lit up with electrical discharge and a flash of electricity split the air in two, and a thick bolt of lightning struck smack in the metal fire pit with a loud, powerful slam. My body went flying and skidding backwards until I landed on my ass several meters from the circle, a ringing in my ears and little black and orange dots in my vision.

My head hit.

My vision went black.

When I regained it a few moments later, I saw we'd all flown backwards. Wilky had been dumped in the lake and was crawling out, and a curtain of orange and silver atmosphere had changed the landscape. In the deepest part of my soul, I believed we were dead. And now we'd join the spirits of all who'd perished here. The drumming, the chanting, all movement had ceased, and the clairs shook their heads, brushed off their thighs and legs of mud and grass.

My head hurt too much for me to be dead. Hell no, I'd hit a tree. My fingers grasped a tangle of roots, and burning heat shot through my palm. I pulled away.

Above me, peering into my face was a hooded, robed figure in white, a man in a mask with two cutout holes for eyes. His breath reeked of whiskey. He looked at me curiously, wondering what I was doing there. He signaled to someone, then other masks appeared above.

What. The fuck.

The man reached down a hand.

"No." I scrambled to my feet.

Imagine the light, the purple light of protection...

My little starshine, sleep, oh, so tight
My little moonshine, dream with the night
When you awaken, Love you will be
My little sunshine Heaven gave me

. . .

FIVE, six hands reached down toward me. *Get up here, you piece of shit,* someone said. They dissipated into thin air, though I could still feel their hate and desire for power. My mind spun a thousand different directions, trying to rationalize what had just happened. When the clairs first mentioned this ritual, deep in my heart I thought nothing would change. I thought we'd perform an occult ritual like the ones on Instagram, offer our flowers, say our prayers, and call it a night. That's what happened in real life, in church after taking communion. We went through the motions. No one actually changed. For a short time, we felt better about our shitty selves and lives, but no one actually ever *transformed*. Not in their soul, they didn't. Everyone went back to who they were before they'd arrived.

Not here. Not this.

Something had changed in *this* sacrament.

Sure, this area was famous for its lightning, weird weather, and all, but this was different. The clairs and I had manifested a clear result. We'd harnessed the elements, bent the laws of physics. And rather than simply "see" a ghost, I'd entered another dimension, walked the hedge between worlds. Instead of the ghosts bleeding into my world, I'd bled into theirs.

I never wanted to touch that tree again. I had a piece of something awful in my memory now. I ran back to the circle, checking over my shoulder to make sure the men weren't following. Their robes and torches would haunt me a long time. I looked down at my hands. The ability I'd had as a child, that for years I'd wondered if it could be true, was more prominent now.

My God, what had I done?

We gathered. The fire had dimmed, replaced by plumes of smoke rising steadily into the night. No one spoke. Maybe the words had fled our mouths and souls, sucked out by lightning. Maybe water had washed our egos free of ever having to speak again. But we were cognizant enough to check each other for wounds, dust each other off, and return to the circle, arms around each other's shoulders.

"I think we did it," Crow breathed.

"Ya think?" Mori chuckled.

In the distance, we heard a scream. We looked up from our huddle.

Cami.

Eighteen

I grabbed my flashlight and clothes, hopped into my shorts, stumbling into the resort. Following the twinge of whimpering, I found Camila crouched on the lobby floor, covering her head with shaking hands. She shot me a glare.

"Stay where you are." Brown eyes flashed in the beam of light.

"As if I would hurt you. What happened?" I squatted beside her. She scrambled backwards on her hands then stood clumsily. I ushered her behind a column where we could talk in private.

"Something touched me." Glassy tears spilled over her lower lids.

"Where?"

"In there!" she shouted, pointing to the ballroom. "Where you left me by myself! What is this place? Who are these people? You know what—doesn't matter. Something effing touched me. I have to go." She crossed the lobby, carefully sidestepped the clairs, then hurried toward the auxiliary door.

"Cami, wait." The others tried following, but I shook my head.

"Are you leaving again?" Crow lifted a broken plank of wood off the floor and twirled it. "'Cause if you are, I'll need you to stay away for good. These interruptions aren't helping our work here.

We spend too much energy resetting from all these emotional interruptions."

Emotional interruptions. Like he didn't have emotions.

"Crow," Mori muttered. "Come on."

"I'm going to talk to her one minute," I told him. "I'll be back."

Slipping behind the counter into the office, I found Cami outside, trying to work her phone between my car and Crow's truck. She jabbed at the screen with rage. "Damn it..."

"The service sucks here."

She pointed an accusing finger at me. "Stay with your bruja friends. I'll have somebody pick me up."

"Cami, I tried to warn you."

"About which part? That you're a bruja? Or that you're a liar?"

"A liar? That's a bit much." My head ached from when I slammed into the tree, and Cami's drama wasn't helping.

"You said you needed space. You said you were in a weird place. You made it seem like you needed a *break*, but the truth is that you're here with these...people...who are in it with the Devil."

"The Devil?" I scoffed. "My Lord...first of all—"

"You're going to deny it? I saw you dancing in your circle, the chanting... I'm surprised you didn't cut off any chicken heads and drink the blood."

I had to laugh. "Would you listen to yourself? I am not 'in it' with the Devil, and neither are they. You have the wrong idea. Nobody in there does anything evil. It's working with energy. That's it. I can teach you about it if you want."

"No, thanks. I'm good. Working with energy—is that a scientific fact?"

"Is God a scientific fact?" I said. "I don't need to see God in a physics textbook to believe He's real, Cami. That's what faith is. The least you could do is use the same logic you apply to God to what you saw out there."

She gestured to the faded exterior of the resort. "What I saw in there was occult, pagan, witchcraft, evil, black magic, brujería, and everything else. *Super* fucking irresponsible of you, Valentina, and you know it. I'm sorry but you can't compare one of the world's major religions to juju dancing under the moon with drugged-out squatters. It's not the same."

"No one's on drugs." Not hard ones, anyway.

"Ah. So, the juju dancing and squatters part is fine..."

"You're being judgmental. You want to know why I left the retreat? That's why."

"Because of me?"

"Because of everyone's bullshit. I'm sick of having to live up to fake standards that nobody else in the church seems to be able to live up to themselves. So damn righteous. You're doing it now."

"See, the important part of what you just said is that there *are* standards. There's nothing wrong with standards. Standards give us something to work towards. Goals make us better people, unlike..."

"Unlike what? Who?" I crossed my arms. Wind Cami up long enough and watch her become sanctimonious.

"Forget it." She went back to trying her phone service.

"Tell me what you were going to say. That my friends have no standards? That they're losers? That your religion is the only correct one? Nothing outside of it matters? You're only further proving my point, Camila."

"My religion? Suddenly, it's *my* religion? *Your* friends? What else is there about you that I don't know? Just so I know who I'm talking to. Or are we back in elementary school, and it's Opposite Day? I forgot?" She cocked her head in that condescending way she did when she got on her high horse.

I breathed calmly. "Listen, there's a lot of misunderstanding here, and that's partially my fault because I haven't told you what I've been going through. You're my best friend, and I should have."

"Finally, you take responsibility."

I held back the urge to defend myself. She was mad. She was allowed to be.

"I know what I'm doing. I've been studying this for the last year, okay? But it's been a secret for this exact reason, because I knew you and everyone would go and judge me for it. There's nothing wrong with learning something new. There's actually some interesting concepts going on in the world of quantum physics and neuroplasticity, if you would just get to know—"

"This is because of Savannah, isn't it?" she interrupted, a light dawning in her eyes. "I remember at the start of senior year, you showed me her Insta. I thought it was weird you were so into her feed. I told you she was a practicing witch, that it wasn't just a goth aesthetic, that you should stay away from her. After that, you stopped showing me her pics."

"Yes, because you said I should stay away from her. What makes you the expert on what makes a person dangerous or safe? Savannah was a nice girl. I'm sorry I never got to know her, because I was too busy listening to your holier-than-thou bullshit."

"I'm sorry for trying to protect you!"

"I'm not yours to protect!"

We stood there, seething at each other.

"It's the same thing with your sister," I went on. "You talk about her like she's so lost. What if Silvie's life is more put-together than you think? What if being with different guys is how she figures out what she likes or who she is? What if, by doing that, she's actually preventing her own divorce in the future?"

Cami scoffed. "This is so..."

"Trust the process, Camila. Stop trying to force everyone onto your path of perfection."

She laughed haughtily. "I knew it was because of Savannah. The Devil works in mysterious ways."

"Stop with that Devil crap already." I smacked the car's hood.

"She's part of what got me into it, but I've been curious for a long time. I've never felt 100% at home in the church. I only went to Mass because my grandfather made me, because I would see you and your family there. For me, church is a social club more than anything."

"Okay, so your whole life's been a lie. Our friendship has been a lie."

"No, not our friendship, Cami. I love you."

At that, she scoffed again, offering no "love you back." She just turned and stared at the empty parking lot reclaimed by tall grasses sprouting all over from within its alligator skin cracks in the asphalt. "You're just like your father."

I bristled. "What do you mean?"

Silence.

"No, you can't do that. You can't just drop a package and not expect people to pick it up. What do you mean I'm just like my father?" I jabbed my face into her line of view.

She was at the end of a proverbial dark hall, turning the corner, begging me to follow. "It's not a secret your dad wasn't big on church. That was a huge point of contention between him and your mom. You know that. Everybody knows that. Even my parents know that..."

Ugh. Every last member of our congregation knew his lack of involvement was one of the driving forces that pushed my parents apart. Didn't make hearing about it from my best friend any less awkward.

"My dad went to church to make my mom happy. Over time, he stopped. He wasn't brought up religious. I never had a problem with it. It didn't make me love him any less. What does that have to do with anything?"

"I'm saying he explored. He took risks, like you say about my sister, and that wasn't enough to prevent his splitting from your mom. You get what I'm saying?"

"No. He tried to make things work with my mom, because of me, so he could be with me and not do the every-other-weekend thing. He didn't want to lose me. That's why he came back to her after their first separation."

And yet, he left after their second. I rarely saw him again.

"Vale, he came home because his side chick didn't want him anymore. She made him choose, just like I told Silvie she should do with her boyfriend. He wanted it both ways. He chose your mom because he was already engaged to her and didn't want to look like a huge asshole to your grandfather."

"He wanted to follow through. How is that so horrible? Whatever you think you know, you don't. Nobody knows the real truth about my parents, except for them. He's not even here anymore to give his side of the story, so just stop talking about him."

"I'm making a point about how he took risks, and here you are, taking risks."

"What risks? Stop talking like you know something."

She shook her head, as if I'd never understand.

"Are you talking about Macy, because she's half Black, because her mother is Black? Does that somehow make my dad a 'risktaker?'" I had to laugh. "What year is it again? Don't be racist, Cami."

"Don't call me a fucking racist, Valentina."

"Then don't suggest he was with her because he was a risktaker. He was obviously in love with her. *That's* why he was with her."

"I'm saying he took a social risk. He wasn't afraid of the consequences, and you're rebellious—*Like him*. I'm not saying it's a good or a bad thing. I'm saying I see where you get it. Look, take me back. I'll stay at a hotel and leave in the morning."

"You can take my car back. I'm not leaving."

Her stare could've cracked open sealed Egyptian tombs. "You want me to go back alone...in your car...after I came all this way to see you."

"I told them I wouldn't leave again."

"And you don't think I should be worried in any way that a bunch of Devil-worshippers you just met are holding you hostage inside an abandoned hotel that touched me."

"It's my choice to stay."

"I see."

"I don't expect you to understand, but we're trying to connect with this place psychically to see its history, figure out lost secrets. Important truths."

"You're ghost-hunting, Valentina." She laughed.

"I knew you wouldn't get it." I could see I wasn't going to teach her anything. "If I go, I disrupt the flow. Take my car."

She stared at me in disbelief. What she was thinking was anybody's guess, but it was safe to say our friendship would probably be over after this. It would take a huge effort on Camila's part to understand that she wasn't the center of my universe anymore.

"It's funny..." She fake-smiled. "You talk about Antoni like what he did to you was so horrible. But look at you, messing with the spirit world when the Bible forbids it. What you're doing is a hundred times worse."

"Worse than what? Than a guy everyone thought was so devout taking advantage of me inside a nasty bathroom?" My chest felt like it was going to explode.

"He didn't take advantage of you. He barely kissed you then took care of himself in the sink. If anything, he avoided touching you. You should be grateful."

"Grateful??"

I couldn't believe what I was hearing. Months of unspoken resentment overflowed into the valley between us.

"That's how you feel?"

"It is." She shrugged. "Sorry I didn't tell you before. I didn't think you'd understand. Have fun with your coven." She opened the car door and slipped inside.

"Wow." So, this was how our friendship ended, with a sanctimonious remark instead of a peaceful parting of ways. My best friend, who should've been on my side, should've sympathized with me after that incident, sat there, smugly ignoring me.

"Also, you lied about Antoni," she said, turning on the engine and starting to drive away. "Everyone knows he's gay."

Nineteen

Tears came rough, complete with uncontrollable sobbing. I sat on the floor of the ballroom with Wilky, Mori, and Fae around me. Crow, too, keeping a mistrustful watch from a distance.

A fight between Cami and me was bound to happen, but it didn't make it any easier to accept. We'd been growing apart for a year, and though I took full blame for not telling her my feelings, she made it difficult to share.

As for Antoni—I knew. My hands had told me that same day. As if a gay guy couldn't still have a sexual experience with a girl, now I looked like a huge liar. But it did happen. I was there. So, fuck Cami.

Mori gently tucked strands of my hair behind my ear. "Friends break up all the time. It's okay. Sometimes they come back. If they love you, they'll learn to grow with you."

"Sometimes they don't, though. Come back," Fae added, scratching a bit of caked mud off my knee. "They can't handle your awesomeness, which is more than okay."

Looking into all their eyes, I felt so grateful to have them here with me, yet I couldn't shake the guilt that I'd traded one set of friends for another.

I'd have to let Cami go, for now. I wasn't about to run after her. Wilky rested his hand, palm up, on my knee, an imploring, hopeful gaze in his eyes. I slid my hand into his, eager for a connection, when my vision darkened, and unfamiliar images began to slide through my mind—a young boy with auburn hair and light skin spitting in my face, calling me racist names. My heart hurt for her.

I let go of his hand.

"What?" he said.

"What just happened?" Mori looked at Wilky, then at me.

"Nothing." Whatever it was, it was personal, plus I had no right to see inside anyone's head without their permission. I grabbed my cross. *My little starshine, sleep, oh, so tight*

"Get rid of that," Crow said darkly from his spot in the corner, smoke curling around him

"No." I cut quickly, glaring at him to the surprise of the others. "It's the only thing I have left of my father's."

"What it represents caused you immense pain today. Today, your whole life, for that matter. Leave it. You'll feel better." His eyes cut through me, intimidating me, but I would not back down —not to Crow or anybody. I was tired of his bullshit.

"Crow," Mori said. "Stop being a dick."

"What, it's true. None of what went on between her and her so-called friend would've happened if it weren't for everything that bauble symbolizes."

"It reminds her of her dad," Fae said. "Are you even listening?"

"I don't care. It's the complete opposite of the work we do here. It's offensive to me; it should be to you all, too." He stood, picking up his camera to check the settings.

"It's just a fucking charm," Wilky muttered.

"It's holding her back. She needs to pick a side. You all do." He stomped away, pushed out the veranda door, which strained heavily under its weight.

"I don't need to pick a side," I said to myself. "I'm sorry about what happened to him when he was a kid, but not all churches are the same. Not all parents or Christians are either."

"I guess Crow told you what happened to him?" Mori muttered.

"Yeah."

"Be nice to Vale!" Fae told Crow through a broken window. "She helped us!"

A URINAL LEAKED AND DRIPPED, the sound echoing across the tiles. Another was cracked like the Japanese art of repairing broken pottery with gold adhesive. Blue light shone through the cracks, rays emanating from within, growing brighter with every pulse.

Antoni stood at the sink, back to me. His right elbow shook, his head tilted back.

His groans were low and prolonged.

The cracks changed to a greenish-yellow color. Then blinding yellow.

I shielded my eyes to protect them. When I reopened them, Antoni's face was an inch from mine. *It's true what they say about you. You're a bitch.*

I'm not.

You are. Look what you made me do. He was gripping himself. I looked away.

You're confused, Antoni. That's why you pulled away. That's why you took me to the bathroom in the first place—to "try" me out.

He hissed like a threatened tomcat. I could smell his rancid breath on my cheek. *You kept pulling from* me, he said, his hand jerking on himself faster now. *Why?*

Because of my hands. My hands see things! Goddammit, Antoni, leave me alone. Why was he putting me through this? Wasn't it enough he'd used me, even though I clearly refused to touch him?

Fuck you, Vale. His hand moved faster and faster, his eyes began to close.

I couldn't move, couldn't leave this situation. I was stuck in the dream, being forced to watch him climax. I looked for an escape route. Beads of sweat formed on Antoni's brow line, as he worked toward his end, and tears stung my eyes. I was frozen in place.

Antoni's open mouth grew wider, taller. *BIIIITCH!* The word morphed into an O, and his voice dropped several octaves, a black gaping maw filling my view. His body stretched tall, taller than the ceiling, which dissolved, replaced by a dark sky where a partially eclipsed burnt orange moon created the illusion of a halo around his head.

Nobody will believe you, he said.

Don't listen, someone else spoke, someone not Antoni, who was still screaming, the walls of the bathroom shaking with his entitled rage. *Truth always comes to light.*

Oversized Antoni fell to his knees to better screech into my face, wind from his cavernous mouth assaulting me. I covered my ears and closed my eyes, begging myself to wake up. Bitterness boiled through me, that this situation still haunted me, that he was still pinning blame on me, that my subconscious was still holding on. The more time I spent at the Sunlake, the more I felt it—rage. Rage for the fucked-up values fed to me, rage over Cami's attitude, rage over Antoni taking up space rent-free in my brain. Rage I'd held in for so long.

I couldn't get away from Antoni's screaming. My muscles seized. All I could do was let his fury come at me. Forcing myself to move, I gave it everything I had and hurled my body upwards to dislodge the sleep paralysis.

Come onnnn... My eyes opened.

A swirling dark mass hovered over me. I gasped, sitting up and shoving my back against the wall. The dark cloud floated closer, curious. Somehow I felt its intelligence. Its consciousness. Whatever it was, it wanted my feelings, all my anger—as fuel. A hole formed in the middle of the mass, widening like the aperture of a camera lens, making space for what I quickly realized was me.

Come in.

"Go away," I whispered.

There was a shift in energy. Something approached from behind it, through it, something alive. It emitted hot breath, and the cloud's focus transferred off me onto whatever it was. Finally, I could make out the shape of a dog—a wolf, *my* wolf—stalking in the gloom. He moved decisively, one paw at a time, closer to the cloud. Lobo lifted his gums and bared yellowed, plaque-filled teeth, snarling at the churning mass.

The formless fog spun like a slow-moving tornado, floated into the center of the ballroom, making the chandelier's suspended crystals tinkle, and disappeared. I gripped the wall behind me, my lungs pumping breaths of air like they were my last.

"Thank you," I whispered.

The clairs were moving in their beds. I didn't want them to wake and be startled by Lobo. I reached out to touch him, but he took steps back onto the parquet floor, claws clicking on the wood.

"Good boy...thank you. Okay, shoo, now."

He stared at me with lackluster eyes, jaw slack, pink tongue bobbing. A drop of saliva dripped as he panted, licked his chops to regain composure, then lolled his tongue again. His silvery eyebrows expressed that he wanted something.

"Coming." I scrambled to my feet.

He led me out of the ballroom into the desolate hallway as

dark as obsidian with the occasional pewter highlights. I crept along one wall for orientation, careful to keep my hands to myself so I wouldn't see into the Sunlake's mind.

Lobo stopped at the entrance to the atrium.

"No," I said.

He panted and stared at me.

"I can't, buddy. I don't like what's in there."

You must, he seemed to say.

"That room doesn't want me. It keeps scaring me out." Hearing my words aloud, I knew it was crazy to think so, but from the first day I'd set foot in the hotel, the atrium had wanted me out.

"Who are you talking to?"

I jumped, my shoulder hitting the wall. I saw a tall, shirtless shape in the diffused moonlight. "God damn it, Crow."

"That's a lot of blasphemy for a child of God." He approached, holding his camera.

"Don't you rest?" I huffed. "You'll see her when you see her. Now that we did the ritual, I'm sure you'll catch a good one of her soon." I was tossing him a bone, I knew, but I didn't want to be here with him. I was going back to bed. "Goodnight."

I started to leave, scanning for Lobo, when Crow blocked my path, showed me the glowing screen of his camera. A self-satisfied smile crossed his lips. "I did. I caught some good ones of, I don't know, something. There's this mist..." He showed me a tall column of what could've been smoke but also may have been a reflection of light off the glass. "And this one..." The next slide was of a giant orb.

"Orbs are dust, I'm pretty sure," I said.

He smirked at me. "There's great moonlight coming in through the windows upstairs. Figured I'd take some night shots." He thumbed through at least ten more beautiful low-light photos, and though they were gorgeous, I fought the urge to tell him I'd seen his Lady. "Ghosts keeping you awake?"

"The wolf did."

"Wolf?" He raised his eyebrows. "Oh, right. An extinct wolf follows you around. Let's see if I catch him." Lifting his camera, he took shots of the hallway, turning on his flash to illuminate the darkness, but thankfully, Lobo had skulked off. "What else do you see?"

"Meaning..."

"Since the ritual last night, do you see anything different? Do you see her?" He put down his camera and crossed his arms defensively.

I stared at him. I didn't want to lie anymore.

"The lady. The Lady of the Lake," he said. "Do you see her?"

Yes, I was sure I'd seen his grass-covered lake spirit last night during our ritual, unless my newly acquired superpower had simply been an overactive imagination. But considering she was his Holy Grail, we were alone, and he seemed to envy me, I lied.

"No."

Crow stood there, studying me. Once he was satisfied that I might be telling the truth, he sighed and took a few slow steps in my direction. "Good, 'cause, no lie, that would've frustrated the shit out of me."

I had no choice but to bump against the cracked wall, he was so close. I didn't like how he was looking at me or how his gaze focused on my lips, or the way he smelled. His time living here had finally infected his clothes and skin, and tonight, he smelled worse.

"What are you doing?" My palms grew sweaty. "Back up."

"I mean, I'm supposed to be the clairvoyant one, right?"

"I said stop."

He reached for my hand. I hesitated. "You're the new one. How would it look to the others if you saw her and I didn't? I'd look like an idiot, wouldn't I? After everything I've done, the work

I've put into saving this place. Imagine if you got rewarded with a full-body apparition instead of me."

I yanked my hand out of his, but he gripped my wrist in a flash, and planted it on his face. His skin felt cold and clammy. "Tell me what you see."

I expected to "see" visions of Crow's childhood or emotional trauma, but only a pair of seafoam green eyes entered my mind. A woman's face superimposed over his, a slender, cracked nose, beautifully formed lips, curved breasts over Crow's body. I smelled a rank stink in the air, like stagnant swamp water and rotting dead fish rolled into one.

I tried to twist my hand from his grasp. "Don't touch me again."

Crow smiled, his fingers tightening on my wrist. "Tell me what you saw."

"She's all you think about," I said. "And she's going to appear to you very soon."

"Don't lie to me, Valentina."

"I'm not." I had no problem lying if it meant he'd release me. I hated these games. Unfortunately, my voice sounded weird when I lied, high-pitched and unsteady.

He held my gaze with those awkwardly light eyes. I looked away, rattled, ashamed. Shoving my hand away, he said, "That's what I thought," and disappeared down the pitch-black corridor.

IN THE MORNING, I leaned against a veranda column watching a large spider build its web. It worked so diligently, even though one of us was bound to ruin it by accidentally smashing through it. Between my fight with Cami, the nightmares, the agonized spirits, and Crow, I felt like a lost soul.

Maybe it was time to leave. I'd done what I'd come to do. I'd helped the clairs. In turn, they'd helped me see life in a new way. For that, I would always be grateful. Was there any reason to stay?

Someone displaced the air beside me, a short body blocking the chirping of birds. I looked. The little boy stood there. Sandy brown hair, bell-bottoms, tie-dye shirt. He ran off so fast, giggling as he bolted, that I felt the icy blast of his wake.

"Hey!" Before I could follow where he went, he disappeared.

I was almost sure it was the same little boy I'd seen in the atrium, staring at the mermaid fountain.

Boo. A giggle.

There he was to my left, holding a yellow tissue paper flower by its green pipe cleaner stem. He held it out as an offering, but before I could take it, he ran off with it still in his hand.

"That's not nice." I smiled, happy to know at least one cheerful soul inhabited this wretched place.

He was gone.

But in his place was someone else entirely. I drew in a sharp gasp from the suddenness of it.

A sickly woman. Hospital gown open. Chest exposed. Large flaps of skin pulled apart and pinned to either side, revealing her ribcage and diseased lungs. I stood paralyzed, watching the flesh sacs fill with air and contract, as she stared at me with vacant eyes.

Something slipped out of a bright red incision in her right lung onto the floor. It looked like a ping pong ball rolling toward me. A small, off-white, plastic-looking ball skittered and rolled, snaking a path toward my feet, disappearing before it could touch me.

I think it's working, the woman said. *I feel better.* She coughed, and blood flew from her lips, spattering onto her gown.

I couldn't respond, I was so shocked by her image and the odd object that'd emerged from her body.

Somewhere behind me, a real voice cried out from inside the Sunlake. Ripping my gaze from the patient, I turned and ran into the hotel, checking the ballroom first, the main hallway, then every room of the ground floor on the way toward the atrium.

I passed Wilky rummaging through a custodial closet. "Was that you just now?"

He shook his head.

I jogged past the atrium, slowing to stare into it by habit. The chandelier bobbed softly between its chains. Back and forth, back and forth. No breeze. I braced for the worst. Didn't wish to see the man hanging there again. Instead, an old-timer with wild white hair hunched over a walker stood there, his hospital shift sliding down his frail shoulders. Attached to the walker was his IV stand. Hollow eyes pled with me.

"What is it now?" I muttered.

I can't move.

"Go to the light, sir," I pleaded. "The light has everything you need."

He looked above my head as though the light were there. Mori was right, these souls needed help. And if I had the ability to see and hear them, to help direct them somehow, how could I, in good conscience, leave the hotel?

I can't... The man continued to stare wide-eyed.

I craned my neck to look up at whatever it was he was seeing, terrified. There was nothing, just the lobby's columns with their scaly tails, ocean wave crown molding shimmering in the morning light, and ropes of green ivy wound around them.

A very real, very loud discussion echoed from down the hall. With a lingering look at the old man, I ran off past the kitchen, wishing I wouldn't run into anyone else not of this dimension. Fae and Mori were in the dining hall, both hunched over Mori's notebook. They marched up to me with a wild look in their eyes, flailing the notebook. "Let's see what Vale thinks."

"I think I'm going crazy," I said, rubbing my temples.

"You, us...it's happening." Mori showed me their notebook.

On one sheet, Mori had written LEAVE LEAVE LEAVE LEAVE LEAVE in their scratchy, trance-writing style. The words took up most of the sheet and were punctuated with pencil puncture wounds through the paper.

I shook my head. "You channeled that?"

"That's not the only one. Look." Mori flipped to another sheet with similar scratchy words that read: YOU WILL DIE YOU WILL DIE YOU WILL ALL DIE ALL DIE.

"I watched them." Fae wiped tiny beads of sweat off her upper lip and twisted locks of hair around her wrist. "I watched them write it, and I'm telling you, I've never seen them do that before. Mori's always calm, Vale. Whoever this was coming through, was not nice."

"Not every ghost is nice, love," Mori said.

Fae insisted. "That wasn't a normal soul. We've been here a year, Mori. When has that ever happened?"

"We opened the portal. We might now be communicating with deities, guides, demons..."

"Demons?" Fae chewed on the dried tips of her hair. "I have enough of those on Earth, Mori."

"I'm not saying it's a demon. I'm saying the amplification *may* have opened another of this building's layers to us where older, non-human entities exist." Mori looked at me, dark circles under their eyes. I wasn't the only one getting shitty sleep.

"Maybe it's a TB patient," I said, thinking of the image of the woman with her chest exposed. "Or a mental patient. Isn't it true that many weren't necessarily mentally ill? In the old days, people were institutionalized for anything—being atheist, believing in angels, seeing spirits, having a vagina."

"TB patients are usually weak," Mori said. "They don't say DIE DIE DIE."

"Then it's someone warning us," I said. "Last night was intense. Did you guys see anything strange during the ritual?"

Mori shook their head. "Lightning, lake water surge, plume of fire...which strange thing?"

"None of those." I checked to make sure Crow wasn't around. "The lady that walked out of the lake into the fire covered in seaweed, looking nearly identical to all the paintings around this place."

Mori and Fae looked at each other. "Ehh...that's oddly specific. I'm not surprised, Vale. You seem to be stronger than all of us combined. Crow know you saw her?"

"I haven't told him, but I think he knows."

With a big exhale, I held out my hand. I had come to the Sunlake to help the clairs, and help I would give, no matter how terrifying this was for me. I had to use my power for good.

Mori handed over the pad, I took a seat on the floor, and they joined me. With the pad between my fingers, I took a deep breath and closed my eyes.

God, keep me safe.

Within moments, a tall and thin figure walked down a dark corridor toward me. A man, wearing a black and red robe and one of those capes that sat only on the shoulders. Broad-bellied, he seemed to float above the ground without feet. His hair grayed at the temples. He wore the Holy Cross around his neck. Where his eyes should have been were sparkling gold coins.

"Gold."

"Gold?" Fae's voice echoed as if from another place.

"A priest," I said.

He moved from room to room, leaving death in his wake, taking what didn't belong to him. Wallets, rings, watches, deeds. He ripped up living wills. He rummaged bags, opened unlocked file cabinets. He took it all.

What are you doing?

I knew his secret. He was searching for rumored gold, taking anything else he could get his hands on in the meantime. He was supposed to be giving last rites to the dying.

The priest bristled and scowled at me. *Leave.*

"You leave," I said. "Walk towards the light. God will decide."

"Who is it, Vale?" Fae asked.

They have nothing left to give, the priest reassured me.

"Then there's nothing to take," I replied. "Leave it."

The gold coins dropped out of the priest's eyes, revealing two bottomless holes where his eyes should be. *You go—you with rage in your heart.*

His words stung. "I have no such thing," I whispered, but he wasn't wrong. Just by being here, anger had been seeping out of my soul for the last week, though it'd been brimming at the edge of my consciousness for years.

She feels it. She feeds off it.

Who? I asked.

He laughed. *YOU WILL ALL DIE ALL DIE YOU WILL...*

"Vale!" Mori cupped my face, thumbs swiping away tears. I pushed out of my trance and dropped the notebook.

He'd seen. He'd seen straight into my heart.

For so long, I'd worked not to let the rage show, to stay even keeled and neutral to everyone around me. I'd mediated my parents, accepted my grandfather's lack of belief in me—*You wouldn't make a good businesswoman, Valentina. Be a teacher. Teaching is a great career for women.* I'd minimized my own hurt to make others feel better about themselves. I'd been the good, Catholic girl. I'd swept pain that was rightfully mine under a rug.

That shit needed to stop—now.

"What did you see?" Fae shook my hands. *Poverty, dirt floor, taunting in school, child services coming for her, a family rumor of riches.* Yet Fae had nothing but love for this earth and everyone on it.

"What did you see?" Mori asked.

Describing the priest might make him reappear. I took back my hands. It was too much, too much. Crow interrupted, rushing in, camera in hand, making a beeline toward one of the front windows. "I fucking knew it."

"What happened now?" Mori asked.

"Your friend you could trust?" he said to me. "Obviously reported us."

Twenty

We peered out the window into the parking lot. A silver Honda was parked. A familiar figure stepped out of the driver's side, hanging onto the door and staring up at the structure.

"It's just Macy," I said, relieved it wasn't a county official.

"Who?" Crow seethed.

"My sister." I made my way through the room, noting Fae and Mori's silent exchange with Crow. I wasn't here to rat them out, yet indirectly, I'd ratted them out.

I hurried down the hall, through the lobby, out the broken auxiliary door. Macy leaned against the car, chin to phone, probably texting me to come out. "Hey," I said, out of breath.

A look of relief washed over her. "There you are. What's going on?"

"What do you mean?"

"Cami came back last night without you in your car, frazzled as frick. I asked what was wrong. She said the two of you had a fight. She said you were in trouble. When I asked how so, she insisted you were hanging around Devil worshippers. I suspected she was exaggerating, but I came to check."

"God." I covered my face.

"I know. But, umm... Look, it's none of my business. I just came because I wanted to make sure..."

"That I'm not actually worshipping the Devil?"

"Making sure you're not in any danger." She pushed a strand of my hair behind my ear.

"I'm not." Though in the back of my mind, I couldn't wrap my conviction around it. Since we'd opened the portal, I'd had a sense of impending dread.

"Cami said you're being lured to the dark side, God is testing you, you're failing." Macy gave a halfhearted laugh. "You're sure everything is alright? I've been giving you the space you need, but you're still my family. I would hate for something bad to happen, and I did nothing to prevent it."

I reached out and did something I'd needed to do for a long time—hugged Macy.

Yes, my hands and arms needed to stop touching people and things long enough to clear my mind, but the hug felt good. Besides, there was nothing bad in Macy's soul. Her all-knowingness slid through me, her willingness to help, to know me as a sister.

"Aww, sis," she said.

In the hug, I also saw her past, her pain, spitefulness she'd received from kids who didn't look like her, how having a sibling meant a lot to her. I saw a teen who worked too hard, who wished she could hang with friends instead of burn the midnight oil.

"You can talk to me, Vale. I know you don't know me well, and I know you're holding back."

Those words made me cry.

Fingertips swiped my cheeks. "But I was just like you once, and trust me, I understand the need to make your own mistakes."

I looked up at the darkening clouds, blotting the snot threatening to come out of my nose with my fingers. "I didn't want to worry you or make you think you made a bad decision by letting me come here. I'm not a troublemaker. I swear I'm not."

"You're not. At all."

"Before I left home, I was drifting farther away from everything and everyone, but I had no idea why. Then I came to visit you, and you're just the air I needed to breathe, Macy."

She smiled.

"But on the third or fourth night, I found this place. I met these people. They've been living here, doing spiritual work." It sounded absurd but at least I was coming clean. "They're clairs."

"As in psychic mediums?"

I nodded and explained how it all began, how I got roped in because of how badly I wanted to learn the skills to contact our dad, but how I'd managed to contact everyone *but* my father. How Cami's visit had been the last thing I needed, because it'd set me back to feeling guilty.

She listened. I appreciated that she wasn't oozing with disappointment. "What spiritual work are they doing?"

This would sound insane. "There's a portal of energy here. The people who built this in the old days believed the land would heal the sick."

"That's how much of Florida got populated," Macy explained, not surprised by my words at all. "Since the Ponce de Leon days, outsiders have been coming here trying to locate healing waters. Always been something alluring about this land. But the vortex, if it's real, makes people nuts, too. 'Florida man' in the headlines?" She snickered.

I was aware of Crow, Mori, and Fae listening in from the dining hall windows. I lowered my voice and aimed it the other way. "So, these clairs can tap into that energy. Well, a few of them can. I can, too, apparently. And because this place might soon be razed, they're desperate to find out all they can. They needed a fifth person to help."

"Find out what?" she asked.

"Stuff that took place here. Stuff that wasn't recorded. Each of them has something personal to gain."

"Ah. I know all about unrecorded stuff." She smirked. "Working for the Department of Tourism, you hear rumors."

My ears perked up. "Like what?"

"Undocumented events, like you're saying. Every state hospital has them."

"Do you know what those are? How can we find out?" If Macy could help me uncover some of the Sunlake's mysteries, the clairs wouldn't have to delve into the dangers of the spirit world to find out.

"I don't know, Vale. Those files are off-limits to me. I'm not an historian for Tourism & Recreation. I just make videos." We stood in silence for a minute. "And that fifth person is you?"

I nodded.

She nodded, too. "I just want to make sure you're getting something out of this, that it's not all for them. I don't want to come to find that you're being taken advantage of."

I thought about that. Maybe I was at first, but since I'd been with the clairs, I'd learned more about myself in two weeks than I had in eighteen years.

"So, something else," I said. "This'll sound crazy..."

"Ah, ah," she warned. "No need to preface anything. Just say it."

I sighed. Macy's superpower was definitely empathy. "Since I was little, I could tell stuff about objects just by touching them. For the longest time, I thought everyone could. Eventually, I learned it was just me. And because that makes me sound like a freak, I ignored it. I stopped touching things. Stopped touching people."

Then I took a risk with Antoni. He was the first sort-of

boyfriend I'd ever had. As terrified as I was of "seeing" things in him, I trusted that God would guide me.

"To the point that people thought I was cold and standoffish," I added.

"When you were just afraid of seeing the truth about them."

Tears leaked out of my eyes. "I've suppressed everything about myself." I'd turned the other cheek at least a thousand times, like my mom had with my dad, like my grandmother had supposedly done with stuff Cuco did behind her back.

"It's okay..." Macy said.

I explained how we were ready to start the ritual when Cami showed up with her surprise visit. "I hated being rude, but I couldn't play hostess. I don't know what she was thinking."

"She was worried about you."

"I get that, but I left home for a reason."

"Why was she so scared, though? She looked like she'd seen a ghost. Well, after what you just said, I suppose she had."

"Macy, that girl can't fathom anything outside her little bubble. I don't mean to villainize my whole community, but the Catholics I grew up with? Even though they're nice and mean well, they cannot see past their noses."

"I wasn't brought up religious, but I know people like that."

Listening to her, I could visualize my dad and Macy's mom's relationship. Dad was probably like me, like Macy was probably like her mom, and if we got along this well, I could only imagine the two of them. Dad must've felt at such ease around her.

We both sighed and gazed around a while. She slapped at a mosquito. "You know what your situation with Cami reminds me of? The Everglades."

I laughed. "Okay..."

"Every summer, lightning strikes from one of these massive storms we get and hits dry brush out there. What happens? The dry brush lights right up—fires. Then people start with the emergency calls. 'The Everglades is on fire!'"

"Meanwhile, it's normal," I laugh.

"Exactly! And so's this, Vale. What happened between you and Cami is a normal brush fire. The land clears the old to make room for the new. It's a natural process. The earth knows what it's doing, and so do you. Trust the process." She jabbed a finger into my shoulder.

What a great analogy. Friendships ended to make room for new memories. Okay, but change still hurt.

Macy sucked in a breath. "Well. It's officially creepy as heck here. Creepy, but beautiful." She withdrew her gaze from the Sunlake and put it on me. "There's another reason why I came to get you. I have someone at home, someone who wants to meet you."

I knew. "Your mom."

I'd seen her when we hugged. The woman was, right now, waiting at the house, nervous about meeting me. I thought about my own mother and the pain she might feel knowing her daughter was being asked to meet the woman my dad had had an affair with long ago. But I also remembered how my mom was grateful to Macy right before I left home for giving me a place to stay.

"Is that okay?" Macy asked.

Despite what my mom would think, I needed to meet this lady, to know what my dad knew, to see the other half of his secret world. I couldn't be the mediator anymore.

"I would love to meet your mom. Let me tell the others."

"They're right there," Macy said.

Mori, Fae, and Crow stood at the auxiliary door, watching us. Mori and Fae gave little waves, but Crow wore his usual scowl and shook his head like I was responsible for the ills of the world.

"Hey, if you guys don't mind, I'm going back to my sister's for a bit. I'll be back. By myself. Promise."

"Damn right you are," Crow said.

"What's his problem?" Macy growled.

"He thinks he owns this place. Let me grab my stuff." I hurried to the doorway in a trot, pushing past the three of them.

"Your sister is heckin gorgeous," Fae said.

"She is." I walked backwards. "Inside and out."

"And intuitive."

"What?" I looked over my shoulder.

Mori smiled but didn't answer.

"*You* seem to be a magnet for bringing in unwanted guests." Crow followed me through the lobby. "Any second now, cops will be here."

"It's fine, Crow," I said. "Lay off me already."

"I'm just gonna say this. If I don't get my chance in front of the historical society about keeping this place up, because of the negative attention you're causing, you'll pay for it, Valentina."

I whirled to face him. "Stop threatening me. It's not like restoring the hotel is your main ambition, Crow. We all know why you're truly here. Since when is opening an energy vortex part of a restoration project? Your only concern is seeing the Lady of the Lake. So just...stop."

"That's not a secret. It doesn't change the fact that I won't get to do what she asked of me. Only by doing what she asked of me will I get to see her. And only by seeing her will I get to ask my question."

"The one about Hell," I said, and he nodded. "You want to know if you're headed there, and only the Lady can tell you. Crow, I know your parents and the church did a number on you, but you're not going to Hell. You haven't done anything to deserve it."

I watched a flicker of sadness, or maybe fear, in Crow's stare. "You don't know that, Valentina. Don't bring anyone else here." He headed off.

But I wasn't done with him. "Or what?"

He stopped in his tracks. "You don't want to find out."

"I may be Catholic, but that doesn't mean I won't send you to Hell if I have to."

A wide smile cracked open his face.

Footsteps pounded down the hall, echoing through the lobby. Wilky skidded into the room with his drawing notebook. His words came out in raspy gasps. "I saw someone."

"Who?" Crow asked.

"A real person or a ghost?"

"Both."

"Both?" Fae and Mori joined us, as we huddled around Wilky who hugged his notebook to his chest.

"I was alone drawing. I heard a scream...I always hear screams. So, I followed it...I followed the scream. Sometimes it disappears before I can locate it, right? Well, this time, I stayed connected. I could hear a man, screaming."

"What did he say?" Mori asked.

"I couldn't tell. But the portal is open, guys. It has to be." Wilky breathed deeply to catch his breath.

So, I wasn't the only one.

"The portal is definitely open." Crow hurled a chunk of concrete against a wall, creating a small crack in the wall. "People don't just fly thirty feet during rituals. The changes since last night are pretty evident. In you guys, anyway."

"Where were you again?" I asked.

"I followed the sound...to the atrium," he said, eyes on me. "I saw the man you saw, Vale. The one with the broken neck, the chandelier guy. I stood in the doorway. I asked if he needed help."

I listened, a tight knot in my stomach.

"When he stopped screaming," Wilky went on, "I was able to get a good look at him. He said the lady wouldn't let him pass."

Crow's face snapped toward him. "Lady?"

Wilky nodded. "He said, 'The lady won't let me through. I can't get through.'"

"Can I see what he looks like?" Fae leaned in for a peek at his sketch.

He turned the pad around. I slid in to see it, curious if it would look at all like the ghost I'd seen with those horrible bloated eyes. Instead, the air inside my lungs evaporated. I clutched Wilky's arm. Touching him didn't help—now I saw both the sketch of the dead man and the image Wilky had seen of the same man in his mind. There was no denying either—it was my father.

Twenty-One

It couldn't be.

I'd seen that same man in my vision, same bulging eyes, same sharp angle of his broken neck, forever embossed on my brain. Blue tone to his face and neck. Shoulders slumped over in defeat. But there was no denying the cheekbones either, high and prominent, chin of a classic actor, the way he styled his hair, flopped over one eye. My mother loved his full head of heartthrob hair. His build, even throughout, was lean and proportional.

Wilky had hashed it all out in charcoal, the likeness was insanely accurate.

Until that moment, no one had noticed my silence. I slipped to the floor and quickly scrambled to my feet when it suddenly felt too hot and stifling inside the breezeless hallway. They hovered around me, while my world imploded, voices alternating from watery to tinny as if from an old-timey radio. Wilky supported me.

I stumbled through the lobby and out of the hotel.

It couldn't be him. How could it? My father passed away of a heart attack. Why would his spirit be at the Sunlake Springs?

"What is it, Vale?"

What is it, Vale?

What is it, Vale?

What if the facts I'd been given about my father had been wrong? What if my dad had died here at this wretched hotel? He'd worked for Volusia County during the separation when he came to meet Macy. Sure, anything was possible, but why would they lie to me?

Outside, the sky had darkened. Macy, who'd been waiting in the driver's seat, looked up from her phone and could see something was wrong.

"Is she alright?" she asked Wilky.

"I showed her a drawing, then this happened."

"Of what?"

"Of a man in the hotel. She'll tell you."

Had he come here for work? An inspection? Urban exploring? Admiring the hotel just for fun? It was possible, given his love of Art Deco and Mediterranean style architecture. Had that been him in the atrium all this time, trying to get my attention?

"Vale, text me." Wilky poked his head into the car. "I'll come back for you, if you need, or want..." Wilky's worry that I might never return after this was not lost on me.

But I couldn't come back. How could I? Wilky's drawing had just filled in a missing piece about why there'd been a closed-casket funeral for my father. If it'd only been a heart attack, his face should've looked normal. My mother said she'd made the decision to protect me from further damage; she didn't want my last view of Dad to be his death mask. I'd believed her. But here was a new truth, assuming the hung ghost in the atrium really was my father —had he taken his life instead? Was the bloated, blue-faced man at the end of that rope my dad?

Macy closed the door, circled the hood, exchanged more words with Wilky. As we drove out of the parking lot back toward the gate, I fought for words.

"What did he say?" I stared ahead.

"He said you stopped talking after he showed you a drawing. What happened in there?"

"It was Dad."

"Dad?"

"The man in Wilky's drawing."

Quietly, Macy drove over the blanket of cracks on the overgrown path. "Dad was the man he drew?"

"Yes."

"How?"

"Wilky sketches. He also hears disembodied voices in the hotel. But I guess, since last night, he can see the spirits, too. And the one he just saw looked exactly like dad."

The longer we sat in silence, the more I began to question my own sanity.

"Vale, are you sure about that?" Macy asked. "Maybe it was another man."

"It was him. I don't understand how. Dad died of myocardial infarction. That's what the doctors said. That's what was on his death records."

"You've seen his death records?"

I looked at her, hoping to find some nugget of truth in her face. "No, but that's what they told me."

What they told me.

A vein in Macy's temple twitched. She cracked her knuckles, then her neck. "I think that might be misinformation. When we get home, we'll sort this out with Lucinda."

"Who's Lucinda?"

"My mother."

I felt like a child lost inside of a fun house, navigating the lopsided rooms. My mother had no reason to lie. The doctors wouldn't have lied to my mother either. However, if my father had died of a heart attack, *why*, like Wilky said, would he have been *screaming*?

We pulled into the street and up Macy's drive where another car sat waiting. On our way to the front steps, she stopped and took my hands into hers. "It's alright. Okay? Whatever it is, we'll figure this out. I promise."

"Is it, though?" I could barely breathe.

Macy's expression, infused with sympathy, softened, then we trudged up the steps. I heard dishes and glasses clinking in the sink. Motherly sounds. I missed my own mom at home. We entered the kitchen, where I prepared to see the woman my dad had had a relationship with before my parents got married.

Lucinda Edwins stood at the window, staring into the yard.

"Ma," Macy said.

Lucinda turned halfway, a sad smile on her lips. "There you are."

She was in her late forties, more statuesque than Macy, expressive deep brown eyes, darker skin than her daughter, but there was definitely a family resemblance. She reached for a towel with long, slender fingers, nails painted lilac, and studied me. She wiped her hands dry.

"Lucinda, this is Valentina," Macy said, adding no further explanation.

Lucinda knew who I was. "Hello, Valentina." A sadness broke across her cheeks, and she offered a hug. I accepted. The moment my hands held onto her wide shoulders, I felt a complicated, textured, unorthodox sense of compassion that nearly broke me.

"Nice to meet you," I said.

"Let's sit a moment," Macy said.

The two of us sat at the dinette while Macy brewed coffee and gave her mother a watered-down version of what I was doing at the Sunlake Springs. She made it sound like I was doing research, which I appreciated. Didn't need my dad's ex knowing, during our first minute together, that I was involved in pagan shenanigans.

"I know this is long overdue," Lucinda said. "But I'm sorry for your loss. When Pablo passed away, I wanted to reach out to you, but circumstances being what they were..." She left it at that.

"It's okay. This is weird." I fought the urge to cry.

"Oh. Maybe we shouldn't..."

"No, it's fine. We need to talk about it," I assured her. Outside, the sky was beginning to spill its own tears onto already oversoaked land.

"I know you have questions," Lucinda said, following my stare out the window. "And it looks like we'll be stuck here a bit, so..."

Macy handed me my usual mug. I stared at it—*Failure Is Not An Option*. When I first arrived here, I'd had visions of my dad while holding this mug, but I'd assumed he was just on my mind. Now I wondered...

Wait.

Wrapping my hands around it, I closed my eyes. *Confusion over relationships. Agony over not seeing my daughter. Wishing I could repair all the damage I'd caused.*

I looked at Macy. "Did my dad live here?"

Macy and Lucinda looked at each other.

Nobody answered the question. I needed the truth. Craved it, like a weary soldier craved home. Macy sat. "In the car," she said slowly, looking at her mother, "we were talking about her dad. Our dad."

Lucinda nodded. "Yes..."

Macy went on, "And I never told her this, but I'm telling her now..." She played with the edge of her mug, sliding her finger around the rim, the way Dad used to do whenever he wanted his whiskey glass to "sing" for me. "I actually met Pablo once before I knew who he was."

I raised an eyebrow.

She measured her words carefully. "He used to rent this house."

"This house," I said.

"Yes. From me," Lucinda clarified.

Fragments of my mind flew all over the kitchen, landing on the floor in sticky, imaginary chunks. "Wait...what?"

"That's how we met," Lucinda corroborated Macy's lost detail. "Miami-Dade sent him this way for work in Volusia—we're talking years back—and they set him up with a temporary place, since he'd be working here for six months."

"So, you're saying...he stayed here? Like, here, here, in this house?"

Lucinda nodded. "I've owned this property for years. My granddaddy left it to me. I already had my own place to live when I acquired it, so I've rented it out ever since. Helps pay the bills. Anyway, your dad was a tenant. Mostly before you were born, but also during his last months."

I popped up and absently walked around the kitchen, trying to imagine my father, walking on these old pine floors, climbing those stairs, ruminating about life, going about his daily life within these walls.

"He was my first tenant before we started seeing each other. I knew he was engaged, Valentina, in case you're wondering. I suppose I'm guilty for trying to change his mind. It's just he was so unsure about getting married, and I was young and so in love with him."

I listened. She seemed to be under the impression that I was upset about their relationship, but I wasn't. I was upset that he stopped visiting me, but not about her.

She went on. "He would tell me how he wasn't sure he could be the man your mother's family wanted him to be. He wasn't a religious man, more spiritual than religious, but you know that. He didn't make enough money to allow your mom to be a stay-at-home mother, which was very important to your grandfather. Your grandpa was a powerful man. Pablo felt small in his shadow."

"My grandfather had that effect on people," I said. Lucinda

was telling me more than my mother ever had. That felt unfair. My mother should've told me this.

"That was the last I saw of him until he came back four years ago," Lucinda said.

"When I contacted him," Macy clarified.

I nodded again.

"The house was available, so he stayed a few months before..."

Before he died.

"But that one night he was here...you remember?" Lucinda asked her daughter.

"Yeah," Macy said with disdain. "I met him and didn't know it was him. My mom sent me here to find Ernest, our repairman who was fixing an A/C leak your dad reported."

Lucinda interjected, "I had a feeling he reported it just so I'd come by and see him, but that ship had sailed. I've been married since the moment this girl was born."

So, Lucinda never got with my dad in the years I was alive. That made me feel better, for some reason.

Macy went on, "So, this lady *sends* me here looking for Ernest, without telling me who the tenant was, right?"

"I wanted Macy to see him for herself," Lucinda explained, eyes welling up. "Maybe there'd be some connection between them, even though I knew Daddy wouldn't like it." She glanced at her folded hands. I assumed Daddy was Lucinda's husband, or the man Macy called her father until that fateful day. "How could I tell you, Mace? There was no easy way to do that."

"By Daddy, you mean...?" I asked.

"My stepdad, technically, though I don't think of him that way. He'll always be Daddy to me." She watched Lucinda wring her hands and dab her eyes. "After seeing him, I just knew. Don't ask me how. I mean, look at me."

Macy was a beautiful blend of Lucinda's dark skin and my

dad's light. I didn't know what her stepfather looked like, but I bet she had questions.

"The moment I turned eighteen, I did it. I took the test."

"And Lord, did the shit hit the fan," her mother said.

Macy smirked. "Anyway, fast forward, Lucinda and I are good now, but we weren't for a while."

"Too long." Lucinda pressed a napkin to her eyes. "Valentina, I want you to know I loved your father, but I respected his decision to marry your mother, which is why it's been hard for me all these years. I didn't want to keep a secret from you, baby," she said to Macy, "but I didn't have a choice."

"You had a choice, but I understand." Macy turned to me. "That's when I contacted him and told him about me. He told your family, and that's when he came to live here for the last time."

"Until the end."

They nodded.

It made sense. He hadn't just come to Yeehaw Springs because it was a nice town in the middle of Florida—he'd returned because Lucinda was here. So was his other daughter.

"He wanted to meet you," I said, swiping my eyes. "I can understand that. My dad never shirked his responsibilities."

"Right." Macy nodded. I could sense the resentment evident between her and her mother. "And then, the Sunlake Springs took him."

Twenty-Two

"Took him?"

Macy grabbed her mug and drank down the entire thing. "When Cami got here all pissed, saying you were spending time at that hotel, that things were getting dangerous, I wasn't sure what she meant. After she left, I called Lucinda. I wasn't expecting her to tell me what she did. Mom?" She sat back in her chair and crossed her arms over her chest.

I knew what Lucinda would tell me.

My father had died *there*—at the Sunlake Springs—not here in the house he'd lived in. And not of a heart attack either. All the time Dad had stayed here, I never knew. He visited me in Miami every other weekend at first, but he never invited me to wherever he was. I always assumed it was because his living quarters weren't up to par. In my mind, I always visualized the sad, empty apartment of a divorced dad, but that hadn't been the case. He hadn't wanted to invite me to Lucinda's house.

He hadn't wanted his two worlds to collide.

"Go on," I said.

Lucinda took a deep breath. "I came by every so often to check on him. We conducted all rental business through email, but he wasn't well, and I wanted to make sure he was alright. Your mother was understandably upset with him. You were upset with him. The whole family was upset. He'd tried staying near you, but your grandfather sent him away. Threatened him if he didn't leave town."

"My grandfather?" I imagined Cuco telling my dad to get the fuck away from his family. He'd always had an overprotective streak. My father and he never got along, but I found it hard to believe that Cuco would outright threaten him.

Lucinda cocked her head like she was showing restraint. "He wasn't nice to Pablo. So, your father figured he'd come here. I suppose this house always felt like a safe space to him. He got a job with Volusia, since he'd done work for them on the side anyway. They gave him a project—at the Sunlake Springs."

"Doing?" I leaned on the sliding door. Every muscle in my core felt weak.

"Surveying, assessing property damage, the usual. Other than that, I'm not sure. I know he was always obsessed with the place since he was a child."

I knew my father was originally from the Orlando area, but I didn't know he knew about the Sunlake Springs, and I definitely didn't know he was obsessed with it. All he ever mentioned was that the Biltmore Hotel in Miami looked like an old favorite of his.

"He never told you about the time he stayed there?"

"What? No."

Lucinda got up and entered the dining room, as I raked my memory for any mention of the Sunlake Springs from my father.

She returned carrying a small box, which she unfolded. What she pulled out made my heart ache in the most agonizing way. In her hands was the little stained-glass sun ornament, the one that hung by his bedside window at home, the one he took with him when he left.

"Where did you get that?" I gasped.

"He left it here. Did he ever show you this?" The next item she pulled out was a yellow flower made of tissue paper and green pipe cleaner for a stem.

My lungs froze. I heard my heartbeat whoosh through my ears.

"He made this as a little boy," Lucinda spoke as though through a tube. Distant and disconnected. The little boy on the hotel veranda had a craft flower that looked just the same. "He was there the night his mother died at the hotel. You've heard about the fire that killed your grandmother, yes?"

"No, I..."

For years I'd heard my grandmother had died in an accident. I never met her. She'd passed away when my dad was little, but it never registered with me. My mom's family was the only family I ever really knew.

Lucinda handed me the flower. "Here."

If I took it, I would see things.

Did I want to see any more? My heart was already breaking.

With a deep breath, I accepted the flower.

Immediately, I "saw" the love my dad had for his mother, her long brown hair in a cascading braid, the halo of sunlight around her head, her blue-green eyes, how peaceful and accepted she'd felt at the Sunlake Springs surrounded by like-minded friends. They'd lived an idyllic life in those last days leading up to her death. Then came the kitchen fire. She, along with several other women, preparing meals for the rest of the guests, were trapped when the double doors locked. She burned to death.

My grandmother was the smiling, waving kitchen ghost.

The flower trembled in my hands. "Why... Why wouldn't he tell me all this? About the Sunlake? About my grandmother dying there?"

"Maybe he did," Macy said. "Honestly, and no offense to you, but maybe you just didn't pay attention. You know how parents talk about family, and half the time, kids don't listen."

No. No, I would've listened. I always wanted to know more about my father's side. He just never wanted to talk about it. He made it seem like there wasn't much to tell.

"Trauma," Lucinda added. "He was there when it happened. The rumor is that he watched his mother die."

"My God." I jumped to the sink, breathing deep to hold down the sickness threatening to come up. Not only did my grandmother die there, but he perished there, too?

What did that mean for me?

"Vale, that place is bad news," Macy said. "Lots of deaths over the years, rumors of malpractice, rumors of arson, theft, patients admitted never made it out..."

Lucinda nodded. "Hate crimes, persecution of Black folks..."

"Hate crimes, persecution of Black folks," Macy repeated. "Not that there's a shred of evidence, mind you, because that's being Black in America."

Wilky's quest. His granduncle. The KKK. Visions of torches out by the Devil's Tree bobbed up and down through my mind. Yes, the place had a terrible reputation. Much too much darkness had enveloped the Sunlake Springs Resort.

"The list goes on," Macy sighed, rubbed her eyes.

"There's no proof at all?" I asked in the hopes I might bring back a "shred of evidence for Wilky and the others.

Macy looked at me sideways. "Sis, listen to me, the state has done a bang-up job of covering it all up to make Florida look good to tourists. Tourism is our primary industry. If people think of our state as a dangerous, racist, misogynist, hate-filled wasteland, they won't come spend their hard-earned dollars. Smiles, beaches, dolphins, and seashells. That's what people want to see."

I nodded.

"So, when you arrived and asked what was there to do around here, I deliberately did not tell you about the Sunlake Resort. 'Cause I did *not* want you going into that historic hell trap."

I needed space to breathe and stepped out, leaving the slider open. The rain was starting to fall in heavy, fat drops. So much I'd never known.

"Vale," Lucinda said. "There's something else. He probably didn't want to talk about it, because your mother's side is so religious. Like I said, he was already on thin ice with your grandfather."

"What is it?" I asked without facing her.

"I heard stories. He told them to me, of course, because I never judged him. He didn't need more accusations of witchcraft hanging over his head than he already had."

Witchcraft?

I searched my brain for the bits of info I had. I knew my dad's mother had been a hippie. I had seen exactly two photos of her in my life, and in both of them she'd dressed like one. I knew my grandparents did not approve of the way my father had been raised, outside of the church, so pagan, practically a heathen. I knew my grandfather had a habit of squashing any belief that wasn't of his own faith.

So, this meant...the little boy running gleefully around the hotel, holding his crepe paper flower, was my very own father—baby Pablo in his happy place where his hippie, New Age mother, had once spent a peaceful summer with friends.

Meditating, moon-dancing witches in their "safe space."

Witchiness ran in my blood.

I sank to the ground and sat there, letting drops of rain soak into my clothes. It felt cleansing. It washed away the blanket of lies. "What else?" I asked. I needed it all at once, so I could absorb it all.

"That's pretty much everything," Lucinda said. "Last I heard, Pablo was visiting the Sunlake every day to take notes. He was adamant the building had to come down. It was unsafe. According to him, it's a time bomb waiting to go off."

"I didn't know that part," Macy said to her mom, glancing at me. "I didn't. I would've told you not to go had I known. Vale, come inside. Please."

But the rain, the rain exposed layer after layer.

"Leave her," Lucinda whispered. "The last time I saw him, I asked why he continued to go there if it was so bad. He said he *had* to go back. He had to double-triple check the measurements. They changed day-to-day. He wanted to make sure he wasn't going crazy. One day, a wall would be nine-feet-three inches, and the next it'd be nine feet, and that's when it happened."

I swiveled toward them. "What?"

Macy was in the doorway. "Vale, let's take a break from this a bit. Why don't you go upstairs, take a nap, while I—"

"No. I've lived my whole life in a fog. I want answers."

Lucinda's gaze held mine. "He didn't come back after that. I didn't hear from him; he never paid the rent, which he always did on time. When I drove by that last time, his car wasn't here. I told my husband, and even though Bill wanted nothing to do with him, he came with me. Together we drove to the hotel to check on him..."

I bit my lip and imagined the whole thing, silently thanking Bill for his act of kindness.

"We saw his car and went inside." She pinched the bridge of her nose. "It didn't take long for us to find him. He was..."

When she didn't continue right away, I entered the house and sank into a chair. Lucinda came over to me. She rested a hand on my shoulder, but I didn't want to see my father through her touch. I didn't want to "see" what she saw when she entered the Sunlake Springs and found my father dead.

I pushed her hand away.

She sniffed. "We called police. They came out quickly, followed by an ambulance. They took him away."

"Why the scream?"

"What scream?" she asked.

"My friend said, in his vision, that he was screaming. Why?" I insisted.

"I don't know. When I got there, he was already gone. I wish I knew more. I would tell you if I did, but that's all I got." Lucinda fell apart on her daughter's shoulder, as I shattered into a million broken dreams.

So, that was it. My father had killed himself at the Sunlake Springs. In the atrium, no less. So, the man I'd seen had definitely been him. My dead, broken father with the snapped neck and bulging eyes. My father's heart hadn't stopped from stress or heartache or any such bullshit. He'd committed a mortal sin by any Catholic standards—he'd committed suicide.

Shame upon my family.

AN HOUR LATER, I stood on the front porch of a little green house in Cassadaga with Macy. I didn't mind her coming along to see Citana. Her story was just as much my story, except from a different side. Our stories had intersected, but we both needed truth.

I kept thinking back. After my father's death, it took a long time for his burial to take place. People kept asking when they could pay their respects. I hadn't realized it then, but I was now sure the church was trying to decide whether or not to allow him a Catholic burial.

Suicide was a mortal sin—an act against God's will. According to our faith, he should not have been allowed into the Kingdom of Heaven. None of this sat well with me. My father may have been upset over the way his family fell apart, but he wouldn't have left without saying goodbye. My father would've given me a goodbye. Even if he was suffering from depression.

At my feet, Bob Meowly plopped onto his back for a tummy rub. Macy bent to scratch him. I kept my eye on the peephole.

"Where are we?" Macy whispered.

"A friend's house."

A shadow appeared through the fisheye lens, then the door opened. The old woman stood there, holding a plate of avocado. "Mori's friend! You need more dinner? I need more time to prepare it."

"I'm not here to pick up food, ma'am. I have questions."

"Oh! Come in. Come in..."

"I'm sorry I didn't call first." I stepped into her airy home.

"Nonsense. You're having a crisis." She opened the door wide. I knew better than to ask how she knew I was having a crisis. "Avocado? I just sliced them. They're from my tree."

"No, thank you." If I ate, my body would reject it. "This is my sister, Macy."

"Hello, Macy. What can I do for you girls? You need a reading?" Citana pulled out chairs for us. Macy and I sat, perched on the edges.

My hands were tense. I opened and closed them to relax. "Last time I was here, you said something about my father. I didn't understand it at the time, but something I learned today made me remember it."

"What did I say?" Her eyes searched my face.

"You said my father was with me. That he's always with me."

"He was stepping forward at the time. I don't see him now, though."

"Do you remember telling me that he apologizes for the way he passed? You said something about him apologizing. I thought that was odd, because he died of a heart attack. Do you remember? Please say you do."

She tapped her chin. "I seem to remember him showing me the way he died. Most of them do. But I didn't want to mention it, because sometimes, the living don't know the circumstances surrounding a loved one's death, and you hadn't come for information about your father. You came for a spiritual cleansing."

"But do you remember what he showed you?" I asked, my body trembling. "I need to know."

"Dear..." She sighed. "His neck was broken. I assume he took his own life."

I stared at Citana, my last hope that maybe all this was a misunderstanding. I kept hoping she'd retract her last statement, tell me, *No, wait, that's a mistake,* tell me my father's heart gave out, just like I'd thought.

Inside, a part of me—the part that believed in miracles and Santa Claus, the goodness in people's heart, and the Universe having my back—withered and died. Macy patted circles on my back.

"And yet," Citana Rose pulled out her tarot cards, shuffled them for focus.

"And yet?" Macy said.

"I'm not entirely sure about that."

The watery swirls in my eyes made it hard to see.

"May I see your hands?" She put the cards back down and stretched her palms across the table.

Oh, God. No. Not her hands, not someone so intuitive. I didn't want to see my father's death in anyone's mind, even if I'd already seen it with my own third eye.

"It's alright," Citana said, slipping her warm hands gently underneath my fingertips. She said a prayer in her language and, with her hand, drew a circle around my head, another around Macy's, and another around herself.

Right away, I saw the darkness, the murky hallways of the Sunlake Springs Resort. Specifically, the atrium where I'd seen the hanging spirit, before I knew it was my father, because my brain couldn't fathom anything different than what I'd been told by my family. "Something else is there."

"At the hotel?"

"Yes. I've told my grandniece many times before. I've never liked her or her friends going. That place has a reputation for the malevolent."

For a moment, I had no idea who she meant. Then, I realized Citana was using Mori's dead pronoun. I forgave her since Citana was a million years old.

"I've felt the same since I got there. Something doesn't want us," I told her.

"Oh, it wants you. Believe me, it wants you. Which is why you must leave, before it gets its wish. It's trapped thousands of other people over its hundred-year history. Same way your father is there."

"But I thought you saw him with me."

"He is with you. But he is also there. He can't cross into the light to his final rest."

"Because he killed himself?" My lip quivered.

"Because the hotel won't let him go."

Macy and I looked at each other. "I don't understand," I said.

Citana's eyelids fluttered. I couldn't see what she saw anymore. I only saw a vast blanket of nightfall covering the resort. "Something prevents him from leaving, the same presence that doesn't want you to leave. It needs you."

"But if my father's soul is trapped there, I have to go back. I have to help him. I have to try. I can't just leave him there." Hot tears rose into my eyes. I couldn't bear the thought that my dad was trapped in an in-between state. "What do I do?"

"Leave."

"But my father—"

"Your father doesn't want you there. He doesn't want anyone there."

"But a black wolf led me there." I was agitated now. "I think he's my familiar or a spirit guide. That's how I got there in the first place. Why should I leave?"

"I'm not sure, dear. I just don't get a good feeling." She rubbed her forehead. After a minute, she reached for my hands again. I could tell she was exerting herself. "At the full moon ritual. You purified yourselves as I instructed?"

"Yes. We did what we were supposed to."

"You were pure of heart?"

"As much as we could be." Although, I had just argued with Cami an hour before.

"Why, were we not supposed to open the portal? Should we go back and close it?" I couldn't squelch the panic in my voice. "We shouldn't have done it, am I right? Crow kept saying that an entity wanted him to do it. I kept wondering why he was so desperate to please her. She told him that opening the vortex would help him finally see her in the flesh."

"You must close it. Tell the others it was a mistake. She's there, feeding on anger, greed, and hate. I couldn't see her before, but I see it now because you are amplified. She longs to escape the lake. She longs to be human."

"Human? What do you mean?"

Citana started shaking. Her face twisted in agony, like she was seeing something horrible. I slipped my hands out of hers. "She's been banished, cursed to stay there forever. That's why she wants out. The hotel will soon be demolished, and she fears it. She wants to return to the living..." Citana was shaking so hard, the chair was scratching the floor.

"What's happening?" Macy asked.

The old woman's eyes opened wide. She shot her hands out and gripped mine.

And I saw. God damn it, I saw.

The immense inky darkness of the Sunlake Springs, only bleaker than I'd ever seen it, like a world flipped on its axis.

Shadows lurking in every corner crouched behind walls, trapped souls parted to let a swirling dark spirit through. The same mass I'd seen throughout the hotel, the one that had woken me up, the one Lobo had snarled at.

With every passing second, I saw further into Citana's vision, the withering patients, the wounded veterans begging for assisted suicide, the doctors who performed them, the women robbed of their babies by doctors who'd deemed them unfit for motherhood, the victims of hate crimes by that awful tree, guests hoping to be healed being dunked into the waters of Sunlake Springs, only to emerge wanting to harm each other.

I saw the Lady of the Lake emerging from the water, long hair fashioned of grass, green, putrid skin eaten by turtles and gators, turquoise eyes covered in algae. She attempted to break out of the lake, fought to become mortal, but she needed more. More what, I wasn't sure.

Energy? Flesh?

Hate.

Where there was hate and anger, there was enough traction to escape her swampy confines. She'd used the corpse of a suicide victim to begin her corporeal reanimation, rotten fingers sliding off bone, feet snapping off as she waded out of the lake, but she was still only a spirit. An entity growing stronger with each death.

"I see her," Citana said. "She is the color of pale aventurine. Sawgrass for hair. She wants you all to die, so she can live. This is what she's done for a hundred years. Feed. You must get the others!"

"I will. But what about my fa—"

"Get them out!" she screamed, "I beg of you!" With a thrust, she let go of my hands and fell off her chair, landing on the floor and shaking on the ground. She looked so frail, every bit her age, an old woman flailing pitifully against the floor.

I felt terrible for coming here and doing this to her.

Macy and I each took a hold of one of her arms. "Citana? God, please, please..." I prayed she wouldn't be gone. I'd never seen anyone die in person and wouldn't know how to begin explaining this to Mori.

But the old woman's chest rose and fell erratically.

"You give her strength," Citana whispered. "You and Crow both. Crow is a fallen child, and she knows what's in his heart. But he can be saved. Remove him from her grasp. It may already be too late."

I thought of Crow the other night, the way he'd looked when he forced my hand on his face. The Lady of the Lake and Crow had looked like the same person. "I don't know how," I said.

"She will manifest. And she'll do it through one of you."

"You're saying she'll become a woman?"

She closed her eyes. "She's no woman. She's a beast."

Twenty-Three

Macy and I worked to get Citana on the couch with a glass of cold water, then promised to tell the clairs to vacate the hotel. Outside, we ducked into my car under the pouring rain and blotted ourselves dry with napkins from the glove compartment.

For a while, we just stared at the watery swirls on the windshield.

"That was the scariest thing I've ever seen in my life," Macy said. "But you're not really going back there, are you?"

"I have to. They're in danger."

"You'd be in danger," she said.

"I know, but you heard her—there's evil feeding off fear and hate, and Lord knows Crow has enough for all of us. We were stupid enough to open the portal to let it through. Now we have to close it back up."

"How do you do that?"

"I have no idea."

Macy's hypnotized voice blended with the rain. "Do you think the beast she's talking about had something to do with Dad and the way he..."

"Yes."

In my heart, I knew my father would not have taken his life. Yes, depression was not always visible on the outside, but Wilky said my father had screamed. Something was blocking his path to the light. Something was there with him. "I need proof he was on duty at the hotel."

"Should I search county records?" Macy said. "I have access to that and more."

"You told me you wouldn't find evidence anyway."

"Of the details of his death? I haven't looked into it. Of the hotel's history?" Macy sighed. "There's a whole slush pile of unpublished accounts of goings-on dating back a century in Florida history. I can use my access as an editor, but I'm not supposed to unless it's for a video I'm designing."

"Will that get you fired?"

"If I'm caught, probably."

I didn't want Macy to get fired. She worked hard enough as it was. I wanted her to reach her next-level dreams, and no amount of information would bring our father back anyway.

"If you can find the free-access stuff, like public records, sure. But don't worry about researching misdeeds of the Sunlake. It's not worth it."

Wilky, Fae, Mori, and Crow needed to accept that their time accessing the untold stories of the Sunlake Springs was over.

"Actually..." I turned in my seat toward Lucinda's box of stuff in the back. "Can you reach that? Maybe there's a work order in there or something."

Macy reached for the box, pulling it forward. There wasn't much in it. Dad's clothes, which I resisted touching. A few thriller novels, a map of historic Florida buildings, a photo of him and Lucinda from a long-ass time ago. As the rain came down hard, I was mesmerized by the photo and the obvious love between them.

At the bottom of the box were the little crushed paper flower and the stained-glass sun.

And something else.

"Can you grab that for me?" I asked Macy.

Macy pulled up an old flip phone. "This?"

"Let me see." I'd never seen it before. Probably an old phone from his younger days.

She handed it to me.

I felt the smooth plastic in the palm of my hand. I closed my eyes. Maybe I'd hear phone conversations between him and Lucinda, or with my mom. Maybe, as happened at Macy's house, I'd hear a woman begging him to stay—Lucinda. I did hear something, but it was a male voice. Deep, baritone, half Spanish, half English.

Loosely translated, the man was saying: *Stay away from her. She doesn't need you. She needs a man who can step up to the plate.*

I can do that.

If you insist, Pablo, I'll make your life a living hell.

You already do, Berto. Cuco—it was Dad talking to my grandfather, Cuco, or Berto Santander. *I'm coming home and making good on my promise to marry her. You'll grant me this, or I'll tell everyone about the students you've been fucking.*

Cuco laughed. *You don't have that kind of power, hijo. There's too many willing to vouch for me, and you know full well, those hijas de puta wanted it. They're all cut from the same cloth as their mothers.*

I dropped the phone and stared out the windshield at the rain swirls now becoming waterfalls. I knew it. Deep in my heart, I knew. I'd heard the whispers, seen the flashes of truth in Cuco's belongings, the glimpses of his secrets in Scary Mary.

"That's an amazing gift you have," Macy said.

I pushed back tears at my lid line. "It's a curse."

"Then I wish I'd had your curse for the first eighteen years of my life. I might've saved myself some heartache."

"Believe me, you don't wish you had this."

I was done. Done being afraid. Done holding back. I didn't care how bad a light it put people I loved into, I needed to know what else my father said to Cuco. I picked up the flip phone again with shaky hands, as voices from beyond spoke.

Give me one good reason why I should let you marry my daughter, Cuco told my father. *You've humiliated her con esa negra, you're a dirty orphan, and your mother was a sinner bruja.*

My father didn't deny it.

He only replied: *Because I love her.*

Throwing the phone into the box, I threw the car into reverse, drove to the lake where the clairs and I had meditated not too long ago, and with hands gripping the steering wheel, screamed my head off. My rage filled the space, my ears, my soul.

The students you're fucking. My grandfather had been waiting for underaged girls to come into his office. The Scary Mary visions had shown me this.

And my grandmother had the nerve to defend him. My church called him a pillar of the community. Did my mother know? Did school administrators? How long had my grandfather been taking advantage of young women?

HOW LONG HAD THEY ALL COVERED FOR HIM?

I continued screaming until my heart nearly gave out, until I realized another scream had joined mine. Two screams filled the car. Macy was screaming with me. Our pains were different, but they belonged together like a chiaroscuro painting. Her hand grasped mine, and I broke into sobs when I "saw" the guilt she felt over Dad's death.

Because of her, he'd left Miami, left me.

Because of her, he'd come back to Yeehaw Springs.

Because of her decision to take the DNA test and reach out to him, he was dead. Macy had been holding a lot inside.

"I'm so sorry." I threw an arm around her.

"No, I am."

We sobbed for a minute.

"Let's get home," her voice cracked. "You go warn the clairs. I'll take care of the paperwork and trying to find his death certificate. But Vale, be careful. If you can't get them to leave of their own free will, promise me you'll come back."

I couldn't even speak, much less make a verbal promise.

"It's not that I don't care about the others, it's that—I don't want to lose you. You're the only family member who's been straightforward with me, and it took a long time to find you."

She, too, was the only one I could trust. "I promise," I said.

And meant it.

I DROPPED MACY OFF, so she could do what she did best—research—while I headed back to the Sunlake Springs to do what I did best—get into further trouble.

Florida people know how heavy summer rains can get. At times, it's all anyone ever talks about. Rain comes down in sheets so thick, you have to pull over on the side of the road because your weak-ass windshield wipers can't handle it. Today's rain was almost there. I managed to navigate my car, almost a boat at this point, up to the hotel gate, where I got out under the deluge to push the metal grate open.

Today, the grate wouldn't budge. Rain was responsible for many things, but I'd never heard of it stiffening up a gate overnight. It seemed, to my puny arms, like its swing angle had shifted, and its bending hinges could not support this new slant.

I dashed back to the car, took the keys out of the engine, and slipped through the open space. The car would have to wait outside. I ran through the deluge, water soaking my shirt and dripping into my eyes.

Behind me was a long, metallic screech. The gate creaked open. My car, which had been sitting on uneven, broken asphalt a moment before, was pushing against it, forcing it open, barreling through the space toward me at an unnatural speed.

What the hell?

I ran from the car, leaping over potholes, smashing down on one knee before rolling out of the way. As the car passed by, I sprang up and grabbed the driver side door, yanking it open and stepping on the brake pedal until it stopped. The car was in neutral. I was certain I'd put it in park before I got out.

I tilted my head back against the headrest to catch my breath. Was the ground that uneven or had my car just tried to kill me? I put the car in park, staring at the "P" to make sure I wasn't crazy. Then I stepped out and dashed toward the driveway, ducking into the hotel through the auxiliary door. I shook off the rain. It felt freezing inside, even though it was easily 96 degrees out, but I was also soaked to the bone. Loose papers and dust vortices spun across the lobby's Mediterranean tile. A hollow cooing sound emanated through the halls. The bird cages rocked, creaking over and over in tune to thunderstorm winds.

"Hello?" I called, reaching out to steady the cages. "You guys here?" I walked past the cages and peered down the hall. Puddles of water dotted the length of it. From above, drops of rain dripped steadily from the lanterns. Armed with new information about my father having died here, I fiercely resented the Sunlake today and wanted out as fast as possible. "Guys?"

I'm here.

I whirled.

The bird cage closest to the atrium was swinging again, vacillating back and forth. How could it pick up momentum so quickly when I'd just steadied it? I imagined at least a dozen unwanted scenarios. I floated over to it. "Hello?"

Dad?

The reason I'd joined the clairs in the first place, to try and communicate with my father, suddenly felt very possible. Meeting little Pablo Callejas on the veranda with his paper flower had been sweet, but I wanted to see my dad.

The cage stopped rocking.

I stared at it, bouncing around in tight circles as if steadied by some unseen force. Something was there. "Who are you?" My voice was hoarse from all the screaming.

Nothing showed. The winds continued to howl. Outside, the thunderstorm intensified. The rainwater collected in larger puddles on the floor, and papers blowing around got stuck in them and melted. Cooing wind whipped past my ears, morphing into words that seemed to be coming from everywhere at once.

...here...

...help...

I turned in every direction, wanting for someone to materialize, and not wanting at the same time. But that wasn't how spirits manifested, not for me anyway. Charging to the bird cage, I gripped my hands around the metal bars and closed my eyes.

"Who...is there?" I demanded.

A brown-skinned man, whose clothes were torn, whose wrists were handcuffed to the cage from the inside, as if being locked inside weren't enough to break him. The rancid smell of filth stung my nose. Uncracked sunflower seeds surrounded him, as well as scattered cigarette butts. On his arms and back were tiny, round burn marks. His eyes, red from exhaustion, implored me.

Tell her I'm sorry.

"Sir?"

My sister.

"You don't need to be sorry. You didn't cause this. You hear me?" My voice grew, as shouts of random men giving orders filled the corridors. I wanted to unleash hell at them for doing this to an innocent person. "This was not your fault!"

I'm next. He bowed his head.

And then I saw what he was referring to. In the other bird cage were three other men, all dark-skinned, all with burn marks, sitting in filth, chained to the metal slats. And I knew, in that moment, that their fate, judging from the jeers and laughter in the background, was to die—at the Devil's Tree.

"Who is your sister?" I asked.

Bernice.

The cage swung once more, and then he, along with the other men, was gone.

As my fingers released the cage, I stood panting, sweating in the cold. Nodding, I tried to speak the woman's name again, for my own sake of remembering it. I backed a few steps, rattled by the vision, and then I broke into a run, strategically avoiding the atrium, tucking into the ballroom. Nobody was there, though their stuff was. I headed out the side ballroom door, craning my ear for human noises, wending my way through each room and out onto the veranda.

As I entered the south hallway through an opened door, my sneaker hit something wet. More water seeping from the ceiling. "Guys?"

"In here!" Fae called back. I wove through the dining room, down through the secret door into the basement, and was shocked to find a pool of water about two inches thick.

"What are you doing?" I asked Mori and Fae. They stood beside the tunnel of death, the one used for disposing expired human bodies, looking into a fissure that had widened.

Fae jumped when she saw me. "Vale, come here, please." She took my hand and pulled me closer to the wall, even as the minor lake by the broken window was still a concern. "Touch here, please. Touch the wall, down near the floor. I've been smelling it all day. I can taste it."

"What can you taste?" I asked.

"The gold!" She clapped in a tiny way, trying to contain her excitement.

Mori shook their head. "Even if it was down there, there's no way to get it without a bulldozer, Fae." They settled into a better crossed-leg position and resumed writing on their notepad.

"I just want confirmation that it's there. That alone would make me happy. Vale, touch it, please. If my nose is going crazy, your hands must be, too!" She shook my hand so hard, I had to pull it out of her grasp.

I didn't want anyone using my hands for their own purpose again, not even Fae.

"Did you know I tasted butter while you were gone? Butter! In the dining room!"

"That's great. Hey, have you noticed the water filling this room? The basement will be flooded in an hour."

"All the more reason I need to know. Before that happens, Vale. I need to know if it's there. Please, right here—touch." Fae tapped the wall, beckoning me. "Please. Just this once, I promise."

Sighing, I knelt on the transitional space between the bottom of the body chute and the concrete step up to the tunnel. I pressed my hands against the bricks and closed my eyes. I saw nothing but loneliness, the occasional roach crawling through the space. Water collected underground, as panicked ants scrambled for dry ground.

"Even the bugs know something is up," I muttered.

"Bugs? Is that it? Oh, Vale, please tell me there's more down there."

I refocused my efforts. Took another deep breath and tried to think of nothing but the humidity in the room, the coolness of the bricks underneath my touch, the cavernous labyrinth between them. This moment.

Nothing but this moment.

Below the concrete foundation, atop natural layers of dry dirt, was a texture incongruously blended with the rest of the earth. Same dull brown, but the items were cloth. Canvas bags, the kind used for carrying sand to block against flooding during hurricanes. The kind you might find holding potatoes, only in this case, something not biodegradable was inside. Dull yellow. Round coins. Not many, but Fae had been right all along—her great grandfather's rumrunning money was under this chute.

"It's there." I took my hands away. "It's been there a while."

"I knew it! I knew it!" Fae spun on the bare balls of her feet, slipping on the encroaching puddle of collected rainwater and landing on her ass. "Ow!" She laughed and crawled her way over to me to kiss me haphazardly on the cheek.

My head hurt with a dull ache. I hadn't eaten much on a stress-filled day. But even through the pain, I could tell something else was down there. I had to see it again to be sure. I put my hands back on the brick.

"You're double checking, yes, good, good." Fae breathed down my neck.

"There's something else."

Again, I saw the canvas bags containing coins, but above it was a crevice stretching upward, opening its maw as it flared toward ground level. Time shifted in time-lapse again, the concrete opening, splitting, yawning apart until broken bricks lay scattered in heaps, unearthing the coins. Complete devastation of the foundation. Underneath one of the fallen piles was a slender broken body, pale hands clutching the bag, skin bloody and raw, skull crushed open by bricks like a coconut. The dead person's hair was long and blonde. And matted.

I scrambled back. "We have to get out."

"What is it?"

"We have to get out," I repeated.

Mori's eyelids fluttered, their fingers nimbly scribbled a message on the paper. I bent to see what it said. There was no message, just the static scratches of a nonsensical drawing. Someone walked by us, someone who hadn't been there a moment before—a man in a white coat.

He didn't seem to know we were there, he simply reached down and pulled on the crank that opened the chute and peered inside.

"Do you see him?" I asked Fae, my words coming out as wisps.

"Yes," she replied, backing away from the wall. "Finally, I do."

Whoever he was began leaving but made sure to beam me in the eye with his gaze as he did. "We'll see you soon." Then he disappeared through Mori who leaned forward in a coughing fit, sputtering and choking, and vomited straight onto the floor. They leaned back to suck in a gasp, eyes wide in horror. "What the fuck was that?"

"We're being warned again," I said.

"We saw a man."

"A doctor."

"He told us he'd see us all soon. I don't like this."

Finally, some concern. I might be able to get them out of here after all. "Guys, I have to tell you something. The Lady of the Lake is real. She's not just a legend or the beautiful spirit Crow thinks she is. She's some kind of abomination. A creature, a...a..."

"Demon?" Mori asked.

"Whatever it is, it's trying to become mortal. It's using us. It's using Crow."

"This is why the spirits can't move on," Mori said. "She's blocking the portal, keeping them from ascending. That's why they cower in corners. How did you find that out?"

"I've had a bad feeling since the day I arrived. I saw her during the ritual, and then I saw her inside of Crow's body last night while you all slept. Today, I visited Citana to ask about my father, and she sensed it, too."

"The portal opening must've affected her, too," Fae said.

"We need to leave. This place isn't safe." I didn't tell them about my vision just now, the one of Fae's dead body amid a pile of bricks. Nor the one of the man inside the cage. We had to find Wilky and Crow to warn them.

"Let's go." As we headed upstairs, something fell behind us, jolting the living shit out of us. A piece of concrete ceiling had fallen, outright disengaged from the rafters and landed at the foot of the stairs a few inches away.

The Sunlake was trying to kill us.

Twenty-Four

"We can't come back to this room, under any circumstances," I said.

"What about the gold?" Fae puffed up the stairs.

"Fae!" I barked. "A few days ago, you said you'd be happy just *knowing* where it is. That would be enough, you said. Do not tempt fate."

"Fine. You're right."

We searched the flooded ground floor for the boys, weaving in and out of every room before eventually stealing out through the ballroom exit. They weren't on the veranda either. Rain pelted us sideways, and Fae paced the floorboards, like a dog sniffing out a cut of juicy meat.

"You smell that? It's sewage." She turned up her nose.

"I smell rain, grass, the lake. Nothing bad." I peered into the silver cascade. Surrounding areas were starting to flood, creating mini lakes on the Sunlake Springs property. If the rain continued this way, the hotel would soon become an island.

"What is that?" Fae held onto a column and pointed to something out by the lakeshore. Rushing water spilled out of the lake and poured into what looked like a fissure in the earth, draining the surrounding pooling water.

"Was that there before?" Mori asked.

"I don't think so," I said moments before the air sizzled, and a crack of lightning hit about a half mile away. I covered my ears. Rain washed down my face in rivers that soaked my neck and shirt.

We heard a shout from the distance. Out by the Devil's Tree, someone stood waving. Wilky cupped his hands around his mouth and yelled something incomprehensible.

"What is he doing out there?" Mori asked.

I jogged the length of the veranda. "I don't think he'd be out there unless it was important. He's calling us. Let's go see."

"And go near that tree again? No, thank you." Fae pressed her back against the outer walls. "I'll wait for you here."

Hunkering down, I hustled into the downpour with Mori following close behind. It took us a minute to navigate the land, as we ran around deep puddles and jumped over a few. On one, I lost my footing and fell to my knees. Mori gave me their arm to help me up.

We reached Wilky, and he held out his arms for us to grab to keep from slipping. "*Why* are you out here?" I chastised. "There's lightning—you're standing by a tree! Come inside," I beckoned.

"Not until I find it." He crouched, raking his open hands through the mud. "Can you guys help me?"

"Find what?" Mori and I screamed at the same time.

"I heard them." His eyes roved the ground. "More shouts. I saw them, a row of Black men, standing right here in this spot, hands tied behind their backs." Wilky's nervous energy was unlike anything I'd ever seen coming from him.

"Wilky..." I knelt beside him with Mori. Together we began digging. "I saw something, too, just a while ago."

"They're here. I know they are." He ignored me.

"Did you hear me? Inside the lobby, inside..." God, I couldn't even say it without feeling sick to my stomach. "The cages. Have you seen what's in the cages, Wilky?" Maybe he already knew. Maybe, by now, he'd filled his sketchbook with renderings of the atrocities but had kept it to himself.

Mori asked, "What's in the cages?"

I didn't want to describe it and hurt Wilky more than he was already. I shook my head at them. Another bolt of lightning within a half mile hit, charging the atmosphere with sizzling heat before releasing its thunderous boom.

"They died by this tree," Wilky said, a maniacal quality to his voice. "They're here, you know. They're here. The screams never stop." He shook his head, as if to dislodge the haunting.

"Wilky, it's not important to find evidence," I tried telling him. "We know it happened. You know it, I know it. You don't need to risk your life trying to prove it."

"Easy for you to say, Valentina."

"We're in danger here. Citana said we are. Please, can we just go?"

"I'm not leaving. I can't stand the screams anymore. I have to quiet the screams!" Wilky raked aside more and more mud, but it was futile. As soon as he'd make one hole, more water would rush in and fill it.

I saw a certain madness in his face I knew I'd never be able to fully comprehend, not until I'd lived a thousand lifetimes in his skin. I didn't know what it was like to hear the screams of people you were powerless to help, day and night.

"It's not your family." His voice broke. "If you're not going to help me, then leave me alone."

He was right. Of course, he was, I only wanted him to be free of his torment. This was how, though, by shutting the hell up and digging alongside the man. But I did have one last thing he needed to hear. "Who's Bernice?"

He looked up, finally. "What did you say?"

"Bernice."

He stared at me through pained eyes. "My great-aunt. How did you..."

I kept digging, scooping up handfuls of mud. "I think he spoke to me, your great-uncle. He probably knew I could see him. He knew we're all connected now. He told me to tell Bernice he was sorry."

Wilky stared at me, chest heaving. "What else did he tell you?"

I wrestled with his great-uncle's last words to me—*I'm next.* Another crack of lightning hit. If I told him, he'd never stop digging, but I realized that even weeks of more of digging would never be worse than not finding closure. "He said he was next."

"Next."

"Next," I repeated.

"Next for...?"

"I don't..." No need to lie. He knew. I knew. "You know for what," I said.

He watched me a few moments longer, as he absorbed the news. Then, he fell onto his hands again with renewed fervor and we dug. We dug until the hole was six feet wide and nearly two feet deep. We dug until our fingers bled, but nothing came up. Mori and I looked at each other but said nothing.

"I need a shovel," Wilky's voice broken.

"There's one in the back of Crow's truck," Mori said to me.

"On it. You stay here."

Mori nodded.

I sprinted off, bounding over puddles, skidding and sliding across mud to get to the veranda, spilling into the hotel, as I left a trail of muck behind me. I ran through the ballroom, soiling parquet floors, cutting across the hallway, blinding my view of the bird cages until I made it to the auxiliary door. Crow's truck was parked away from the covered driveway. I ducked back into the rain.

Reaching the truck, I searched the flatbed, rummaging through hoses and plastic chemical buckets filled with rain. I found a coil of rope that sent a jolt through my mind the moment I touched it.

Fight through it, I told myself.

I curled my fingers around the rope again, afraid of what I might "see." Crow used it to rip coconut palms growing too close to backyard pools out of the ground.

I grabbed it and searched the cab of the truck. Still no shovel. I slammed the truck door and sloshed back to the auxiliary door, dripping into the hotel like a wet towel. Cutting through the hallway into the ballroom, I slowed when I felt another presence, caught a whiff of something putrid on the wind. Shadows flitted in my peripheral vision.

I hurried to the end of the room, to the corner that opened onto the veranda, when I heard a scraping sound. Checking behind me, I saw Crow there when he hadn't been a moment ago. In his hand, he held the shovel.

"Looking for this?"

"Yes." I held out my hand. "Can I borrow it?"

Crow stared at me a long moment, his bioluminescent eyes scanning my muddy clothes, his sweaty face the color of algae. The smell was getting stronger, wafting off of him in sheets. Pooling underneath his feet was lake water with a greenish tint. Goosebumps broke out over my arms.

"What are you looking at." It wasn't a question.

"I'm worried about you, Crow."

"I can say the same about you. Where did you go today?"

"I told you, I had to deal with personal issues."

"You told authorities we were here, didn't you?"

"What? No. I swore I wouldn't."

"It's a matter of time, Valentina. You brought your friend, you brought your sister. I know your sister, by the way. Yeehaw Springs is a small town. She works for the state. Any moment now, code enforcers will arrive."

"She's not going to do that, Crow."

"We'll see."

His skin had taken on a wrinkled appearance like crepe paper in the rain. He seemed taller somehow, his purple hair looked slicker, shinier, gelled with some slimy product. Citana's warning echoed through my mind. "Crow, I'm sorry to tell you this, but this building is falling apart. As we speak."

"It isn't. It's just water. Water dries. The sun comes out."

He wasn't making any sense. I shook my head. "No, Crow. It's over. The basement is flooded. Chunks of ceiling are falling. One nearly hit Mori, Fae, and me."

"We only have to keep it open long enough for the historical society to approve a restoration budget. We only have to—"

"No, Crow." *It's not going to happen,* I wanted to say, but felt Crow's cold, dead stare, like a fish after it's stopped gasping for water on the deck of a boat. His feet were bare and red, almost scaly. He lifted one foot and used the toenails to scratch the top of the other.

A beast becoming flesh.

"Okay, we'll talk about it later," I said in the hopes of appeasing him temporarily. I held out my hand. "I need the shovel, please."

"Are you sure you don't need the rope instead?" He gestured to my other hand holding the coil of rope. A wet cough bubbled up in his chest and exited his mouth as frothy foam.

My nostrils flared. He was making fun of my father. "That's not funny."

"Oh, I'm sorry. You don't like my father-daughter joke?" He laughed so low and long, he coughed again. I prayed he would choke on his spit.

"Don't fuck with me. I've been through too much today."

"Only today? Try a lifetime," he sneered.

I wasn't about to have a pissing contest over whose life was worse. We both knew it'd be his. I'd been lied to repeatedly, but I wasn't about to let it turn me into a hateful asshole.

The thought of charging at him and pummeling his face into a pulp ran through my mind, but I knew it was what he wanted—for me to fall apart at the seams, let my rage get the best of me. It wasn't him underneath the exterior. It was half him, half someone else, Crow on emotional steroids. Crow...infected.

"Give it to me." I reached out to snatch the shovel.

He pulled it into his chest. "Come and get it."

"Put it there against the wall." I pointed behind him. "And then walk away."

He laughed. "You don't trust me?"

"No."

"The feeling is mutual."

"Crow, we don't have time for this. The building is not safe."

"You keep saying that, Valentina," he hissed. "As if I don't know. As if I'm new here and just seeing the deterioration for the first time. As if I haven't dedicated the last year of my *life*," he yelled, "to studying this building. Of course, it's not fucking safe here!"

"Then come with us."

"I *can't* do that!" His eyelids fluttered.

"Why not?"

"I live here."

"You can leave, Crow."

"I've lived here forever."

I stared into his seafoam green yes, no longer blue. Someone new was talking to me, someone not Crow. I backed away slowly. "She's just using you to get what she wants."

"God, I hope so," he chuckled. A flash of craving in his smile reminded me of Antoni, of the lecherous sneer he'd worn in my dreams. "What do you think my Lady wants?"

"To be alive again. To find beauty and youth. That's what Citana Rose said."

"Citana Rose doesn't understand the complexities of necromancy."

"Necromancy?" I recoiled.

"Communication with the dead."

"I know what necromancy is. And we all communicate with the dead here."

"Not my way, you don't. I don't 'see' visions like you guys do." His nostrils flared. His handsome smile was back. "I raise the dead from their hallowed ground to ask them important questions about the afterlife."

Wilky and Mori were out in the driving rain waiting for the shovel, so we could dig up God knows what, close a door behind us, and get out of here. It was clear I wasn't going to be able to get Crow to do the same. "Just give me the shovel," I said.

"So demanding. Trade you for the rope." He laughed, extending his arm, and held the tool out to me. I threw the rope at him and snatched the shovel. No lightning bolts shot from his hands, no unintelligible phrases poured from his lips.

I turned on my heels without uttering as much as a thanks and ran without stopping to look back until I'd almost reached the Devil's Tree. By then, Mori and Wilky had managed to dig another food of depth. Forearms caked with dirt, they looked up at me with rivers of water cutting through the grime on their faces and scrambled, devoid of energy, to their feet.

I handed Wilky the shovel.

Necromancy. Black magic. Raising the dead.

Maybe opening the portal had served us in some other way. Revealing truths in each other, exposing the colony of ants simmering underneath the surface.

We took turns with the shovel for the next forty minutes. I still had no idea what we were digging for, but each time my fingers plunged into the muddy soil, I caught a flash of the past. A boot here, a cigarette filter there, a dark-skinned cheek being rammed into the earth.

Laughter.

Struggles for power.

Fear of losing it.

I hated this spot, this tree, I even hated the fine root system that had snaked its way through the earth, making it difficult for us to get the job done. I hated when the shovel's tip cracked into something hard and bony. I hated the way Wilky's fingers curled into the mud to scoop it out. I hated the pain in his eyes when he cradled it to his chest, and I hated seeing the bullet hole in the forehead.

Most of all, I hated that Wilky had to go digging by the Devil's Tree to find a truth he already knew existed, that he'd unearthed his answer, and that he did not seem any more or less satisfied for having uncovered it.

He sat on the ground a long time, cradling the skull, whispering to it. And the rain fell from a gunmetal sky for a long time, washing away his tears.

Twenty-Five

"Where do you think she went?"

Fae had left the veranda but wasn't in the ballroom. We needed to find her so I could drive the three of them away from the Sunlake Springs. I would try to convince Crow to leave, too, but that would be harder. Regardless of who came with me, I had to go. I'd promised Macy.

"Probably in the kitchen," Wilky said.

Wilky, Mori, and I hurried down the corridor through the double doors into the kitchen where we found Fae's flip-flops floating in a river of rain. Mori bent to pick them up. "Wait. Tell me again why you think we should leave?"

"Especially tonight?" Wilky added. "In the middle of this storm? We still have so much we want to accomplish. That skull was just the beginning."

I looked at both of them, still so anxious to begin the work they'd waited a year to do. "First of all, the flooding. Second, Citana warned of an evil presence, and third, Crow's not right in the head. Do you know what he said to me tonight?"

They both shook their heads.

"He asked if I needed a rope. As a joke. As in my father hung himself, so I should use a rope on myself, too. Does that sound funny to you?"

"Definitely not," Mori said. "And we know there's a dark presence at the Sunlake—that's why we're here. To find out what havoc the presence has caused, so we can help trapped souls. The only way to help them is to rid whatever is blocking it."

"Mori." I placed my hands behind my head. "To be honest? Had I known there was an evil here, I never would've stayed to help. I know you want to help the spirits of the Sunlake find passage to the Light, but I'm pretty sure this is a bigger battle than we thought."

Mori held my gaze a moment then moved to the corner kitchen doors to peer through each one. "Fae?" They ignored my plea to leave the building.

"I was hoping to keep digging," Wilky said. "The more I uncover, the more I might be able to find peace for other families."

"I get it, Wilky, but at what cost? It's using us for our pain. That sounds like more than we bargained for, doesn't it?"

"She's scared, Wil," Mori said.

My jaw dropped. "Is that what you think? That I'm being chicken shit? It's not *only* about what Citana said. It's also about the building. Mori, you saw the size of that concrete chunk that fell from the ceiling when we were leaving the basement. What if that'd fallen on our heads?"

Mori paced into the dining room, and we followed. "So we stay out of the basement. There's other stuff you may not have considered, Vale. I always have a couch to sleep on at Citana's, if it came down to it, but Fae has nowhere to go. Her family's completely abandoned her. We're her family."

"She can stay with me. I know my sister wouldn't mind, though I'd have to ask."

"She can stay with my family, too," Wilky said, eyeing me. "You all can."

Mori considered it. For a moment, I thought I'd convinced them. "Thanks, but you know her heart is set on finding that gold," they said, sloshing through the dining room's puddles. "That's the whole reason she's here."

"Mori, if the county gets its way and the building eventually get demolished, maybe we can request a special permit to search the foundation once the rubble is cleared and leveled."

"Can we do that?" they asked.

"We can try. My father worked for them, and my sister works for the state. But for now, we should leave. Isn't it a waning moon? Influences passing, time for goodbyes and closures? We've already done all we can do here. It's time to let this place die a peaceful death."

Mori thought about it. "Everything has its time," they whispered.

I remembered Macy's Everglades story. "Yes. The old burns down to clear space for the new. It's just the natural cycle of life."

Fae came running in just then, wild excitement in her eyes. "There you guys are."

"Where were you? We've been looking for you," Mori said.

"The basement. I need your help. The concrete foundation connected to the opening of the death tunnel is cracked. I wonder if there's a way to open that up more, maybe using the shovel. We should try!"

"Love..." Mori took Fae's hands.

Wilky and I looked at each other.

"I hate to say this, but...I think you're going to have to settle for knowing that gold is down there. Yes, Vale saw it, but there's no way to get to it, not unless this place is torn down."

"No, Mori, Mori, listen...the wall is literally breaking apart from all this rain. It's like a miracle!" Fae leaped in the air like a ballerina. "Come! Come see it!"

"It's severe structural damage is what it is," I said. More water began creeping into the dining room from the hallway. "See? For there to be water moving in here, that means the whole parking lot must be flooded, too. At this rate, we might not even be able to drive out of the gate."

"She's right," Wilky said. "This is getting bad. We should go—tonight."

"What? No!" Fae cried. "That's so easy for you to say, Wilky. You found what you were looking for!"

Wilky paced up to Fae and cupped her chin. "Let's be clear on one thing. I will *never* find what I'm looking for. Okay? That skull, that body we found? That was only the tip of the iceberg." He let go of her chin and exited the room.

"I agree we should go," Mori said. "The basement's in bad shape. We can always come back after the rain dies down. After the property is razed, whenever that is."

Fae yanked her hands out of Mori's. "Then, go, all of you." She backed into the hall with tears in her eyes and cheeks red with anger. "I still have work to do here."

"That's the spirit." Through the corridor's gloom, Crow's silhouette emerged. "Sounds like Fae and I are only ones who understand the meaning of the word dedication."

"Crow, we're leaving," Wilky blurted. "Vale says we're in danger."

"Of course, Vale says we're in danger. She was born and bred in the Catholic Church, the petri dish of fear."

I bristled at Crow's menacing presence.

"Meaning, the building is falling apart as we speak," Mori clarified.

"Of course, it is. That's why we're here, to accomplish goals before it does. But Vale's been hesitant to help since the day she arrived. There's a cautious energy about her that blocks us from accomplishing those goals. Or has no one else noticed?"

"It's called intuition, asshole." Wilky stepped up to him.

Crow held out his arm to prevent Wilky from coming any closer. "It's called cowardice. The moment you give into your fear, you've lost. A real witch attracts the result they want by envisioning nothing less than the result they seek."

"I don't have time for this." I shot forward and moved past Crow.

"We are *going* to get the county's approval," he insisted in a loud voice. I paused to gape at him. "And then we're going to refurbish this beautiful landmark hotel. And *then*, people will return from everywhere, near and far, for the healing waters of the lake, for the splendor of this building's architecture. The Sunlake Springs will enjoy another hundred-year reign."

When the lightning illuminated the hall, we could see Crow's arms had grown scaly and itchy like his feet earlier. His skin was mottled and veiny. He looked sickly and pale.

"Whatever you say, bro. I'll be in the ballroom—packing." Wilky turned and blew past Crow, passing me. "You coming?"

"You're not wrong about the waning moon symbolism," Crow said, his head twisted back so I could hear him. "The end of an era brings the beginning of a new one. This hotel's loneliness *is* ending. But soon, it will enjoy a revival."

"Because the Lady of the Lake told you?" I snapped. "She's lying. She's only telling you what you want to hear, because she wants you to do her bidding, so she can be reborn into flesh, and she's using you, Crow. Look at you—you're putrid, like the lake outside. It's already begun."

"You know nothing," Crow hissed.

I felt the air, filled with his stink, reach my nose as he charged at me through the gloom. I lifted my arms, ready to shove him back. I'd never been struck by anyone before, much less a man taller than I was, but I was Latina, full of fire, and pissed as fuck.

"What? You're gonna hit me?"

"Crow? Stop it!" Mori shouted.

"You...are a liar." He rushed at me, his form growing larger as he stomped toward me. I hadn't noticed how much taller he seemed to have gotten since I'd been alone with him in the ballroom earlier. I braced for the shove, but ended up tripping and landing ass-first in a puddle anyway.

Wilky's hands were on Crow in a blur, knocking him into the wall and lifting a fist to ram into his face when a white light flashed off the walls, lighting up the Lady of the Lake painting in the lobby. We all stopped. Another glint flashed off the bird cages, this one red.

White-red, white-red.

The electronic sound of a voice speaking through a police radio sounded out of place and echoed off the walls. Outside, car doors slammed shut. Crow shoved Wilky back with both hands. "And there they are. Everyone hide your things. I'll handle this."

"What is it?" Mori shuffled past the lobby.

"Cops. Let's pick up and move."

I'd never gotten in trouble before. Not at school. Not at home. I'd been the goodiest good girl the world had ever seen. Leave it to me, on my first time away from home without my parents, as an adult, to get arrested for squatting in an abandoned building.

Wilky, Mori, and Fae split off in different directions.

I followed, or intended to follow Wilky into the dining room, intent on collecting my things and telling the truth, should a police officer ask me why I was here, when suddenly, a muscular bicep curled around to gag me. As I watched Wilky enter the ballroom without noticing what Crow was doing to me, he dragged me, kicking and muttering, down the corridor.

"Hello?" Beams of light criss-crossed through the lobby, reflecting off the atrium glass.

Crow unlocked a door to one of the small offices between the grand rooms we never used and shoved me inside. He navigated the dark, windowless room with one arm, as he dragged me then pushed me into an armchair, my muffled screams evaporating into nothingness.

He let go of my mouth, and I sucked in a deep breath. Before I could scream, he'd shoved a rope, the rope I'd given him in exchange for the shovel, into my mouth. I heard one of my teeth chip and kicked blindly in the dark, aiming for his groin. He caught my foot between his knees where he held it still.

"I can't trust what you'll tell them," he muttered, his thick, fish-smelling sweat falling on my face, as he worked to wind the rope around my wrists behind the chair. "I'll be back."

I fought against the restraints, but Crow had tied me tight.

"Your father came to close this place down, too," he said, testing the knot around my wrists. "The Lady harassed him every time. Like you, he couldn't resist the building's beauty either. He'd come back. She haunted his ass until he couldn't take it anymore. She made it look like a suicide. I'll do the same to you later."

What? NO.

I reached out with one leg and clocked him in the knee. He buckled, restrained a cry, then reached out and yanked a good chunk of my hair.

"Watch my stuff," he breathed into my face, indicating a pile of stuff on the floor.

He left, closing the door.

I sat in pitch darkness, breathing through my nose, hearing the police officers calling throughout the building. I couldn't tell if they'd found any of us or not, if anyone was hiding or coming clean. In my mind's eye, I watched them creep with their flashlights, as they stepped through puddles. Deep in my heart, I knew the cops were here because of Cami. She had reported us. She was trying to "save me from myself."

I heard talking.

What would Crow tell the police? Probably how the rest of us were squatters, and he was here on assignment. I could hear it now. Would they notice his changing appearance?

As I sat in complete darkness, I heard the officers giving each other orders, directing to search different areas. The hotel was so sprawling, it would take a while. As footsteps scrambled past the office I was locked in, I screamed against my gag, working myself up to the point I could barely breathe.

How had I gotten into this situation? From the moment I first arrived, I knew this place—I knew Crow—was bad news and still, I delved deeper into it every day. Was I so desperate to feel anything at all that I'd risked injury, even death, to know what living was like?

Yes.

Closing my eyes, I focused on trying to settle down before I choked on tears. I breathed evenly, calmly. I worked to clear my mind, envision that I wasn't in danger; I was safe inside this room. In the distance, I heard more radio calls, more orders being given.

But in this room, I was safe.

In this room.

I sank into deep meditation.

His shadow entered my mind before I saw his face, my Lobo of deep pewter fur, my lupine spirit guide. He filtered into the room quietly and circled the chair, his tongue lolling. In front of me, he sat on his haunches and stared. *What did you get yourself into?*

Hey, I wouldn't be here if not for you.

Snarky wolf.

Through the darkness, another shape emerged, a dark cloud blending through the wall. I couldn't deal with another ghost right now, not when I was the one who needed the help. Quickly, it took the shape of a woman with long hair and curvy shape. Her cheekbones were high; her smile told me everything would be okay. I couldn't see her eyes. Half her face was missing. Half her hair. Around her waist was a charred apron.

Kitchen ghost?

When she reached out and touched my cheek, I felt a love that transcended time and space. My grandmother. Though we'd never met, I'd only seen her in that one photo of her wearing hippie clothing, I knew she loved me. The seed of her adoration had been planted inside my father's heart, then passed on to mine, waiting for the right moment to germinate.

My little starshine, sleep, oh, so tight
  My little moonshine, dream with the night

Only it was her melodious voice, the same song she'd sang to her little boy night after night before she'd perished in the fire, a song he'd kept in his heart and passed onto me many years later. My grandmother sank to her knees, transformed into a column of twinkling blue lights, and pushed something toward me.

When you awaken, Love you will be
  My little sunshine Heaven gave me

In the light she emanated, I could see what she'd pushed Crow's laptop bag. Papers slid out. It could've been my imagination—all of it—a vision borne from distress. I couldn't be sure, but the next thing that happened I would remember clearly as long as I lived. A leather laptop bag that toppled from the top of a pile of Crow's stuff, was explainable. My chair rising off the floor, however, was not. I rose a few inches before my grandmother's column of light disappeared. The chair tumbled onto its side with me in it.

The fall loosened my bound wrists, enough so I could wriggle my hands out of the knots. Once a hand was free, I was able to pull the hemp cord out from between my teeth. I lifted the papers to my face, adjusting my vision as much as I could in the darkness. I smelled phosphorus, and a flame sprouted out of thin air. Blue-green orange at moments, the light hovered, flickered, a ghostly ball of fire to illuminate the papers.

Code enforcement forms.

As a child, my father had given me blank or used ones to play with, to keep me busy while he worked. I'd pretend I was a code enforcer for the county, like him. On the forms, I saw words penned in my father's handwriting—*stress cracks, uneven settling of foundation, copper pipe breakage, floors sinking*, etc. Words to decree this building condemned.

"How long?" I looked at the spot I'd seen my grandmother, now empty. "How long until it collapses?"

The ball of flame grew wider, flew straight at me, as if hurled by human hands, catching the edges of the papers, eating its way inward, erasing my father's writing, his memory and hard work, no matter how hard I tried to blow out the flames. The survey was charred, blackened, gray ashes flittering out like dead confetti.

A reply echoed from another place and time—my father's voice: *Now.*

Twenty-Six

Outsider voices carried through the corridor, as I slipped into the shadows. Police officers talking to Crow, Crow fielding police officers' questions, mumbles, blips of walkie-talkies, reports of their findings.

"Squatters at the old Sunlake. They've been here a while," one of them said on a radio call, as flashlight beams swiveled through the hotel. "Yes, the old sanatorium."

I melted into the shadows, thought of the farthest place I could get without being seen, and dropped into the south stairwell near the dining room toward the sound of rushing water. The basement was flooded. My feet sank through two feet of rainwater, and my flip-flop dislodged and floated away. I held onto the wall.

Great minds think alike, because Mori and Wilky were here, too, huddled halfway inside the body chute. "Are you going to stay or escape?" I asked.

"Wilky is going to check the bottom grate in a minute to see if it's unlocked," Mori said, pointing through the chute.

"That goes down, though. It's probably flooded at the end."

"Better than climbing out a window where the cops will see us."

I wasn't concerned about the cops as much as I was about the lower levels of this building, especially after the vision I'd had down here and the papers I'd found in the storage room. "Where's Fae?"

They both pointed. It was then I realized she was below them, deep in the foundation's crevice, and they were in the body chute waiting for her.

"Guys, no. She shouldn't be down there."

"Tell that to Fae," Wilky murmured. "We're just here making sure she's safe."

"But she's not safe." I sloshed through water halfway up my thighs, feeling the ground uneven beneath my bare feet. The room felt off-kilter, as though the walls themselves were angling inward. Water seeped in thin, trickling mini-falls from every corner of the ceiling. I waded up to the platform and climbed up.

"She only needs a minute," Mori said.

I reached Mori and Wilky and peered down Wilky's flashlight beam. The foundation of the basement where it met the platform on which the tunnel was built had ripped apart to expose layers of brick underneath. At the bottom of this spontaneous ravine was Fae opening bags of gold coins in a pool of fetid water.

"Vale, you were right!" she cried, holding up a gold piece—an actual gold doubloon. "Ha! My great-grandfather really was a rumrunner. Holy shit! Behold ye treasure, mateys!"

"Get her out of there," I said, holding onto what was left of the rim of the brick foundation. My earlier vision of Fae deep in the ravine barreled full-force into my head, and I had to forcibly shake my head to dislodge it. "Now!" I screamed.

Mori caught the panic in my eyes. "Fae—out. Now, let's go." They splayed on their stomach, reaching down into the crevice which was quickly filling with groundwater. Anything could've been down there, from old sewage to dangerous debris from the building itself.

"Hold on, I'm making sure this is the only one," Fae replied, feeling around with her hands.

"Fae, get up here!" I was fuming. How could she come back to the basement when I specifically warned her not to?

"I'll get her," Wilky said, handing Mori his flashlight. He climbed into the ravine, using the exposed bricks for foot anchors, like an inverted rock-climbing wall. He reached down as far as he could for Fae's hand.

"Okay, I'm coming." Fae wrapped the canvas folds of the bag around her wrist and stretched her skinny arm up to meet Wilky's. Wet strands of long hair plastered to her face, she looked like a trapped cave diver emerging for the first time in days.

I backed away to give them space to hoist her out, still angry that Mori had allowed her to go down there. There was such a thing as too much empathy. Now we had to wait while she climbed out of this godforsaken hole before we could run out to safety.

But then, the basement floor began shaking. It took me two seconds to realize there'd be no way out of this if we didn't act quickly. "Hurry!" I screamed, as the entire tunnel began to crumble, a loud sickening crash filling my ears.

Without much foundation left to support the curved passageway, the center arch began to fall away slowly, brick by brick plummeting to the ravine below. The flashlight fell into the earth's crack. Wilky used his one free arm to protect his head from the falling bricks, while his back and feet pressed against the ravine wall, holding him in place by tension. His other arm continued to reach down. "Come on!" he screamed.

"I'm trying!"

I covered my head, too, and winced when a brick hit me square in the shoulder. Wilky managed to grab Fae's arm with one hand and tugged as she screamed.

"Get her out!" Mori screamed.

Fae's foot slipped from underneath her, however, and she fell a few feet, unable to get a footing on the wall, now slick with cascading water. Wilky couldn't lift her out, no matter how differently he positioned his feet or knees for better leverage. He would have to let go, drop to the bottom to reach her, risk being trapped himself.

I struggled with the idea of leaving them all here to die while I saved myself, but there was no way I could, not even to keep my promise to Macy.

As the bricks continued to fall, Mori screamed and scooted back on the platform, allowing space for the bricks of the death tunnel and its surrounding wall to land around them. The collapse caused the floor to tilt, as all the water that had pooled in the basement rushed into the gorge, filling it to the brim. The floor began to cave.

"Get out!" I screamed and scrambled out of the tunnel, reaching back to offer my hands to Mori and Wilky.

There was nothing we could do for Fae. Though my heart longed to help her, as I was sure Mori longed to die with Fae, she was gone. We knew it. If the bricks hadn't gotten her, the rushing water filling in air spaces would. Her only chance at this point was to swim upwards.

Mori and Wilky made it out of the collapsing tunnel, and we waited a moment in the hopes that Fae had found her way out. But the bricks began to pile atop the ravine break, the ceiling began to cave, and plaster and concrete rained down in chunks.

Mori reluctantly ran toward me, pulling me along, as Wilky ran to catch up, the three of us glancing back to confirm the worst —she wasn't coming out. We reached the stairs and waited another second. When the rest of the tunnel collapsed, my entire soul did, too.

"We have to keep moving," I said.

"Fae, my Fae," Mori cried in the stairwell, their wails

consuming them entirely. I felt their pain as if it were my own, deep in my chest where the heart chakra exploded with black, roiling fire. Here, Mori had found someone who so completely accepted them for who they were, and now she was dead.

I tugged them by the hand. "Come on. Please, or the same will happen to us."

"No, no, no..." they cried.

"Yes, we have to." Between Wilky and me, we managed to get Mori to climb up to the ground floor where the landscape had changed. Because of the collapse in the basement, the dining room had caved as well. I tried to push away the images of Fae being crushed by tons of brick and concrete.

The moment we stepped into the main hall, a beam of flashlight shone into our faces. "Hey," someone said. "Hold it."

"The basement is collapsing," I breathed.

In front of us were four police officers, one of them holding Crow by the arm, and what looked like two county inspectors.

The vein in Crow's temple pulsed with contempt. "*Nothing* is collapsing."

"No?" I was aghast at the lengths he'd go to deny the inevitable. "You want to go down there and check for yourself? We just watched Fae die." Then I saw his sallow skin in the dim light and knew it wasn't him doing the talking anymore.

An officer used his radio to call an ambulance. In my mind's eye, all I could see was Fae, pathetically clutching her gold coins inside of that gorge, as an avalanche of bricks collapsed on her, head cracked open like a pumpkin.

Mori fell apart against Wilky's shoulder. "No, no..."

"Where? In here?" One of the cops, a female, peered into the depths of the stairwell, as the others began giving orders to evacuate the building.

"Yes, the death tunnel's already gone. That's why this floor is collapsing," I explained.

"Death tunnel?" she asked.

One of the other cops explained. "She means the body chute of the hotel from the hospital days. Alvarez, ambulance *and* backup."

"When was the last survey on this place?" an officer asked.

"Last one was filed six years ago," the inspector flipped through his clipboard.

"Wrong. My father completed one just four years ago condemning the hotel," I interjected.

The inspector shook his head. "Last one filed was six."

"He never got to turn it in." I seethed at Crow, taking slow steps up to him. The officer holding his arm jutted out his hand to keep me at a distance. "He died here. Killed by something who didn't want the report filed. I saw the report myself inside a storage room down the hall."

"Show me," one of the officers said, leading me away.

"There's no time," I replied. "My father said the building would collapse now."

"I thought you said your father died." Crow laughed, and the cop looked at me sideways, as if *I* were the liar.

"Excuse me." I brushed past them all to leave, but the officer reached out and told a solid hold of my arm.

"Nope. You can't go just yet. None of you. Alvarez?" The cop gave a secretive nod to his partner. "Trespassing."

"For real?" I said. "You're going to detain us for trespassing when we're warning you about the building? This is ridiculous. Let go of me." I yanked my arm, but Alvarez had a firm grip.

"Hey, my guys. Can we answer questions after we get out of the building?" Wilky pleaded. "You all are making a huge mistake by keeping us standing around."

"Kaspian, we'll be outside," Alvarez said to the rest of the team. He and his partner began leading me, Mori, Wilky, and Crow down the hall when one of their walkie-talkies crackled on.

"Wait in the hall," the woman officer said. "On our way."

We all had to stop and wait for the rest of the team to catch up, while two officers held four of our arms. Wilky, busy holding Mori up, gave no resistance, and Crow, towering over all of us, watched my concerned face with amusement. He was shirtless still, and his arms and chest had changed into a deeper blue-green. His face was dry, crackled like alligator skin, and his neck had what looked like flaky scales growing on it.

"Buddy, you okay?" Alvarez said.

"Oh, I'm perfect," he chuckled.

Wilky and I exchanged looks. "Let me go," I said quietly to the officer. "I'd rather resist arrest than die here with all of you. Please."

"Don't let her go." Crow chuckled. "I need her."

"That's enough," Wilky cut Crow off. "I'm tired of your shit."

"Nobody cares about you, Wil," Crow replied. "The only one with any real power here is Valentina. Hers is the gift we need. Hers is the anger—"

"Who the fuck is 'we,' asshole?" Wilky asked. "You, only you."

"Crow and I," Crow replied.

Mori looked at him curiously.

"Hey," a cop tried intervening. "Save it for the station."

The obvious finally dawned on Mori, Wilky, and me—Crow wasn't himself anymore. I tugged on my cross. *Heavenly Father, please help us.*

Crow's filmy gaze fell on the cross, as it always did. "God keeps so many secrets from us, doesn't He? For a deity who claims to love His children so much, He's pretty stingy." About me, he told Alvarez, "This one's the most deluded of all. Been driving us insane since she arrived a year ago."

"What?" I yanked on the officer's arm. He pushed my elbow behind my back and reached for my other wrist. "Crow's the one who's been here a year, working on a stupid portfolio. He thinks he can bring this hotel back to life so his demon girlfriend can give him secrets from the underworld. He's a pet."

Crow laughed to himself.

"Vale, don't," Wilky murmured.

"Crow, you're the one who dragged us here," Mori said in a grief-stricken voice. "Telling us this place needed us. Telling us we would all get something out of it. What this place needed was more death! All so your Lady could grow in strength. Because of you, Fae is dead!"

"Fae is dead, because she was greedy," Crow hissed.

Mori ripped out of the officer's stronghold and plunged into Crow, knocking him against the wall, pounding their fists into his cracked cheeks. Crow took each punch, but with each strike, Mori grew weaker until they were sobbing, and Alvarez pulled them apart.

"Alright, people, let's finish this outside. Come on." Alvarez gestured us further down the hall. At least he wasn't treating us like criminals anymore.

But Mori collapsed to their knees, face in hands. "I'm staying. I have no one."

"Not true." I offered my hands. "You have Citana. You have me..."

"You have me," Wilky said, squatting beside them.

As Wilky tried talking Mori off the ledge, and the two officers met with the rest of the team on their way back from inspecting the damage, Crow shifted his weight against the wall. A spasm rocked his body, then another, and another. A raving mad look crossed his eyes. He began sweating profusely, agonizing over some unseen force. The haze of purple-silver light I'd seen in the ballroom emanated from his eyes, nostrils, and mouth. Dark cracks formed in his cheeks. His eyes darkened to pure black.

He looked to me for help, but I froze.

How could I help? Crow wasn't Crow anymore.

To my horror, he was growing taller, limbs cracking and stretching, as he writhed in pain. One of the officers noticed it at the same time Wilky and Mori saw it, too, and watched agape, as Crow's torso thickened. A layer of slime covered him, oozing out of his pores.

"Wilky...Mori...time to go," I said.

"We are not...going...anywhere!" Crow screamed, his mouth opening into a wide tunnel. My eyes widened to absorb the horror. Like the Antoni of my nightmares, Crow shrieked out his rage. "I never should've let you in *heeeere!*"

Hot wind blasted from his elongated throat, lifting flaps of clothing and hair on everyone, his gaping mouth firing squall after squall of tainted green miasma. Loose papers, fiberglass, even wall sconces detached from the walls and flew around us, as Crow released suppressed rage. Years and years' worth.

The worst part was I understood it.

I could've easily become the monster.

We tried to run, getting as far as the atrium where pieces of ceiling had begun falling, whole panels, fiberglass, and stucco raining down on our heads. My vision blacked momentarily when something hard hit my head. I fell on my back and covered my head with my arms. As I scrambled to find a hiding spot underneath a cypress tree, a dislodged painting fell at my feet—the Lady of the Lake as her mythical, legendary self, her beauty a ruse to earn human sympathy.

His screams—*her* screams—assaulted us. With each shrieking gust of wind that came out of his mouth, I watched Crow's skin change to a deep aquamarine, as swags of lake grass grew from his head and got caught in the whirlwind. Smooth, scale-covered breasts formed on his torso, his waist cinched into an hourglass shape, and his legs lengthened then fused together to form one.

Two of the cops drew their weapons and fired round after round at Crow's periphery, a misguided attempt to scare him off without hurting him. It was clear they didn't know what to make of him, having been a young human a moment before. The two inspectors were gone; two other cops ran off in opposite directions.

The one, fused leg of the creature that was no longer Crow had formed a fish tail, the mass of which supported its upper weight, and its lake grass hair had morphed into thin tentacles at the ends, feelers that covered a multitude of square footage at once. Its luminous eyes covered by filmy membranes appeared blind to light. The creature reached out its long arms, quickly stretching into tentacles, and caught each of the two, fleeing officers in its coils.

They were crushed on capture, their bodies quivering, nerves outplaying their remaining actions. The fine tentacles of hair stretched behind it, into the repressed gloom of the hallway, and plucked out the two remaining police officers. One slipped from its grip and fell to the ground, where the creature promptly crushed it with its tail, and the other slapped the female officer with its mermaid tail until her skull smashed into the Sunlake's dissolving walls.

The beast plucked the two county code enforcers from behind the columns of the lobby and raised them to the ceiling. It inspected them casually before popping each one into its maw then ripping the heads off one, then the other. As blood rained down around me, spattering my arms, I winced and tried my best not to breathe, so it wouldn't find me.

At times, the creature looked like Crow, helpless and remorseful. At others, the Lady of the Lake. But it was neither. The creature was something else, something from the depths of the lake we never could've seen coming, something ancient that had lain dormant for centuries, awaiting its perfect moment of rebirth. When it was done devouring the five or six bodies it'd smashed to pulp, it turned its attention to us.

Wilky and Mori scrambled to share my hiding spot. Our arms

embraced each other as one. In their touch, I "saw" their fear wind its way through my veins, turn mostly black with flecks of scant specks of light, like tourmaline. The creature turned its rage on us.

Death by evil mermaid, headed this way.

"*Run,*" I breathed.

Twenty-Seven

Mori and Wilky took off, slipping past the creature undetected, as it let out another wail. I'd started out as well, but then the walls of the Sunlake reverberated, releasing tatters of wallpaper, Mediterranean light fixtures, and artwork, the hotel's remaining shreds of dignity. I sank back again.

The creature narrowed its sightless eyes in my general vicinity and screamed with words I couldn't hear. *I've waited centuries...*

Every warning I'd ever heard from my family, church, or friends echoed through my ears. *Don't mess with the spirit world. You'll be sorry.* I tried again to run, managing to get a few feet into the hall, when the subterranean siren's tail came thrashing toward me, a rush of sulfurous air preceding it, powering its muscled flesh against me. I retreated at what felt like hundreds of miles an hour against one of the atrium's outer walls, heard a crack, and tumbled. My bones screamed in agony.

Along the glass, a fissure spiked upward, spitting sharp fragments raining toward the ground, as my vision wavered in and out of darkness. Vaguely, I heard Wilky's voice imploring me to reach out and hold onto him, but then that massive whooshing tail swept the floor once more, slamming Wilky into one of the great columns.

He slumped with a thud, writhing in pain.

"Wilky!" Mori ran to him. "Vale, let's go!" they screamed across the hall, but there was no way I could span the distance without getting scooped up.

"Just go!" I screamed.

Mori kept shouting, but I couldn't focus on their words. A roaring boom from the creature's depths groaned in a voice that didn't translate as human, but I understood just the same. It needed one more.

One more what?

One more soul to make the transformation complete. Then it would rise from this forsaken nest where it'd spawned and seek eternal life in the natural world.

I would've liked to reply, *Like hell you will,* but I was only one tiny life. If the beast was going to take anybody, it'd be me, not Wilky, not Mori, who had already suffered enough for one lifetime. I'd lived a good life, despite the lies. They were just lies, not physical pain, not harassment, not abandonment, not hate.

I had a family.

I measured the distance between the spot where I lay hurt and the auxiliary door or even the closest broken window. I'd rather cut the hell out of my skin jumping through one than provide the last soul the creature needed. If I couldn't make it, so be it. I'd already done what I'd come to do—save the others.

Give yourself, the creature told me, its tentacles curling and whipping.

"You won't survive out there," I replied.

Yes. There is enough hate to sustain me.

"There's more love than hate."

In the distance, I heard the ambulances navigating toward the Sunlake. They wouldn't make it past the gate, I knew. But who would? Macy. I could hear her voice calling for me from the back of the building. The veranda. She'd found the same path I'd used to first come here.

"Vale!" she cried.

I could see her and Citana pounding on the atrium glass. "I'm alright! Go home! Get out!"

"It's a sinkhole!" Macy screamed. "Vale, did you hear me?"

Yes, I could hear her, but there was nothing I could do. The atrium I'd feared for weeks had become my terrarium, and the creature was my captor.

The stress cracks, the squashed columns, the gate that had shifted on its axis, the sunken foundation, the ravine in the basement, the fissure through which the lake water poured... It wasn't only a crumbling, decrepit building, but a literal pit of death opening beneath us. An eroded limestone foundation about to suck the dying and unstable into its earthy depths.

Through the glass, I could see Macy's mouth open when she saw what I faced. All the creature needed was one more soul. It could easily break out of the crumbling building and take Macy, Citana, or Lucinda, too.

Macy, please, I tried telling her. *GO.*

But sisters don't leave when sisters need help, and so she remained at the glass, pounding and searching for a way in. When the creature shifted its attention to Macy, I jumped from the foliage, leaping over rocks and fallen palm fronds to distract it. It coiled a tentacle underneath me, lifted my flailing body to its scaly face. Its mouth was an explosion of teeth. Its eyes, no pupils, no soul, just two gaping holes of blindness.

When I looked into them, I saw reflected back at me the woman who'd crashed through the atrium, whose dead flesh the creature had used as a starter to its new form. It was Crow, purple hair sprouting from its massive, shiny shoulders. It was the woman holding her womb, furious at what had been done without her consent. It was the priest with the dire warning. It was Wilky's grand-uncle and the other men in cages. It was Fae, clutching her gold. It was the little boy who'd witnessed his mother's death.

It was no one and everyone at the same time, every soul who had passed without dignity in this cursed place.

The creature wheezed open its jaws. What if...after I died, there was nothing on the other side?

No Heaven, no Hell, no in-between, no duality.

What if "spirit communication," the gift of sixth sense, the psychic ability to "see" another dimension was all natural brain phenomenon that would end after we drew our last breaths?

This was my ultimate fear.

Macy kept pounding and pounding at the glass, and the creature, distracted, loosened its grip on my torso. I wriggled out of its grasp and fell twenty feet to the soil below, rolling into the bushes behind the tree. I watched it thrash with anger, searching for me in the plants. It upended trees left and right, slapped its tail, and toppled the fountain. The mermaid fell on her stone head and cracked at the neck. Her eyes gazed at the creature.

As more debris rained into the hallway from the floors above, the creature blocked the entrance to the atrium considering its next move, while I prayed for a way out. Closing my eyes, I imagined the purple light washing over me. Nothing existed but now, this moment. I imagined running past the beast and spilling out the front of the hotel. Nothing else. I could do it. And if I couldn't, I'd die in peace knowing I'd tried.

The creature slowed, its tentacles curling beautifully around it. I pitied its need for fury. It would not survive in a world overdue for healing. Though plenty of anger remained, the old establishment was on its way out. The new establishment was about love, joy, and acceptance.

Hail Mary, full of grace, the Lord is with you.

Old habits died hard. I sucked in a breath, stood, rubbing the tips of my fingers together—and ran.

Blessed art thou among women, and blessed is the fruit of thy womb, Jesus...

Straight towards the creature, ducking through plants, aiming for the right side of the hall where it hopefully wouldn't see me. I leapt through small spaces, flew through the air, landed on the other side of the beast. But the lobby column with the fishtail began crumbling, its crown molding raining down in chunks, and one hit me square on the temple.

I cried out.

The mercreature heard me. It shifted, swept its tail along the lobby floor, and curled around my body, squeezing tight. I punched against its slimy, giant scales with my fists, but it lifted me to its mouth, sniffed me once, then to my shock, catapulted me across the air back into the atrium.

As I flew, I reached out and caught the tangled mess of the loose chandelier's old wiring. Why had it let go of me? Was it playing with its food before it ate me? As the creature spotted my dangling limbs, it slithered toward me and peered into my face with iridescent blind orbs. Someone was inside.

"Crow?"

The ground began to shake. It rumbled so furiously, I knew this was the end of my human experience on Earth. I wasn't afraid anymore, but the creature was. It howled at what was happening, just as I heard another howl from down below.

My lupine familiar stalked the atrium, searching for a way to reach me.

"Lobo, no."

Every few seconds, I caught his beautiful golden eyes looking up worriedly, saw his silky black fur reflecting dim light. He stepped over rocks and wooden planks. He was solid, as solid as any animal that roamed.

From underneath us, the atrium floors began to crumble into the inky fathoms below. The creature looked at me. Why wasn't it crying anymore? For one split second, the creature's iridescent eyes turned luminous blue. It cast a glance at the cross around my neck.

Crow always looked at the cross around my neck.

"Crow, it's okay," I said. "I forgive you."

None of it had been his fault. He was just a kid when it happened.

"It's over," I told the entity controlling him. "This place is coming down, and you're coming down with it."

I'll be reborn, it spat and hissed.

"You won't. You'll be trapped here."

Hold your charm, I heard Crow say.

"My what?"

Your father's protection charm.

I could barely hang onto the chandelier, how could I hold onto my charm?

I switched to my other hand and hung with renewed determination. With the little energy I had left, I pressed my palm, not against my charm, but against the creature's cheek. Closing my eyes, I "saw" its pain, a hurt older than this hotel, a deep hole in the earth, the passage through which it'd been born. I saw its fall from grace, the moment it was cast into hiding by the universe.

Consumed by hate.

Helpless and hurting.

I opened my eyes. "I'm so sorry," I told Crow, trapped inside it.

Its blind eyes blinked once.

And then, it opened its mouth.

Twenty-Eight

Some places couldn't help but be miserable. They festered, steeped in the lingering effects of human wrath, fury, and pain. They never should've been born in the first place and held onto their wounds like a pacifier. The Sunlake Springs Resort was one of these places.

And it was ready to die.

I touched my father's charm.

My little starshine, sleep, oh, so tight
My little moonshine, dream with the night

As the bottomless tunnel of teeth wrapped around my body, I smelled its foul breath and punched a serrated tooth so hard, my free hand cut open. The earth began to fall away. I heard Lobo cry. The creature spun its head to see what was going on, and my body flew out of its mouth. I swiveled, grasped for the chandelier's chains and hung on. The same object had touched my father.

The walls of the hotel came crumbling down.

Lake water rushed through the halls, and the land and lake merged as one.

I felt a squeeze of muscle around me. The entity tried pulling me off the chandelier chain, but I held on. With a roar, a chasm opened in the floor beneath the atrium. Plants, rocks, discarded benches tumbled into the tunnel. The chandelier swung back and forth, two of its chains loose. I contemplated letting go. To keep itself from falling into the chasm, the creature released me and clung to the chasm's edge instead, roaring angrily.

I heard Lobo whimper. I wanted him gone and safe. Instead, he'd climbed onto a mountain of broken debris and began howling at the creature.

"Lobo, no!" I appreciated he was trying to protect me, but there was no way for him to help.

More of the floor fell away, concrete and tile tumbling, eroding closer to the wolf. The creature swung one of its long, coiling arms toward Lobo, which he artfully dodged as he sailed from one pile of debris to another. The sinkhole yawned open. If I didn't jump now, I'd be sucked into it.

My little starshine, sleep, oh, so tight
My little moonshine, dream with the night

I swung, gained momentum, then soared through the air, aiming for the other side of the earth's opening. My feet hit ground, my knees cracked, and pain radiated through my leg. When the mercreature saw what I'd done, it tilted its head back and bellowed into the atrium. Glass shattered and showered down.

Lobo skirted the outer edge of the sinkhole. He whimpered and limped.

"Come here, boy. Come on," I called to him.

But the Sunlake gave its last breath. Water and plaster rained all around, as it begged to put itself out of its misery. The creature hung on, blindly grasping at plants, tree trunks, and rocks.

It wrapped a slimy coil around Lobo.

The wolf squealed.

"No!" I screamed.

The last of the standing walls crumbled. The ceiling fell to pieces—plaster, pipes, dust plummeting all around me. Debris smashed onto my shoulders, as I wrapped my arms around my head to protect myself. As the Sunlake Springs surrendered to the earth, its resident evil leapt over the chasm right at me, falling short, holding onto the edge, clinging with the same tentacle that held Lobo.

Calm, golden eyes watched me.

Nothing to fear.

The creature squeezed its coil to gain leverage, shutting the light in Lobo's eyes out forever. My heart filled with rage so deep, my bellows rivaled the mammoth's. It hung off the chasm's edge, pulling itself up with two appendages, flinging them at me in a last-ditch effort to survive.

At that moment, our bodies collided in a wave of heat, followed by a tsunami-like surge swelling high above me, filling me with rage the likes of which I'd never felt before.

It wanted inside me, to consume my anger like it'd done with Crow.

And for a moment, I closed my eyes and let it.

Fuck, it felt good to hand that burden over, to allow this beast to take control of me, releasing me of the obligation to squash it. It was mine to feel. Anger made me real, made me human. There was no denying it. But I wouldn't let it consume me for long.

I opened my eyes and took back my pain, staring into the beast's eyes. "Unlike you, I remember how to love." I grasped the cross around my neck.

Though I hadn't uttered the actual words aloud since the day he died, only thought them in my mind, I sucked in a deep breath and spoke them aloud, giving them power.

"My little starshine, sleep, oh, so tight...my little moonshine, dream with the night; when you awaken, Love you will be; my little sunshine Heaven gave me."

The beast laughed, its chest shuddering. *Your father is coming with me.*

It was a lie. Because that's what demons did.

I imagined the creature surrounded by the same purple light that protected me. "My little starshine, sleep, oh, so tight," I repeated. "My little moonshine, dream with the night; when you awaken, Love you will be; my little sunshine Heaven gave me."

I watched it recoil as though I were covering it in acid. As it writhed in pain from my words, the precipice gave way again, a blast of heat shot up from the chasm, and the entity tumbled in, taking my beautiful, loyal, protective Lobo with it.

"Goodbye, little one."

I wasted no time.

Dragging my broken body through busted walls and piles of debris, I trudged out of the hotel as fast as I could, adrenaline coursing through my veins. The earth's crust finally surrendered its hold, and the whole of the Sunlake Springs Resort and adjacent lake cried out with dismantlement.

In a matter of seconds, the entire hotel had plummeted. Gone, swallowed by nature, reclaimed by earth, clouds of ash and dusty memories rising from the newly-formed crater.

The parking lot eroded behind me, as I race-limped across the gray expanse toward the gates. I wasn't safe as long as the parking lot continued to dissolve. I ran, blindly, with everything I had in me toward the highway, slowing only when the rumbling ended, when the land quieted, and something inside my soul told me it was done.

I collapsed on the dirt path into a foot of water. Currents of rain washed my grit, blood, my wounds. Someone licked my knee and nudged my head, sniffed my ears. My fingers dug into soft, wet fur. I inhaled the scent of my wolf, my sweet Lobo, whimpering over me.

How had he survived? For him—only for him—I forced open my eyes to acknowledge his presence and unwavering protection.

But my sweet, beautiful wolf wasn't there.

My dad was.

Twenty-Nine

I heard helicopters and sirens. A mélange of voices melded with my dreams of being asleep outdoors. Funny, this dream, it felt real—the warmth, humidity, the chirping birds, the dumped rain I was stewing in.

When I opened my eyes, I was surrounded by shoes.

"You get that side. I'll get her feet." The shoes shuffled into awkward positions around me. I felt tugging, pulling, as they jostled me into a sitting posture.

My lashes fluttered, as muted, clouded light brought me to my senses.

"She's waking. Vale? Thank God, you're okay." Familiar voice. Someone named Mori? Maybe Macy. "Your knee is torn up pretty bad."

Around me, five faces peered into mine—Wilky, Mori, Macy, Macy's mom—what was her name again? Mori's aunt. My father and Lobo were gone. But I was sure I'd seen them. My father had stroked my hair for so long, sang to me, and told me the darkness was gone. The souls were free because of me.

I sat up and stared at everyone smiling and crying. Overnight, I'd been gifted a new family. My forehead pulsed. I sat on the dirt path, the driveway leading into the resort. Piece by piece, everything came back—the building, the atrium, the battle, a creature as horrible as the kraken of ocean lore but borne of a wretched, dying swamp.

We'd lost Fae and Crow.

We'd lost so much. But these people—they were still here.

"How long have I been out?" I squinched my eyes against the soreness.

Macy raked her fingers through my hair, wiped my face of dirt. "Since last night. After it happened, we came looking for you, but a crew told us to steer clear of the area."

"When what happened?"

"Don't you remember?" Macy asked.

Images of wide chasms, festering heat, and destruction came barreling into the forefront of my memory. "A sinkhole."

Macy nodded. "They're saying it's the biggest one Florida's ever seen. Five hundred feet wide. They're all arriving now to confirm, but they let us in to look for you. We have to get back."

Wilky's face was covered in bloody scratches. "The whole damn thing, just...swallowed up, Vale."

I know. I saw.

Behind Lucinda was the iron gate to the property, and behind that...the sun coming up on a flat horizon. No looming hotel. No shadows stretched across the land. Just an old landscape, washed away by the rain.

"We should get out of the way, so the crews can do their work," Macy told the others.

"We need to close the portal is what we need to do."

Everyone looked at her—Citana.

"Before the inspectors arrive, and we're not allowed back in. Hurry." Citana rose to her feet with Wilky's help, and they began walking toward the gate, the whole bottom corner of which was submerged in mud.

Mori looked like they'd been crying a long time with puffed eyes and red cheeks. I took their hand and squeezed it. They nodded, biting their bottom lip. With their help, I scrambled first to my good knee, then to a semi-standing position, wincing.

"Ready?" Wilky scooped me up and carried me.

We followed Citana to the gaping sinkhole. I wasn't sure I wanted to see a crushed hotel in its depths. As it was, I'd have nightmares about this for the rest of my life. But I needed to. We had to finish what we started.

"Will it work, Tata?" Mori asked.

"Of course, it will," Citana replied without batting an eye.

Faith was everything.

It took a while to reach the edge of the precipice, as we now had to navigate lifted sections of old pavement and cracks that had formed last night. As Wilky huffed and puffed while carrying me, I thought about Lobo. Was he Dad all along? He'd known the area, known the clairs were in danger, known I was protected by his charm, the only explainable reason why he'd send me into a dangerous situation.

The devastation was intense. Not only was there a hole in the earth one-tenth of a mile wide, but the adjacent Sunlake Springs Lake had emptied, rivulets of water seeping from its edges into the chasm like mini waterfalls. No sign of the Devil's Tree either. Silence permeated the air, as if the sinkhole had taken the cries of the resort's souls with it.

We walked as far as we could, several feet away from the actual edge.

"Don't go any further," Wilky said, setting me on my feet.

Even from where we stood, there was no glimpsing the bottom. I was grateful for that. No need to gaze into the final resting place of Fae, Crow, and countless others. It was hard enough knowing their broken bodies were down there.

Mori dropped their chin. I put my arm around them.

"Let's do this quickly," Citana said. "Everybody, hold hands."

"Does it matter that we're six?" Wilky asked.

"Only matters that we love." Citana glanced at Mori, still shaking against my shoulder. She reached out to take their hand.

On the edge of this cliff, the six of us stood in a circle. Mori to my left, Wilky to my right. A collective sigh spread over us, as thoughts of sadness assailed my brain. Citana began with a chant in her beautiful, haunting dialect that was as natural to this land as the trees, dirt, birds, and breezes.

"Let us pray," she said, same words uttered in cathedrals, mosques, and temples around the world. So much division when we were the same.

I envisioned royal light surrounding us and the chasm. In my vision, I watched it spread over the land. I sent the light into the ground to surround Fae, Crow, and Lobo, though I was sure they had already ascended. I felt no gloom. No heavy mass of anger breathing down my neck. No lingering resentment tugging at my sleeves, like needy children.

"We close this portal, sending energy back into the universe," Citana proclaimed. "Love into Heaven, Hate to be transmuted. We hereby end the curse that has plagued this land..."

Though I was glad we were doing this, I was sure the entity had already returned to where it came from, weakened like a hurricane split by island mountain peaks. Whether it would reassemble and try again, I didn't know. But for now, it was gone.

"As above, so below," Citana said.

"So mote it be," we finished.

"This place is now unblemished," Citana announced. "Let us go in peace."

During Mass, we all said, "Thanks be to God," said goodbye, and left. We'd worry about getting out of the parking lot on time or whether or not we'd arrive in time for Sunday brunch. Mindless and onto the next thing.

Today, in this place of quietude before the masses arrived, nobody moved. We stood there, arms around each other, welcoming a new day. Mori in tears, Wilky holding down the fort of emotions for us all, the ladies looking melancholy at best. The power of prayer meant nothing without intention.

Without love, words meant nothing.

Without love, *we* were nothing.

Thirty

Once upon a time, the smell of alcohol, wiping of blood, or buzzing of needle would've been enough to repel me from ever getting a tattoo. But this felt amazing. Earned, like a badge of honor. I didn't ask anyone's permission. I just did it. I couldn't "see" the tattoo artist's thoughts in my head either. Closing the portal had dimmed the psychometry in my hands.

Macy sat next to me, getting her first tattoo also.

Every so often, I'd snap photos of our progress with my new phone, but mostly, I stayed in the moment, in awe that the last couple of months had led me here. If a year ago, someone had told me I'd spend the summer away from home, getting to know and be accepted by a new family, realize the truth about my dad, all while learning that the seeds of manifestation lay inside each of us, I'd have said they were insane.

It *was* insane—in a good way.

I didn't feel powerless anymore. Our lives were canvases. We could create whatever tattoos we wanted onto that blank slate. This was only the beginning, and this artwork on my skin was a testament to that power, always within me.

Macy got a beautiful, sparkling sun dreamcatcher. Mine was a full moon with tiny hanging crystals, the silhouette of a wolf in the middle. Day and night, solar and lunar celestial energy. One and the same, made of the same stardust. Sisters forever. When we were done, we took a slew of photos and posted them online.

Immediately, I started getting snide messages from friends I'd known in the past, friends who were confused about the new Valentina.

What does the moon mean? Are you a werewolf now?

Funnily enough, it didn't bother me. They were frustrated with their own lives, stuck inside their boxes, unable to break out or make sense of their confused feelings. I felt sorry for them and even sent God a message that night, asking to please help them on their journeys like He'd helped me.

Send them dancing wolves on ceilings.

I thought of reaching out to Savannah, the girl who'd started it all for me, whose IG account I'd become so obsessed with at the start of my senior year. So many of our classmates had written her off as weird or evil. I hadn't known what to make of her then either, but now I understood her more than ever. She was a child of the moon—like me.

The next morning, I messaged her.

She replied: *Omg a Ministerio buddy?!* With a laughing face, as if—what were the chances that a classmate from her private school past had reached out to her in this new life?

She'd been living in New Orleans, working at an occult shop and a praline store (not at the same time). She asked if I wanted to come visit. Of course, I couldn't. Summer was almost over. I was about to start college, I told her. Besides, how awkward would that be to just show up in New Orleans and hang with a girl I barely knew?

Then, I remembered—I'd done that with Macy.

And here we were, living in Yeehaw Springs, getting matching tattoos. We'd never learn what life had in store for us if we sat around waiting for things to happen. You had to go to the creaky hotels, explore the haunted woods. Sometimes, you had to touch the Devil's Tree to find out what was buried underneath.

Sometimes you lost friends along the way.

I longed to heal the rift between Camila and me, but the time wasn't right. Like Wilky had said, friends break up. You go your separate ways, and sometimes you come back. Sometimes you don't. Both are okay. Both a part of life. I just never expected that to happen with Cami. I still loved her, and always would. We were just on different paths.

And I loved my new one too much.

THE NEXT MORNING, Mori and Wilky showed up at the house, as I was throwing my bags into the trunk. We stood outside, between the cars, talking about random things, though our underlying sadness was palpable. We were forever changed. You couldn't battle an evil lake mermaid back to the depths of Hell and not be. But we would survive a year apart, no doubt.

I had to go. I had things to work out with my family. I hugged them each and bit back the tears, promising to come back and visit next summer.

"Fae says goodbye." Mori pulled me into another hug.

I smiled. "Tell her I say hi. I love and admire her, more than she'll ever know."

Mori smiled, dimples deep and beautiful. "She knows. Love you, Vale."

"Love you, too."

Wilky was harder to let go of, because with Wilky, there was so much unexplored territory. Under different circumstances, I would've loved getting to know him, what made those deep eyes so sad, why he made people work for his smile.

He handed me a rolled-up piece of paper. "I made you this."

"Aww." I unrolled the scroll, and there, behind a layer of wax paper, was a gorgeous charcoal drawing of The High Priestess tarot card, triple moon goddess for a crown. Instead of a black cat at her feet was a black wolf.

"It's you," he said.

It was—my face, my likeness, serene and powerful, looked out from inside the dark robes. "I love this, Wilky. I'll treasure it forever."

"Come here." He pulled me into a warm, delicious hug. After a minute, I pulled away from the pounding of his heart, and he tapped my nose. "Stay wild, moon child."

His voice, his smile, his lingering look as he retreated to his car made me think twice. I'd loved every minute of the last two months I'd spent with him. Especially the last four weeks, when he, Mori, and I had tried to normalize by couch surfing, researching abandoned locations with weird pasts, and ordering takeout every day. My leg cast from the hairline fracture I'd gotten wouldn't allow for much else. I couldn't believe I had to drive home after that.

Finally, I turned to Macy. "Guess this is it."

"What am I going to do without you, huh, little sis?" She smiled, holding me by the arms, pulling me into a warm hug.

"Get back to normal? I bet you're like, damn, finally, she's leaving."

"Bullshit," she said. "I wish you would stay. We'll make up for lost time, cross the globe, rule the world together." She laughed, shaking her head. "Right after I finish my work, right? Ah, jobs."

"You could get a new one," I said. "Something more fulfilling than editing."

"I guess so. But for now, paying bills feels nice," she said. "But I like the way you think. Maybe I ought to get back into that world-ahead-of-me mindset, like you."

"Say goodbye to your mom for me. It was really great meeting her." This, I couldn't expand on, though my heart tried. I wouldn't be able to do it without crying. She'd never understand what it meant for me to finally get to know another woman my father had once loved.

"I will. Don't forget your orange juice," Macy said.

"Got it. And the snacks. Thank you. I owe you—huge."

I got in the car, started her up, and pulled out of the driveway, as the three of them stood there, watching me leave. Why did my heart ache so bad? I hadn't known them for long. I shouldn't feel so attached. Not like this. I had been through a terrifying experience this summer—I should've felt relieved I was leaving.

I waved out the window, honked the horn. They smiled. Perfect—I captured them in my memory like potions in bottles to keep my heart beating another year. Heading to the highway with the window open, warm air tangling my hair, I swiped at my eyes.

Yes, I had to check in with my mom, but hadn't I done that over the last four weeks with my calls? We'd talked about my father, his death, and my family's secrets. We'd talked about Abuela and her old school ways. And yeah, we'd talked about my grandfather.

We hadn't gotten to the bottom of things, because let's face it, that would take a while. But we were talking. Healing. We'd started the process.

As for school, I had no clue what I wanted to study. No idea where to go from here. I'd enrolled at FIU at the beginning of the summer, because I hadn't known what else to do. It seemed, at the time, like the right thing. You finish high school—you go to college. You start with humanities. You figure it out. That's what all my family members had done. But there was no reason I had to start right now.

Was there?

The red light at the south onramp waited.

My heart pounded.

What if I didn't go back? What was the worst that could happen? My mom and grandmother would get upset with me? *Pfft.* I'd already jumped that hurdle. The worst was over. FIU would have one less freshman to deal with? Camila would consider me lost forever? That might've been true anyway.

What if I spent the next year getting to know myself? Macy, Wilky, Mori... What if I sent Savannah another message, telling her that would be so great if I could visit her, explore a new city, learn more about the craft? Find new ways of blending my old beliefs with my new one? What if I could finally allow myself to get close to Wilky? Or anyone, for that matter. See what it would feel like to linger in someone's arms?

To kiss. And more.

The light turned green. I didn't move. Behind me, a car honked. I inched forward. It was time—turn onto the onramp. *Go home, Vale.* Nice thoughts, but I couldn't push fate. I'd already spent enough time here. The car honked again. I stuck my hand out of the window and told them to pass.

The driver went around, like I was annoying him for the hundredth time today. The guy even raised a hand, cursing me, but I had a counter to his curse—patience of steel. New mindset. New possibilities. You know who'd given that to me? My friends. My sister. My father. My coven.

My mother would understand.

I needed a gap year all to myself.

I drove through the intersection past the south onramp, a sneaky smile plastered on my face. I would not be driving six hours back to Miami today. I'd be driving five minutes. I did a one-eighty at the next U-turn and headed home to Yeehaw Springs.

Dear Reader...

If you enjoyed this book, please leave a review on Amazon and Goodreads and join my newsletter at GabyTriana.com to receive updates on new book releases, free chapters, and giveaways.

Thank you!

Acknowledgments

I'd like to thank my Women in Horror Critique Group for beta-reading early drafts of this story: Angela De Groot, Sara Tantlinger, Q.L. Pearce, Miranda Hardy, and Michele Brittany. These amazing women are all fantastic authors, podcasters, and academics in their own right, and you should check out their work.

Special thanks to Alejandra Amaris Fernandez, who read my tarot cards while I was still outlining the concept and told me I was about to go deeply personal with a new book, more than I ever had with any other novel. I hadn't told her about *Moon Child* yet. Indeed, at the time, I was trying to figure out how much of my own life experiences I wanted to inject into Valentina's story, and decided, after speaking to her, that I had to go all in. Thanks, my witchy friend.

I send huge love to my family—Michael, Noah, Murphy, and especially my husband, Curtis, for listening to me agonize over imposter syndrome night after night. There comes a time, usually halfway through writing a book, when I tell myself I suck, I don't know what I'm doing, I don't understand plot, I'm going nowhere, everyone else is better than I am, and I should quit to go sell balloons at the Magic Kingdom instead. Night after night, Curtis would slap me upside the head and insist that I was a rockstar. Thank you, bebe. I needed that.

Finally, I thank my readers. Without you, I'd still be teaching (a beautiful, noble, thankless career) instead of living my bestselling author dreams. <3

About the Author

GABY TRIANA is the bestselling author of 21 novels for adults and teens, including Moon Child, the Haunted Florida series (Island of Bones, River of Ghosts, City of Spells), Cakespell, Wake the Hollow, Summer of Yesterday, and Paradise Island: A Sam and Colby Story. Her short stories have appeared in Don't Turn Out the Lights: A Tribute Anthology to Alvin Schwartz's Scary Stories to Tell in the Dark, the Classic Monsters Unleashed Anthology, and Weird Tales Magazine (Issue #365).

Also the host of a YouTube channel, The Witch Haunt, Gaby writes about witchy powers, ghosts, haunted places, and abandoned locations. She's ghostwritten over 50 novels for bestselling authors, and her books have won IRA Teen Choice, ALA Best Paperback, and Hispanic Magazine's Good Reads Awards. She also writes Paranormal Women's Fiction under the pen name Gabrielle Keyes and lives in Miami with her family.

Also by Gaby Triana

MOON CHILD

PARADISE ISLAND: A Sam and Colby Story

ISLAND OF BONES

RIVER OF GHOSTS

CITY OF SPELLS

WAKE THE HOLLOW

CAKESPELL

SUMMER OF YESTERDAY

RIDING THE UNIVERSE

THE TEMPTRESS FOUR

CUBANITA

BACKSTAGE PASS

And as Gabrielle Keyes:

WITCH OF KEY LIME LANE

CRONE OF COCONUT COURT

MAGE OF MANGO ROAD

HEX OF PINEAPPLE PLACE

Printed in Great Britain
by Amazon